Sweet Amy

a novel

LYNN ABELL

ISBN 978-1-66782-181-8 (Print)
ISBN 978-1-66782-182-5 (eBook)

This book is dedicated to my husband, Kevin, who thinks Reese Witherspoon would enjoy this book, so he is sending a copy to her. And to my sons, Ryan and Craig, who may not *read* the book but promise to listen to it if it is made into an audiobook. I'm holding you to that, boys.

PROLOGUE

I don't drive anymore. Not since the accident. Subways, taxis, and buses move the empty shell of my body from place to place. I adhere to schedules that aren't mine. The loss of freedom is part of my penance. I wait, standing on platforms, on curbs, in three-sided glass boxes covered with peeling flyers. I board, stepping carefully over the gap, sliding into backseats, holding the handrail as I climb the black rubber steps. I submit, handing over all control because I need to keep searching. I need to find deliverance. I look desperately out the windows, but I can never see past my own reflection, my translucent ghost keeping me from focusing on the things that lay beyond the glass.

I could drive if I wanted to. I'm still alive. The only survivor of a trinity of souls. Physically, I have healed completely. There's just a little aching in my hand before it rains.

CHAPTER 1

September 1980

"Amy, please slow down," my mom begged, her high heels slipping on the marble steps, a holdover from when the elementary school building had been a grand public library. I rushed ahead of her and pulled the heavy glass door open with my two small hands.

"I know where I'm going, Mom, you don't need to come with me," I said, but as I looked down the hallway, it seemed impossibly long. Longer, wider, taller than all the times I had come here with my older sister. A kaleidoscope of a view that, until today, had been unintimidating. The sound of a locker clanging shut startled me like a car backfiring, and bigger kids seemed to be everywhere, blocking my path. The din of their voices became oppressively loud and unwelcoming, as disturbing as hearing laughter in a nightmare. I stopped mid-step, recoiling unexpectedly with fear, and reached back for my mom's hand, moving my arm around, trying to find her grasp in the empty air. She placed her hand in mine and gave it a comforting squeeze. With her touch, the hallway shrank back to its appropriate size and the noise level returned to normal. As we walked down the hallway together, my metal lunch box banged against my shin in a rhythmic pattern, as reassuring as a heartbeat.

"Welcome, welcome," the teacher greeted us. "I'm Ms. Chapwell." She reminded me instantly of an apple, round and shiny, her plump cheeks flushed red with excitement. "Please, have a seat while we wait for the rest of the class." I looked around at the checkerboard of empty desks. The kids who had already arrived were sitting on a large oval rug that was ringed with the letters of the alphabet and pictures of corresponding words in happy primary colors: 'B' on a bumble bee; 'U' on an umbrella.

Then I saw her. The princess. I had seen her before, sitting on the front stoop of one of the newly built townhouses across the street from my own. I watched her from my window, mesmerized, as she played with her Barbies, her hair the same color as the dolls. It reminded me of the girl with spun-gold hair that I remembered from a Russian fairy tale in an oversized library book with strangely sketched pictures and a cracked spine. The beautiful girl in the fable had a long braid made of gold that reflected in the water and made the lake beneath her shine like the sun, but the braid was so heavy, she could never leave her spot by the lake. Daringly, I sat down next to the princess, imitating her crisscrossed legs so that our knees almost touched.

"Okay," Ms. Chapwell said, stretching out the word in a sing-song voice. "It is time for all mommies and daddies to say goodbye to their big children." She made a shooing motion toward the door with her hand. Reluctantly, parents filed out into the hallway. My mom turned and blew me a kiss that I caught with my hand under my knee, where the other kids couldn't see it.

"Welcome to your first day of kindergarten!" Ms. Chapwell's voice chimed as the last of the parents shut the door behind them. Surprisingly, the princess reached over and grabbed my hand.

CHAPTER 2

November 1996

O'Sullivan's Bar was a landmark in my hometown of Bell's Lake, Pennsylvania. Inside, the tables were dark pine layered with years of furniture polish so thick that you could carve into the soft wood with your fingernail. Names, dates, and quotes graffitied the tabletops and the backs of chairs, solidifying O'Sullivan's as the place that you could always come back to when you wanted to remember where you came from. Tonight, my best friend and I were meeting early so that we could catch up before everyone else that was home from college for the Thanksgiving holiday arrived and the bar would be transformed into a loud makeshift reunion.

I was chatting with Steven, an old classmate and current bartender at O'Sullivan's. I had just started telling him about my favorite dive bar at college when he abruptly stopped listening, his eyes fixated over my shoulder at the entrance where Anna Kildare stood in front of the heavy wooden door, blinking as her eyes adjusted to the low lighting. She wore a white sweatshirt with her sorority letters embroidered across the chest, fashionably dark jeans, and chunky Doc Martens boots. With her long blonde hair pulled into a loose ponytail, she looked like she had just walked out of a picture in a college brochure. I called her over and stood to give her a hug, stretching up on my tiptoes slightly so that my height matched hers, a habit from long ago. She said hello to Steven, and they exchanged pleasantries, a quick rundown about their lives after high school. When Steven excused himself to greet new customers, Anna and I grabbed a table at the back of the room.

"You lost weight," Anna said with a sly smile. "Is there a man is your life?"

"The only man in my life is Henry Gray," I said. Noting her confused look, I added, "He wrote our anatomy textbook. It's a common joke at the school of nursing. 'I'm sleeping with Henry Gray. I was up all night with Henry Gray.' It's a lot funnier when you're running on fumes. Nursing school doesn't leave any time for dating, I've told you that."

Anna pulled out her chair and angled it next to me at the small table so we could talk more privately. "Or food, apparently." It was true that nursing school had stressed me down a size or two from our high school days, especially now that I was facing finals for the semester and the ever-present licensure exam looming after graduation. A flicker of fretfulness crossed Anna's face as she looked me up and down, although I wasn't sure why. Anna certainly never had to worry about her weight, she was naturally thin with just the right amount of curves. I had always envied this about her. I gained weight easily and knew I was going to have to be vigilant if I wanted to keep the weight off.

"So, what's your news?" I asked after appetizers had been ordered and our first round of drinks was nearly gone. When we had spoken earlier in the day, Anna mentioned she had something to tell me. I imagined she'd been offered an internship in journalism, a career she had decided on when we were just about nine years old, and that decision had never wavered. I had always been impressed by her resolve. Indecision haunted even as I applied for college. I was torn between the liberal arts degree that would sustain my interest in photography and a practical job-oriented degree as a registered nurse. Practicality won.

"Well, it turns out," Anna exhaled, "that dear old dad has been sleeping with receptionists up and down the eastern Pennsylvania sales territory. I know, I know, no surprise there, but Mom has finally had enough. They are getting a divorce." She poked at the ice cubes in the bottom of her empty glass with the flimsy drink stirrer that bent under her grip.

"What?" I was completely taken off guard, not because of the divorce itself, but because I was so off base with Anna's news.

When I first met Anna, her parents, Renée and Jackson Kildare, were the very definition of young, modern love. Renée worked for Doctor Benjamin Phillips, a sought-after pediatrician in Bell's Lake, who was called Doctor Ben by everyone except Anna's mom. Renée would clarify to anyone who mistakenly called her a secretary that she was the office manager, pulling herself up to her full height, making her presence as big as her petite frame would allow.

Renée met Jack just after his pharmaceutical company, Prime Laboratories, relocated him from Columbia, South Carolina, to Philadelphia. Jack was a detail man. In the early '70s, detail men were typically somber and unassuming, ready to provide the doctors with facts and statistics that they gleaned from the articles in the medical journals, but Jack was different. He wore his dark blond hair longer than his colleagues, all of whom were several years older, but he kept it cut just above the collar of his shirt. Jack also had a moustache, his nod to the current trend, but like his hair, he kept it well groomed.

Instead of sitting patiently in the waiting area, Jack preferred to lean through the small window as Renée sat at her desk, checking patients in and out. He'd stolen Renée's heart before he finished his first sales call.

In elementary school, Anna's dad was every girl's secret crush. Even the teachers sighed when Jack came to parent–teacher night. It was shortly after Anna and I started middle school that Renée had her first suspicion about Jack's infidelity. Anna called me late one night and I could hear her parents arguing in the background. Anna relayed Renée's accusations to me between sobs. I reassured her that her mom was wrong, Jack would never upset his perfect little family and to me, Anna's family was indeed 'perfect.' At the time, my older sister Samantha had just started high school, and I could feel the sisterly bonds that had always united us, straining under the weight of her full transition from childhood to teen. Her near-constant arguing with my parents made her the center of attention, pushing me into the background, an afterthought in my family's priorities. But this was Anna's first time experiencing a family shouting match so vicious it could make the paint peel off the walls, an event that had become practically a weekly occurrence at my house, and it would be a long time before Anna's family had another one. Although I didn't fully realize it then, I was jealous of Anna's lack of a sibling who refused to play by the rules for the sake of family harmony. I was sure this was a one-time event for her that would be resolved when Renée was proven wrong. Yes, *omne trium perfectum*, as my Sunday school teacher would say, her use of Latin making the phrase indisputable—everything that comes in threes is perfect.

But when we were older, Jack's affairs were harder to deny. And as Renée grew resigned to them, Jack's dalliances became something quieter. Not the elephant in the room, but the mouse that scurried behind the cabinets, smart enough to never let itself be seen in full daylight. But still, three became four, as obvious as the empty seat at their square kitchen table.

"I'm so sorry, really," I said to Anna after her words had time to sink in, but secretly, I wondered how Renée had remained married to Jack this long. I placed my hand comfortingly on Anna's shoulder and waited for her to look up again.

"Well," said Anna, "that isn't the only thing. Dad moved to some crappy singles' apartment complex with a weight room and a Jacuzzi. A Jacuzzi!" she said with disgust. She pushed her glass across the table. It left a wet trail in its wake, condensation filling in the words etched in the wood. "He's pretending it's fun to be single again." She rolled her eyes and then looked down at the table. "Mom is seeing someone," she said quietly. "She's started dating Doctor Ben. His wife died a year ago. Oh, god, Doctor Ben could be my new daddy!" Anna said sarcastically, looking up and meeting my eyes.

"You better get free lollypops," I deadpanned, and Anna, taken off-guard, barked a laugh.

"I'm serious, Amy. I mean, Mom and Doctor Ben, well, everyone saw that coming. They would have gotten together twenty-five years ago if Dad hadn't gone into Doctor Ben's office. But my dad, he's going to be lost without Mom. He may seem like a playboy, but actually, he needs her."

"So, what are you going to do?" I asked.

"What can I do?" she asked rhetorically, shrugging her shoulders. "Go back and finish my last year at Penn State, spend Christmas driving back and forth between them, oh god…." She put her head in her hands, and the reality hit her, her eyes growing soft with tears.

"Let's just get through Thanksgiving," I said, giving her an awkward hug across the table.

"Is that you, Amy? Amy Sheppard?" Megan, a girl I hadn't seen since graduation, interrupted us as she approached the table. "And Anna! Oh my god, can you believe we're back? This place never changes."

Anna quickly wiped a napkin under her eyes. "Megan!" she said with false enthusiasm. We each hugged her in turn and spent the remainder of the night lost in conversations about life after Bell's Lake High, Anna masking her emotions with aplomb.

• • •

My parents' house was dark when I got back a little after two in the morning. I moved quietly through the familiar kitchen, leaving my purse on the table. The smell of cigarettes clung to my hair and clothes, more obvious since leaving the bar, and I was longing for a shower. Bits of conversation with old friends replayed in my head as I walked upstairs. Anna was as popular as ever, and it seemed that people hovered near us, talking to me while waiting for their chance to ask Anna about her life and brag to her about their own post-graduation accomplishments.

I silently opened my bedroom door. Nothing had been changed since I left for college. The walls were still the bright yellow that I had woken up to for seventeen years and the matching flowered comforter was worn pale from washing. My poster of Morrissey, the lead singer for the English band The Smiths, hung over my bedframe. Unframed snapshots from high school littered the mirror, held in place with scotch tape that was beginning to curl at the edges. I pulled one of the pictures off the mirror and looked at it closely. In the picture, Anna and I were standing on the lawn outside the high school, clutching our diplomas and leaning our heads intimately toward each other, graduation caps touching. Memories of that day came flooding through me. Moments after the picture was taken, Anna's dad arrived late to the graduation. From a distance, we could see he was carrying two bouquets of flowers wrapped in green tissue paper. There were bright white daisies with yellow centers as big as quarters in one bundle and carnations dyed garish shades of purple, red, and orange in the other. Renée, who had been saving an empty seat throughout the ceremony, let out a sigh, but whether it was from exasperation or relief, it was difficult to tell.

As Jack came closer, we could hear that he was crooning lines from "Daisy Jane," a song by the band America that was popular the year Anna was born. It was his song for her, the lyrics describing the simple longings of a man in love. He reached our small group, my family and Renée, and kissed Anna tenderly on the cheek. He continued singing and handed her the bouquet of daisies.

"Dad, stop!" Anna said, but her smile betrayed that she was flattered.

"Aw, I know that you're a big high school graduate now," Jack's southern drawl was more pronounced than usual, "but you'll always be my Daisy Jane." He scooped Anna into a tight hug then without letting her go, he looked directly at me, his crystal blue eyes, so much like Anna's, shooting straight into mine. "And you," he said, pulling me into their embrace. "You're my second favorite flower." Leaning back, he handed me the bouquet of carnations, then replaced his arm around my shoulder, swaying us back and forth as he sang promises to his Daisy Jane. As the lyrics implied, he may not be perfect, but he loved his girl with all he had, and he was desperately hopeful that was enough. I could smell the sour-sweet scent of alcohol as it drifted off his warm breath.

I replaced the picture on the mirror, smoothing the tape until it held fast in its spot.

• • •

May 1997

The phone was ringing as I opened the door to my off-campus apartment. Remembering that Gail Bishaw, my college roommate, was gone for the weekend, I rushed to answer it before the answering machine picked up.

"Hello," I balanced the phone on my shoulder and kicked off my shoes. The phone cord stretched as I continued moving forward, dropping my backpack on the sofa. Mentally, I was still at the hospital, reviewing the discharge paperwork I filled out before leaving, wondering if I remembered to include the request for an increase in pain meds for the woman being transferred to assisted living. As a fourth-year nursing student, I was assigned six patients under the supervision of a senior nurse. Today, it seemed more like six hundred. My stomach growled, reminding me that I had skipped lunch. I couldn't wait to graduate in three weeks.

"Amy?" I recognized Anna's voice, the hoarseness of it snapping me to the present.

"Anna? What's wrong?" I asked, stopping and sitting on the sofa. When Anna didn't answer right away, I could feel my pulse thrumming in my ears. Thoughts of work and hunger disappeared into the ensuing silence as my mind raced through a barrage of tragedies.

"It's... my dad. He... he...." She inhaled loudly, her breath catching.

"Anna, what happened?" But in the quiet that followed, I knew something was terribly wrong. I knew, and I felt my heart breaking for Anna.

"He died," she finally whispered into the phone.

"Oh god," I whispered back, my stomach clenching with anxiety. It was even worse than I was anticipating.

"I can't believe it, but he's gone, Amy," Anna sobbed into the phone. "My dad is dead." She said those last four words as if she needed to say it.

"How?" I asked, but Anna's wracked breathing was my only answer. As I waited, my thoughts traveled back to images of her youthful dad bursting with life. Memories of him pulling into the driveway of Anna's childhood home filled my head. Jack stepping out of the car in his wrinkled suit, bending over with outstretched arms to catch a running Anna and hold her. Anna giggling when he pretended that his arms were stuck, and he couldn't let her go. Eventually, she'd wiggle free and come back to playing with me, a smile toying at her lips for the rest of the afternoon.

"It was an accident," Anna choked into the phone. I wanted to know more, but I realized Anna was in no condition to talk and the details could wait. I mistakenly assumed she was referring to a car accident—I had seen too many at the emergency room. It was an all-too-common form of sudden death.

"Oh, Anna, I'm so sorry." The inadequacy of my words was tempered by the anguish in my voice. "Where are you?"

"I'm home, at my mom's house." Anna paused, exhaling a long breath, gaining composure. "Doctor Ben drove Mom to school so she could tell me."

"Okay, I'm coming to you as soon as I can. Let me make some arrangements. I'll call you right back and let you know when I can be there. Oh, honey, will you be alright?" I asked. Anna didn't answer; she didn't need to. I knew the answer was 'no,' but I didn't know what else to say.

Two days later, I arrived in Bell's Lake. Anna opened the front door to her mother's house wearing an oversized pullover that I assumed had belonged to her dad. Even though Anna had inherited Jack's height, the pullover overwhelmed her slim frame. The knit fabric, far heavier than was needed for the spring weather, looked as if it was physically weighing her down. Her face was red and blotchy from crying. She began shaking when she saw me and then collapsed into my arms.

"Where's your mom?" I asked, releasing Anna slowly and walking her to the living room.

Anna gestured upstairs with her head as we sat together on the sofa.

"So, what exactly happened?" I asked. Anna had given me an abbreviated version of Jack's death in our many phone conversations over the past two days, but it always ended with her hard sobbing that made conversation impossible. She was able to convey that I had been wrong about the car accident; an even more insidious demon had caused Jack's death. Now that we were together, she relayed the story again, the final version uninterrupted.

"He was always a drinker, you know? The life of the party." She threw a used tissue on the floor where it joined a pile of others. "He couldn't handle being alone." She bent her knees and gathered her legs toward her torso, making herself small enough to fit on a single sofa cushion. "We don't know much, just that he was alone and drinking heavily. His TV was on, the volume was turned up loud, and sometime after midnight, his neighbors at the condo called the police to complain about the noise and to say that no one was answering the door. The cops found an empty bottle of Johnny Walker Black next to his hand. He was sitting in his reclining chair, leaning back." She drew in a breath and swallowed before continuing. "He choked on his own vomit," she said, looking at me with puffy red eyes. She looked like she was drowning in her tears. "Oh, Amy, there was no note, but I can't help thinking he did this on purpose."

"No," I replied in a hushed tone, "he wouldn't do that." I paused, feeling Anna's conclusion take root in my head. "He wouldn't do that to you," I repeated the words without feeling conviction behind them.

"You're right," Anna said, shaking her head as if to clear it. "My dad wouldn't have done this on purpose." Her words were unconvincing, but still, once said, the words negated the implication of suicide. Jack's death was an accident. Period. Anna would never say words like that again.

Platitudes rose to my lips and dissolved there like sour candy.

"I don't know what to say," I said simply, opening my arms wide. Anna let go of her legs and leaned into me.

"There is nothing to say," she mumbled, crying on my shoulder.

Eventually, her tears slowed, and she sat back, giving me the details of the funeral. She talked about the blundering funeral director that recognized her. We had gone to elementary school with his son, and he wanted to know where she was going to college. When she answered, he seemed impressed and asked her how she liked Penn State.

"As if I could think about making small talk." Anna spat out her words, her disgust obvious. She told me about how when her mom identified Jack's body at the morgue, she wouldn't let Doctor Ben come in the room with her. Anna recalled getting a note from her residence advisor in the middle of class that her mom was coming to school and that, without explanation, she should go and wait in her room until her mom got there. Anna's thoughts tumbled out in half-formed sentences that drifted, not tethered to a timeline. The disbelief she felt, even as her mom cried that her dad was gone. Her last conversation with him, how she'd been late for class and promised to call him back, but she never did and how that felt so clichéd now. She talked about how when she went to buy a pair of nylons to wear to the funeral, she cried as she stood in line to pay, stunned that the world had kept on spinning, people buying clothes, cash registers ringing, radios playing, when it all should have stopped. The world should have stopped and acknowledged that her dad had departed from it, but it didn't. I listened. It was all I could do.

Anna touched my shoulder as I turned to leave. "Thank you, Amy, I'm lucky I have you," Anna offered me a forced smile, but I saw it fade as the front door closed.

• • •

The gravesite was quiet except for the sounds of Anna's tender crying. A group of about thirty people stood uncomfortably close under the black funeral home canopy, hushed, waiting for the service to begin. The air was mild and warm, smelling vaguely of fresh dirt and budding flowers. Sweat bees, thin as needles with their tiny wings fluttering, were swatted away surreptitiously. The minster began speaking and his solemn words, sounding stanch and rehearsed, rolled off my ears. My parents stood on either side of me, my mom's arm around my shoulders and my dad firmly holding my hand. I couldn't bring myself to look at the closed casket. While my family wasn't flawless, the thought of losing any one of them was just too difficult to fathom. Instead, I watched Anna. She alternated between leaning on her mom and standing up straight, pushing her mom away. Doctor Ben stood with them, looking miserable and awkward, occasionally patting Renée on the back, but not daring to touch Anna.

The minister ended the service by inviting friends and family to take a bouquet of Jack's favorite flowers and approach the casket to say their final goodbyes. That is when I saw them, the unbearable tribute to father and daughter. Bouquets of two and three daisies held together with shiny black ribbons. Anna saw them too, her eyes opening wide, a stabbing pain shaking her to her core. She was his Daisy Jane. I broke free from my parents and grabbed Anna, turning her away from the flowers and holding her fiercely as she cried.

"It's okay," I whispered, not knowing what else to say. Tears streamed down my own face. I closed my eyes and pulled her closer. "It'll be okay," I said, using the very words I swore I wouldn't. The words I knew weren't true.

CHAPTER 3

December 1997

My family was never one for subtlety when it came to Christmas decorations, *and this year is no exception*, I thought to myself as I stepped outside my car and stopped to admire the lively, blinking spectacle that was my parents' house. The entire street seemed to be in competition giving the suburban neighborhood an air of festivity so sweet, you could taste it, like bits of candy cane stuck in your teeth. Behind me, Anna's childhood home was the single outlier. The sparse decorations, each window demurely lit with a single plastic candle and the homemade wreath of pinecones on the door were the Kildare family's traditional holiday decorations, but this year the effect was solemn. The burned-out bulb in a string of lights, which I wished I could fix.

I shook off the sadness and headed to my parents' front door. Once inside, the first person I saw was Charlie, Samantha's husband, balancing a platter of sliced turkey on top of a can of Coors.

"Hey, Scrubs," he greeted me affectionately. I had earned the nickname when I showed up for a happy-hour blind date with one of Charlie's college friends wearing my hospital scrubs. His friend later joked to Charlie that contrary to the sexy nurse he envisioned, he was greeted with an actual nurse, and 'sexy' wasn't the word he would use to describe the indistinct stain he saw on my shoulder.

"It's the reason I was late," I had told my date when he asked. He laughed but glanced uncomfortably at the stain while we drank cocktails and did not suggest we transition the date from drinks into dinner as I'd hoped.

"Hey, Charlie." I kissed his cheek carefully so as not to throw off his balancing act. "Am I the last one here?"

"The usual suspects are in there," he said, gesturing with his head toward the kitchen as he continued walking to the dining room, the aroma of turkey drifting behind him making me feel like a cartoon character who could be lifted off her feet and dragged by the smell.

"Merry Christmas," I announced, walking into the kitchen, hugging my mom, dad, and Sam before settling into a chair at the table. The room held the pleasant warmth from the overloaded oven. I shrugged off my cardigan, stowing it on the back of my chair, and joined in the chatter while my mom bustled around us, brushing off our offers to help her.

At dinner, my mom asked conversationally, "Will you get to see Anna while you're home?"

"No, Anna's going to spend the day with her family, but she is leaving tomorrow on a vacation with her new boyfriend, Paul. They are going skiing in the Poconos."

"Have you met him?" Sam asked.

"Not yet,"

"I'm sure Anna could use the time away," Mom said, "although I know Renée would have loved to have her stay home at this time of year, considering…." My mom's voice drifted off.

Anna had been living with her mom since the funeral. As far as I knew, Anna returned to Penn State only once, a few days before graduation, to pick up her things. She had been doing well in all her classes, and her professors waived her final exams. She didn't even walk in her graduation ceremony, something I hoped she wouldn't regret one day.

"Well, you know, Anna and her mom, it's…"—I searched for the right words—"it's hard for them to be together now that Anna's moving out. Anna's mom wants her to stay, but neither of them are really happy, especially in that house."

Anna's mom had been planning to redecorate after the divorce. "New paint and new furniture for her new life," she had declared to her daughter. Anna and her mom shared a weakness for interior design. Back when Anna was still in high school, the two of them could spend hours together holding paint samples against throw pillows, debating the perfect base and accent colors for each room. Now, Renée refused to change a thing. She went through Jack's belongings at his apartment, carting home bags of his things like found treasure. She put their wedding portrait back on the living room mantle where it had stood for more than two decades. Even Jack's keys, hanging from his weathered leather keychain printed with the Prime Laboratories logo, were returned to the ceramic bowl in the foyer. If any of these things made Doctor Ben uneasy, he didn't say anything.

"Anyway," I said, turning to Sam, "what's new with you guys?"

Sam and Charlie exchanged knowing smiles. "We have a special present for the family this year," she said.

My mom squealed excitedly as I said, "No way," in a low whisper, not wanting to jinx what I thought she was implying. Sam grinned, looking down at her belly for the slightest second before confirming the good news.

"Yes, we are having a baby!" The happiness in Sam's voice was undeniable, but she sounded like she'd been practicing that sentence for a bit longer than she'd been pregnant.

"Oh, oh, a baby." My mom's hands flew to her face, her palms cradling her cheeks. "I'm so happy for you," she stood and threw her arms around my sister. Her eyes glistened as she pulled back to kiss her cheek. My dad joined in, embracing Sam from the side without standing up, saying, "Well, isn't that something."

"Aw, I'm going to be an aunt!" I was already pushing my way around the table, waiting for my turn to congratulate my sister. I hugged her and gave Charlie's shoulder an affectionate pat as I squeezed behind him on my way back to my seat. "Congratulations, you two," I said, sitting down again. "When are you due?" I asked.

"July 27."

I quickly did the math; it was still early in the pregnancy. "How have you been feeling? You're taking prenatal vitamins, right?"

"I feel a little nausea," Sam said. "I can't seem to keep anything down in the morning, but I'm starving by lunch. My doctor told me to stop eating tuna, something about mercury? And lunchmeat. I don't know. Anyway, what do you think, Amy? Can I still eat tuna? You know how much I love it."

"Oh, tuna is fine. I ate it all the time with both of you," my mom said as she took a sip of her water and rolled her eyes.

"Well, not really, Mom, they've discovered that—"

"Maybe you'd like to switch seats?" Charlie said, and I realized I was leaning over his plate, practically touching his green bean casserole with my elbow to talk to my mom and Sam.

"Yeah, sure," I said distractedly, standing up again and picking up my plate.

"I wasn't really serious," Charlie said in the direction of my dad, who was the only person at the table paying attention to him, "but, okay, I guess I'll—"

Dad stifled a laugh.

"Move," I said, nudging Charlie without looking at him. "Mom, tuna isn't safe, it *can* have high levels of mercury." I continued talking as Charlie and I clumsily changed places.

"Just eat," my dad said to Charlie as he settled in his new spot. "And get used to it." Dad knocked his beer can against Charlie's and saluted him with it before taking a sip.

After dinner, we insisted that my mom take a break while the rest of us cleaned up. Charlie and my dad brought the dirty plates into the kitchen while Sam and I washed them by hand, not trusting my parents' wedding china to the old dishwasher.

"Any luck with the house hunting?" I asked Sam as we finished drying the dishes. After she graduated college, Sam had moved to a small apartment in Havertown, Pennsylvania. Havertown was bigger than Bell's Lake and close enough to Philadelphia to have the runoff of big-city amenities that our hometown lacked, including entry-level job opportunities. When Sam and Charlie got married, he moved into her apartment and commuted to his job in Center City, Philadelphia. I knew they had recently hired a realtor and now I understood why.

"Not yet," Sam said, sounding a little frustrated. "Mom said that you're going to keep rooming with Gail?" Sam looked to me for confirmation, and I nodded. After I graduated from college, I knew that I wouldn't move back to Bell's Lake. The only hospital in town was stiflingly close to my parents' house and the pool of other nursing jobs was frighteningly shallow. Moving to Philadelphia was the logical choice, but it was an elective class in photography that sparked my love affair with the City of Brotherly Love. My class took a field trip from Bloomsburg, our small college town, to Philadelphia. Our assignment had been street photography, candid photographs of public places. The three-hour drive began before sunrise, and the coming of day mirrored the change in landscape from country roads to highways to Interstate 76, the Schuylkill Expressway—known to the locals as the "Sure-Kill Expressway." We sat in the morning traffic before descending into the city's heart via its concrete arteries, the cars starting and stopping like pulsing blood. Once we arrived, I remember walking the length and breadth of downtown, seeing it in a different light than my previous trips to the city. Class trips to see the liberty bell or my family's annual excursion to watch the holiday light show at Wanamaker's always centered on getting to a landmark, making Philadelphia feel like a destination, not a place where people lived the everyday. But that day changed my perspective. As I photographed everywhere from the expensive brownstones near Society

Hill to the graffiti-covered abandoned warehouses at the waterfront, each picture made me more certain. For the first time, I felt it. I wanted to live in Philadelphia. I was overjoyed when I landed a job at Philadelphia Hospital.

When I suggested to Gail, who was also offered a nursing position at Philadelphia Hospital, that we rent a place together, she reluctantly agreed. She was hoping to move in with her boyfriend, but he wasn't quite willing to take their relationship to the next level. I was working under the assumption that when Anna was ready to leave her mom's house, Anna and I would be roommates, so Gail and I negotiated a six-month lease instead of the usual year. I was surprised when Anna told me that she had found a place of her own. The deadline on my lease with Gail was rapidly approaching, and since she was still in the same slow-moving relationship, we recently extended our lease.

Reading my mind, Sam said, "I kinda thought that you would be getting a place with Anna."

"I know," I replied, realizing again how much it hurt that Anna hadn't thought of it. "Anna's been so distant lately. She didn't even tell me that she was looking for an apartment, but Gail and I made it through the last six months together. We make a good fit. Besides, Gail spends a lot of time with her boyfriend, Quinn."

"Speaking of boyfriends, when are you going to get one of those?" Sam said, teasing me.

"Why? Does Charlie have someone else in mind?" I asked eagerly.

Sam laughed. "No, I think you scarred him for life; he'll never set someone up again." Sam smiled prettily as she remembered the story that had become family lore.

"Sam, your skin looks great. I can't help it, I have to use the words: you're glowing."

"Prenatal vitamins are the real secret. My hair actual shines," she said, flipping a curl dramatically off her shoulder. "I should start modeling now before the vomiting stage ends and I actually gain some weight. I could make some big bucks."

I laughed. "Let's take some pictures of you and Charlie tomorrow. We can go to the lake," I said. "Around four? The lighting will be perfect."

"I'd love that. Thanks, Ames," Sam said with genuine gratitude. I nudged her affectionately as we carried the plates to the dining room and stacked them in the china cabinet.

Later, drifting in and out of sleep in my old bedroom, memories of the months preceding Sam's wedding popped into my head. Sam had been a diva as a bride, stressing over every detail, calling my mom multiple times a day with demands. When I tried to talk to my mom about asserting herself to Sam, my mom was not, after all, being paid to be Sam's wedding planner, my mom brushed it off. "Sam has always needed more consideration," she explained, as if attention from one's mom was based on necessity. During that time, Anna was there for me, taking my side when I complained that the wedding was getting out of hand. After the wedding, Sam calmed for a while, seemingly content to go to Charlie to fill her bottomless demands for attention. But with a baby, would Sam again monopolize my family? I quickly pushed this thought away. I was happy about the baby and as a new mom, Sam *would* need help. That was an undeniable fact and I chided myself for being selfish. Sam and I had gotten along so well tonight. But with Sam it was always one extreme or the other. I was either the best, couldn't-live-without-you sister or a nuisance to be cast aside. Restless, I rolled over and willed sleep until new images worked their way into my subconscious. A glimpse of my plate with half-eaten turkey from dinner folded seamlessly into a memory of Anna and I dressed as American Indians, waiting to be ushered on stage with our classmates in our second grade Thanksgiving play. As I became submerged in the dream, I could feel my stomach flip-flopping with the anticipation of standing on the stage, all the parents' eyes on us, eagerly waiting to hear our song. In that moment, Anna, terrified, had grabbed my hand the way she did that first day of kindergarten. I woke with a jolt, clenching my empty hand but still feeling how my own nervous anticipation dissipated when I focused on her.

• • •

A storm passed through during the night. I would say that it woke me up, but I wasn't sleeping. I don't sleep well anymore. It was an angry summer storm, sharp cracks of lightning followed by rumbling thunder. The rain sounded like broken glass thrown against the windows, as if demanding to be let inside. Breaking tree branches and howling wind added to the cacophony. No, I couldn't sleep.

I prefer winter storms. Quiet snow that falls peacefully and covers the dirt in layers of pure white instead of washing it away. Trees frozen in place, their branches slick and heavy with a coating of clear ice that melts in the sun and drips soundlessly back to the ground. When a winter storm passes through, everything stays in its place.

I have fond memories of snow days in elementary school. School closing would be announced on the radio. Anna would come to my house right after breakfast. My dad would answer the door and announce that the other half of the "double-A battery pack" was here. Anna would wait for me on the entryway rug, not wanting to drag snow farther into the house while I finished zipping my boots. Year after year, she wore her favorite pink earmuffs, the same bright color as the flying saucer her dad bought her on one of his business trips. The earmuffs perfectly framed her delicate face. I wore whatever coat my sister had outgrown and forced my unruly hair under a knit hat.

There was a hill nearby that was popular for sledding. It started with a moderate slope, plateaued, and then fell off into a steeper slope that ended perpendicular to Farmer's Hill Road. Kids would sled down the hill, laughing as their stomached dropped like a roller-coaster ride. At the bottom of the hill, we took turns keeping watch and yelling a warning if a car came down the road. From the top, you could see the markers of our shared childhoods. The public swimming pool that was covered in blue tarps for the winter; the top of the flag that flew in front of the elementary school was just visible over the trees. Behind us stood the deep, dense woods, where we played endless games, building forts and treehouses. Later, we used the same structures to hide while we smoked and drank in the twilight years between teen and adult life. But memories of snow days were wrapped in the happy mist of cottony white nostalgia. Except for one.

I was eleven years old, and school had been cancelled due to the weather. Anna and I spent the morning sledding, but by lunchtime, the tedium of trudging up the hill for the momentary thrill of sledding down was wearing thin. Even at that young age, Anna knew how to draw people to her, and she had been flirting with a boy I liked all morning. He obviously shared the attraction with Anna, and I pretended not to care, but the feelings inside me festered. It was the first of many times that I would be jealous of her, but in that moment, the feeling was unfamiliar to me. An irritation, like sandpaper on my skin that had turned raw and itchy under my wet clothes.

Anna climbed on my sled and called for the boy to watch her. I stood, self-consciously feeling my body looking short and square next to Anna's long, lean frame. Anna gracefully folded herself on the sled and asked me to give her an extra hard push. My built-up annoyance came out in one fluid motion as I shoved her fiercely down the hill. I regretted it as soon as I felt Anna slip away from me, my hands releasing from her back. For a moment, my outstretched hands hung in the air like I was casting a spell. That is when I heard the refrain of "Car!" from the bottom of the hill.

Anna looked at me over her shoulder for the briefest moment on the plateau between the slopes; she was going too fast to stop and she was paralyzed with fear. Her blue eyes were wide and unblinking. Her mouth dropped open and her neck constricted, preparing for a scream that caught in her throat. She clutched the sides of the sled with her gloved fingers and ducked her head at the last second as she started to descend the second slope, her body tensing and preparing for a crash. She disappeared over the side.

The oncoming car skidded and swerved, missing Anna by inches. As I looked up at the darkening sky, the clear blue from earlier now *obscured by lead-colored clouds, I let out a childish-sounding sob. My only thought was,* How could I live without her?

CHAPTER 4

March 1998

Anna and I sipped our beers as we sat at the outdoor tables for Slackers, a bar on South Street. South Street ran east to west on the southern border of Philly's Center City district. It hosted a mix of local shops, restaurants, and bars that tried to keep their authentically alternative vibe alive against the influx of wealthy hipsters and upscale chain stores. Although we complained that it had too many tourists, South Street had quickly become our go-to meeting place and Slackers was our bar. It was a gritty hole in the wall that had survived gentrification without raising the price of beer and offered little in the way of ambiance in return. There were four outdoor tables, two on either side of the doorway, fitted snugly against the building to allow for the flow of pedestrians up and down the sidewalk.

It was a rare warm March evening, the kind that promises spring after the interminable Philadelphia winter. Anna and I sat on chairs facing the street, our backs against the brick wall. Anna was looking impatiently for Paul Callaghan, her boyfriend, whom I was meeting for the first time today. It was almost seven in the evening and the eclectic blend of South Street patrons were just beginning to arrive. By eight, the street would be crowded, but for now, there was little blocking the cityscape of hand-painted signs hanging on the brightly colored townhouses-turned-businesses lining the street. It felt to me as if Anna and I hadn't met for drinks in ages. Anna had been reclusive all last summer, held captive by grief, preferring that I visit her in Bell's Lake rather than traveling to see me in the city. She started coming to Philly more frequently in the fall, meeting Paul on one of her visits. Their relationship started out as long distance, seemingly not too serious until late December. After their vacation together, Anna took a job as a proofreader that barely covered her rent but got her out of her mom's house and moved her to the city. Still, it bothered me that she'd been dating him for nearly five months, and I hadn't met him yet.

But tonight, I could feel things slipping into place like the interlocking pieces of a puzzle. I was happily in my element, hanging out at Slackers with Anna, who was looking brighter than she had in months. As the sunlight faded to ginger bands across the sky, street-lights popped on in the shadows. The golden hour was giving way to twilight.

"Man, I wish I had my camera," I said, looking longingly at the storefront for the Garland of Letters bookstore. The vibrant colors of the sunset lingered artfully on the glass, mixing with the abundance of silk flowers in their window display. Anna smiled but didn't answer, her thoughts distracted as she searched for Paul in the ever-growing hum of people.

A few weeks earlier, on a whim, I took my camera to Giovanni's, the family-owned pizzeria in my neighborhood. Gail and I ordered pizza from there so often, I just had to call and say, "Hey, it's Amy," and "Hey, Amy, the usual?" was the predictable response, the words as comforting as the food. In a city of neighborhoods, I was grateful Giovanni's was nestled in mine.

When I asked Antonio, the owner and patriarch, if he minded if I took some pictures of his family while they worked, he replied, "Us? Sure! Me and my boys, Amy, you ain't gonna find no better beefcake in this city." He gestured with his hands as he spoke and his accent, a blend of Italian and Philadelphian, chopped his words, hitting the consonants hard, mimicking the sound of his knife knocking deftly against the cutting board. As I put the camera to my eye, his three sons started posing, flexing their muscles under the bleached white T-shirts that served as their uniform, and hamming it up for the camera. I took a few shots before the phone rang and the door chimed as a family with two small children walked in. They were greeted with plastic-coated menus and directed to their seats. As business returned to normal, I continued to take candid pictures.

I hung my favorite photo from that afternoon in my kitchen. In the photograph, Antonio was spinning pizza dough behind the glass counter. The dough was high above his flour-covered fingers, his muscular arms stretching upward. He was looking up, his head tilted back; his curly black hair, slicked back with Brylcreem, was just starting to show streaks of gray. Wiry black stubble coated his neck and chin, and his faded red apron was dusty with flour. In the background, his oldest son, also named Antonio, was standing in front of a tower of empty pizza boxes, expertly folding one in his hands. He looked directly at me as I snapped the photograph. He was smiling, his straight teeth gleaming white against his olive skin. In his eyes was the expression of a man who knows he's sexy, flirting with the camera.

Still waiting for Paul to show, Anna's knee bounced impatiently under the table, making it rattle, a habit of hers I had learned to tolerate. I looked down the street to where musicians were busking, their music gentle and unobtrusive. The male guitarist sat cross-legged on the sidewalk strumming tenderly, his attention solely on the woman in a long peasant skirt who sat next to him, her hand on his knee. She sang with her eyes closed, the words taking her back to a time marked by peace signs and tie-dye shirts, a wistful longing for an era that ended well before her life began. The guitar case was open in front of them. Inside, the dollar bills shook as if they wanted to escape on the breeze but held fast under a strategically placed rock.

"There he is!" Anna said, startling me with her sudden outburst. She pointed to a man walking toward us and gave him a quick wave. He was tall, about six feet, and his posture was rigidly straight. He was wearing a tight black T-shirt that stretched across his wide shoulders and hugged his flat stomach above his camouflage shorts. His hair was dark and cut military short, mostly hidden under a baseball cap. Anna had told me that Paul was around five years older than us, but his boyish face didn't show his age. The blue-black ink of a tattoo peeked out from beneath the sleeve of his shirt on his bulging bicep.

"Hey," he said, leaning down to greet Anna with a quick kiss on the cheek. He extended his hand to me. "I'm Paul. Nice to meet you."

"Amy," I said, smiling and returning his firm handshake. I resisted the urge to make a joke about him breaking my fingers. Paul turned his chair backwards, spinning it on one leg, and sat with his legs in a straddle, his arms resting over the top of the chair. The waitress who had been leaning against the doorframe, admiring Paul as he approached, came directly to our table.

"What can I get you?" she asked. Her eyes were lined with heavy black eyeliner and mascara so thick and clumpy, her eyelids drooped under the weight.

"What do you have on tap?" Paul asked, and the waitress recited the list from memory, a shiny silver ball on her pierced tongue clicking against her teeth as she spoke. Paul ordered a Miller. He took off his baseball cap and put it on the table, running a hand through his unmovable hair.

"Why were you late?" Anna asked, sounding a little annoyed.

"I'm not late," Paul replied looking at his watch for conformation. "We said seven-fifteen." I was sure that Anna told me that we were meeting Paul at seven, but it didn't seem worth it to argue. I felt Anna tense, so I started talking before she could reply.

"Interesting tattoo." I gestured to his arm.

"Yeah?" his voice rose slightly, assessing my interest and pulling his sleeve up so that I could get a better look. The tattoo was a pair of wings joined by a parachute with the letters AA in the middle. Above the wings the words 'Desert Storm' were written in clear block letters. The waitress reached around him and placed his beer on the table, hovering for a second more than was necessary as the sticky froth ran down the sides of the glass.

"Army Airborne," he said, answering my unasked question when the waitress left. "Joined the army straight out of high school and served for two years before becoming a paratrooper. First combat jump," he said, pointing to the words. "I was in the 82nd Airborne Division," he said with obvious pride.

"Army Airborne, wow!" I commented before taking a sip of my beer that had warmed and tasted flat. It suddenly occurred to me that Anna had told me little about Paul.

"Yup, five years. I didn't stay in," Paul volunteered.

"Oh. Why not?" I thought it was a harmless question, but Paul's face changed so quickly that I regretted asking.

"After Desert Storm, I was stationed in Fort Bragg in North Carolina. Some liberal jackoff at a bar saw my tattoo and started in on us, asking us how it felt to bomb innocents." Paul paused, raising his glass and taking a sizeable swallow, his Adam's apple bouncing up and down. He lowered the glass and continued. "I don't even know what the hell he was doing there. It was an army bar, a place for us to go to blow off steam without having to watch our 'political correctness' and all that bullshit. Anyway—"Paul was getting agitated by the memory—"it got heated. It came down to respect, and this guy wasn't showing it. So, I punched him. The guy completely overreacted. He pressed charges, and I was out of the army." Paul shrugged as if he was long past the resentment, but the muscles in his arms were tight and his fists were clenched with his unspoken denial.

"I had no idea the army was so strict."

"Yeah," Paul said. "Fucking zero tolerance," he added with disdain. He picked up his beer and took another agitated swallow that left foam trapped in the late-day stubble of his upper lip. He put his beer roughly back on the table and wiped off the foam with disgust, flicking it off his fingers onto the grimy sidewalk.

"Paul's working for a security firm now," Anna said, clearly wanting to change the subject. "But he still jumps on the weekends for Blue Skies Skydiving, doing jump training and tandem jumps. I'm thinking of doing a tandem jump with him."

"You're kidding," I said, a bemused smile breaking across my face.

"No," Anna said giving me a questioning look. We exchanged confused glances until I couldn't hold back any longer.

"You *hate* to fly! You freaked out riding Flying Dumbo at Disney!" I blurted out.

"Oh please," Anna retorted as if this were ancient history. "We were kids!"

"It was a graduation trip," I countered, "from *high* school. We were adults."

"Well," Anna said, "luckily, if I jump, I'll be attached to *Paul*, who is *not* a two-ton metal elephant. Amy, those things were destined to crash. I could feel mine giving way." She laughed self-effacingly at the memory. I looked at Paul to get his attention, but he didn't react.

"Paul, she screamed so loud, she made the little boy in front of her cry." I reached out and touched his arm, snickering. Paul looked down at my hand, and I quickly removed it.

"Which kind of set off a chain reaction with the other kids," Anna said, blushing slightly.

"They stopped the ride!" I added, leaning toward Paul with a boisterous laugh that he didn't return.

"I was glad that I had my mouse ears on so I could cover my face," Anna said, and my mind traveled to the memory of Anna stepping off the ride, pulling the ridiculously childish hat down low over her head.

"Unfortunately," I added, giggling with anticipation at the next part of the story, "the ears had 'Anna' embroidered across the back. So, all the kids knew her name. Well, the ones who were old enough to read." My words were broken up with laughter and Anna continued to snicker, shoulders shaking.

Paul gave me a weak smile and drank what was left in his glass. He seemed to be waiting for us to finish. I felt suddenly uncomfortable, and my laughter died away.

"So," I said clearing my throat, returning my attention to Anna, "are you really going to jump?"

"I think so," she said, giving Paul a pert, excited look.

"If you do, you'll have to take it seriously, Anna," Paul said.

"Oh, of course." But her voice had turned as flat as my beer.

"Sounds like fun," I said but neither of them acknowledged the sarcasm. An awkward silence filled the table, and I wondered what Anna saw in this guy. The pierced waitress came over and took our orders for a second round and I hoped that the night would get better.

• • •

January 1999

"Where are you going, all dressed up?" Gail, my roommate, asked as I walked through the living room. She was curled up on the sofa painting her nails a pale pink that complemented her warm brown skin. Her tight corkscrew curls were held behind her ears with a headband. Gail considered makeup necessary only for special occasions. Today obviously didn't qualify, but her pretty features didn't need it.

"Huh?" I said, looking down at my long-sleeve T-shirt, faded jeans, and worn boots. I was decidedly *not* dressed up.

"You're wearing lipstick," Gail said. I laughed and rubbed my lips together.

"C'mon, am I that bad?" I asked.

"Yes. Yes, you are."

"Well, I'm meeting Anna and Paul to watch the Super Bowl," I told her as I put on my coat. I wrapped a scarf around my neck, took it off, and rewrapped it, buying time.

"You? Wearing lipstick and *voluntarily* watching football?" Gail sat up straighter, careful not to smudge the polish.

"It's Paul," I said. "Now that they're married, I need to make an effort, you know? I barely saw Anna over the holidays. Actually, I've barely seen Anna at all since they got married in September, and that was months ago."

I thought back to the day Anna told me she had eloped with Paul. We were meeting for what I thought was going to be a quick uneventful lunch near her office. We planned to sit outside and enjoy the crisp autumn day, but when I got to the restaurant she had picked, the outside dining area was closed. The inside felt inappropriately dark for lunchtime, a narrow room dominated by an oak bar that ran the length of the side wall. I took a seat in a booth facing the door. There were only a few other patrons, seated in seclusion, steadfastly ignoring one another, and looking stubbornly sad, like they had somewhere important to be but were drawn here instead. The sound of pool balls colliding reverberated from the back room. I was just about to leave; my intention was to intercept Anna and find a different place for us to have lunch. But before I could stand up, Anna arrived. She came directly to me without saying a word and held out her left hand. I instantly saw the diamond ring on her finger as the door behind her edged closed.

"You're engaged?" I asked, astonished.

"Not just engaged," she said with a sly smile, "Paul and I got married!"

I stood up and lifted her hand toward my face to get a better look. There they were, the double layer of rings, one for the engagement and one for the marriage, looking large and cumbersome on Anna's slim finger.

"What?" I said, my voice deep with disbelief.

"It's true! We did it! Call me 'Mrs. Callaghan.'"

"Get out!" I was frozen in place, blinking at her with my mouth gaping open. I was utterly stunned, and I could feel worry building inside of me, making my stomach burn. Something about this didn't feel right. I was still digesting the news while Anna bounced excitedly up and down and talking rapidly. As she spoke, I was reminded of Anna as a little girl, dancing around my bedroom in my communion veil playing 'wedding' with me. We would take turns wearing my veil because Anna's mom wouldn't let her play with hers. We walked down an imaginary aisle holding plastic flowers that we stole from a vase in my parents' foyer. After we each had a turn being the bride, we'd collapse on my bed and talk about the real weddings we would have someday.

"We decided to just, you know, do it. Once I start my new job, I won't have much time off," Anna continued talking, taking a seat on a barstool that was conveniently nearby. I followed suit, still in denial. Anna had just accepted a job as a writer at a small magazine called *Back to Basics*, or *BTB* for short. It was a self-help magazine with a bent toward simpler living. Anna had written a freelance piece on vacationing on a budget, featuring free and almost-free attractions in Philadelphia area. I helped Anna with her research, going with her to book readings and After-Five Fridays at the Philadelphia Museum of Art. The article was well received, and when the editor asked Anna to join the *BTB* staff full time, Anna leapt at the opportunity.

"And I'm moving into Paul's brownstone apartment, which is closer to work and walking distance to you!" she said, squealing with happiness.

"What about your lease? I thought we were going to find a place to live together when our leases are up at the end of the year."

"Were we?" Anna tilted her head. I couldn't believe that Anna had forgotten.

"Yes." I answered exasperated. "We talked about doing it sooner when you got the new job, but you told me you couldn't break your lease."

"Well, I did have to pay an early termination fee, but it wasn't that much. Besides, it's not as if my *husband* and I are going to live apart."

"Even so, you didn't have to get married; you could have just moved in together," I said thinking again of the wedding day plans we made as girls down to the smallest details. White ball gowns with sequined heart-shaped necklines and long trains. Our moms would cry during the father–daughter dance. That's when it hit me. Her perfect wedding would never happen without her dad, and the elopement started to make sense.

"Live together before marriage? Mom would never approve, you know that. She's a traditionalist, well, when it comes to *my* relationships. Go figure. She was sad enough that we eloped, but she's planning a small reception for us in a few weeks. Aren't you going to ask me for details?" she said. A little of the hurt that she'd been trying to hide at my lack of enthusiasm broke through her voice.

I struggled to rally behind my words. "Yes, of course! So, how did he propose?"

"Well, you know how Paul was planning that weekend scuba diving trip in Cancun with Evan?"

I nodded, although I'm sure I wasn't aware of Paul's plans at all. My mind twitched with foreboding, but I locked a smile on my face as I listened.

"Well," she continued, "Evan had to back out at the last minute. They already had the plane ticket and hotel, so Paul asked me to buy Evan's share." Without thinking, I raised an eyebrow questioningly and Anna stuttered, "I mean, to come along instead. Anyway, after looking at the pictures of the resort, I commented that it would make a beautiful honeymoon spot, but I wasn't hinting, I swear. Paul looked at me and said, 'You know, you're right. Marry me, sweetheart,' and I said yes!" She paused for a moment to flag down the bartender. "Two glasses of champagne! We are celebrating!"

Unfazed, the bartender nodded and turned away from us.

"So," Anna continued, "I knew I would tell you if I saw you and that's why I cancelled lunch last Tuesday. You told me you had to work through the weekend, but I was still nervous that I would run into you before that and spoil the surprise. We were officially married by the magistrate on Friday, and we drove straight to the airport. We didn't make a big deal out of it, but I did wear a white dress and a clerk took our picture." She carefully pulled an envelope from her purse, slid out a picture, and handed it to me. For the first time, I noticed that her nose was freshly sunburnt and peeling slightly. I studied the picture. Anna's dress was unembellished, simple and understated, accentuated with a delicate white silk wrap, a concession to the changing season. Paul was standing at her side in his typically rigid military posture, but his face was relaxed, and his smile looked genuine.

"You look beautiful," I said truthfully, handing the picture back to her.

"I wish you could have been there, Amy," Anna said, her eyes tearing suddenly. "It was just—" She trailed off as I cut in. I put my hand over hers. It was already done.

"So, this is going to be one hell of a party that your mom is throwing, right?" I said, in an attempt to bring Anna out of her descending melancholy.

"Yeah." Anna looked up and wiped her index finger swiftly under her eyes to stop her mascara from running. "Yes, will you help us plan it?"

"Will Renée let me?" I teased. Calling Anna's mom by her first name was something I only dared to do behind her back, an old joke that seemed to help lift Anna's spirits up, placing the conversation on familiar ground again.

"As long as you agree with her plans, we'll be fine." The champagne arrived in wine glasses instead of champagne flutes. Anna seemed not to notice as she raised her glass and we toasted.

"To the happy couple," I said as our glasses clinked clumsily.

"Oh," Anna said after swallowing hard. "I brought a notebook so I could write down some ideas." She pulled a pink journal from her purse. It was held shut with a silk ribbon tied in a shoelace bow. Anna unraveled the knot in one pull of the ribbon's end and opened the book to a fresh page and so we could begin planning.

At the time, Anna had said she wanted to wait until after the holidays to have the party, but it was now the end of January, and she still hadn't settled on a date. I was concerned about her dwindling enthusiasm whenever we talked about the it. Maybe I could bring it up again at the Super Bowl party tonight.

"So, how are Barbie and GI Joe?" Gail's boyfriend, Quinn, asked as he walked in from the kitchen carrying a bag of chips and two bottles of beers. He sat down next to Gail, putting the beers and the chips on the coffee table. They exchanged a quick look that told me they were happy to have the apartment to themselves for a while. Gail began blowing feverishly on her nails to dry them.

"You realize," I said authoritatively, "that if Barbie's proportions were real, she wouldn't be able to walk upright because of the weight of her boobs."

"Anna seems to be doing just fine," Quinn said, wiggling his eyebrows.

"Hey!" I yelled.

Gail, holding her hands still, playfully leaned back and kicked Quinn in his side, saying, "Bad dog! Bad dog!"

Quinn winced and laughed guiltily.

"Where are you meeting them?" Gail asked. "Slackers?"

"No," I said mournfully. "A bar near Chinatown. A *sports* bar! Oh god, I don't wanna go! We had to reserve tickets just to get in! This place is going to be packed. And everyone there but me will be, well, you know, sports fans."

"Maybe you'll meet someone," Gail said. I stopped her with a look. "Or not," she amended. "Hey, at least there'll be commercials to look forward to."

"Yeah." I unenthusiastically pumped my fist in the air. "Let the good times roll."

"Do me a favor," Quinn said lightly. "Ask Paul to show you his kung fu grip." He did a fake karate chop into the air in front of him.

"Ha, ha," I said without expression and walked glumly out of the apartment.

• • •

It took several trips around the block to find a parking space. When I entered the bar, it was even more densely packed than I had anticipated. I scanned the crowd for Anna and spotted her at an empty table with coats draped over the seats. Anna had been vigilantly watching the door, and she waved me over. I jostled my way through the people and took a seat next to her. Paul was standing with one hand on the back of her chair talking to two guys. Their mannerisms and build were similar to Paul's, and I guessed that they were some of his buddies from the army.

"Paul, Amy's here," Anna said pulling at his sleeve.

Paul turned and gave me the briefest nod and a small 's'up?' before turning his attention back to his friends.

"Paul," Anna said, irritated, "introduce Amy to the guys and sit down. I'm tired of trying to save these chairs."

Paul said something to them, and the three men took seats, all facing the massive projector screen that covered the bar's windows. The resolution was poor, but it was large enough that most of the people in the bar could watch the game with little obstruction. Paul introduced me to Drew and Evan, and I shook their hands. Just as I was about to attempt some small talk, I was saved by the announcement of the kickoff. The men leaned forward, hands on their knees, eyes riveted on the screen.

"So," I said to the table, "who's playing again?"

Paul made a disgusted sound. Drew, however, took pity on me. "Denver and Atlanta," he said.

"Oh," I said unexcitedly. I could think of nothing else to add, which must have showed on my face because Drew let out a small laugh. He had a nice smile and a strong jawline. His light brown hair was buzzed close to his scalp, like Paul's. He moved his chair a little closer to mine.

"If you don't have a favorite team, you gotta root for Atlanta," he told me.

"Okay," I said, "and they would be wearing…."

"Black," Drew said, and Paul gave me a sharp look that no one else saw. Stunned, I drank my beer.

"So, why Atlanta?" I asked.

Drew started to answer but was quickly sidetracked by the game. After the play was completed, he turned back to me, blinking as if trying to remember what we were talking about. Before he could start talking, the ball was back in play and his eyes glanced guiltily to the screen.

I gave him a forgiving look and lightly touched his arm. "It's okay," I said. "Watch the game." He turned to face the game, relieved.

I stared at the television for a while, trying desperately to get into it, but football has never interested me. Anna sat with her hand on Paul's knee, commenting appropriately, her cheerleading days to her benefit. She was wearing a Falcons jersey, and I wondered when she bought it, thinking that either Paul had given it to her or the buyers for Ann Taylor had completely lost their minds. By the time the Broncos scored an 80-yard touchdown in the second quarter, the alcohol that I was consuming too quickly in response to the lack of conversation was hitting me hard. All three men yelled at the screen, arms flailing with indignation.

"You know," I said drunkenly to Drew during the three or four replays of the touchdown. "I'm getting the impression the game's not going as planned." Anna spit out some beer with a laugh and a snort. Apparently, that was too much for Paul. He violently pushed his chair back as he stood up, nearly knocking it over as he stomped away from the table. Drew looked surprised, his eyes following Paul as he walked away. Then Drew looked back at me and started to say something, but I ignored him and leaned conspiratorially toward Anna. I felt uncomfortable that I had egged Paul on with my comment and I didn't want her to feel embarrassed at his childish reaction. Although, oddly, Anna didn't seem to notice.

The game resumed, and I stretched my neck to see the game clock in the corner of the screen. "This has been the longest eleven minutes of my life," I whined quietly to Anna.

Anna moved her chair closer to mine, and we abandoned any pretense of watching the game. Finally.

"It's been a long time since we've hung out, stranger," I said.

"I know," she admitted apologetically. "Listen, I was thinking, what if we started walking together? It would be a good way for us to catch up, and we could sneak in a little exercise at the same time."

"This is an idea from *BTB*, isn't it?" I said, referring to the magazine where Anna worked.

"It is. I have to write an article on bonding with girlfriends in today's hectic world, so if we walk *and* get a latte, I can charge it to the magazine."

"Wait, did you steal that idea from *Martha Stewart Living*?"

"Dah-ling," Anna said in her best high-society accent. "We steal everything from *Martha Stewart Living*."

"Actually, walking sounds like fun. You're on." We decided to start that week. Anna and I passed the rest of the game catching up, gossiping about mutual friends, and trading work stories. The game ended with a score of 34–19, a win for the Broncos. The bar was clearing out, and Paul's mood was foul from the Falcons' loss. Evan and Drew were telling anecdotes about their army days, trying to draw Paul out, but he was inconsolable.

While our group was waiting to settle the tab, I saw Paul looking at a short, stocky guy sitting at the bar in a Broncos jersey. The man's hairline was receding on top, and his face was flushed with alcohol. He was excitedly reliving the game with his friends, high-fiving and gesturing enthusiastically. He met Paul's gaze and shrugged politely as if to say, 'Win some, lose some.' Paul's face abruptly became hard. He rubbed his hand back and forth over the hair on the top of his head while staring the guy down. The man watched Paul's hand movement, curiously at first, then with understanding. Paul was referencing the man's receding hair. Shocked, the guy sneered at Paul and looked away.

"Well, time to call it a night," Drew said, signing his credit card receipt. He stood and stretched, his untucked shirt riding up for a second to reveal a toned, flat stomach and I found it difficult to look away. I caught Anna's eye, and she gave me a mischievous wink. Evan drained the beer from his glass, leaning his head back to catch the last drops even though it was mostly foam. As I put on my coat, I caught sight of Paul in the mirror behind the bar. Paul was standing ramrod straight with his jacket zipped to the top, the ribbed collar looking uncomfortably tight around his thick neck. He was glaring at the Broncos fan and slowly, deliberately, moved his hand across the top of his head again, baiting him. The Broncos fan had had enough.

"What the fuck is your problem, man?" the man said as he threw a chair out of his way and walked toward Paul with long, angry strides. Next to Paul, the man appeared even shorter, but his chest was puffed out and he was not about to back down.

"What's going on?" Anna said anxiously. She had been oblivious to Paul's incendiary actions. She gave Paul a questioning look, but he completely ignored her. He was looking over the man's head into the middle distance, his face devoid of emotion. Evan stepped between Paul and the enraged man joining the face-off as the man's friends started walking toward us and the air thickened with tension.

"Whoa, listen, we're leaving," Drew said to the men approaching our table, holding up his palms, gesturing for them to stop, "all of us. No one wants to start anything." Everyone's eyes returned to the standoff. The Broncos fan leaned over to look around Evan at Paul and pressed his lips together, making them white with the effort. He raised his eyebrows and widened his eyes, waiting for Paul to make the next move. Paul was perfectly still. The atmosphere was strained and silent, except for the highlight reel playing in the background. I saw the bartender holding the phone in his hand, ready to call 911. Suddenly, Paul broke into a grin.

"I got no problem," he said, stepping back, and put his arm carelessly around Anna's shoulders. He moved her in a long, slow circle toward the door. Anna tucked her head under Paul's arm and avoided my eyes.

"Anna?" I called to her questioningly, but she pretended not to hear me and positioned herself closer to Paul. I wanted to call out again and stop her from leaving with him, but her reaction had me stunned. Anger flooded through me as they opened the door and walked out, letting in a blast of the frigid night air. Evan was right behind them.

"What the hell was that?" I said to Drew as we followed them outside into the bitter cold.

"Paul's had a bad night," Drew said dismissively, his warm breath turning to smoke.

"Paul *caused* a bad night. I don't want her around him."

"Her? You mean Anna? She's his wife. Why wouldn't she go with him?" Drew scoffed, as if I was completely misreading the whole situation. "It's no big deal. He's already calmed down and this has nothing to do with her. They're fine. Anyway, are you okay to drive?"

Dumbfounded I said, "Sure." The near brawl and my anxiety about Paul had my adrenaline pumping, and I felt oddly sober. "I'm parked right over here, so you don't have to walk me," I said, gesturing to my car under a streetlight, but hoping he still would.

"Okay, then. 'Night," he added over his shoulder as he jogged ahead to catch up to Anna, Paul, and Evan. I walked back to my car feeling rejected by both Anna and Drew. I wasn't sure which one bothered me more.

• • •

The bus passes under a billboard showing a group of beautiful young people in a bar, holding up their bottled beers, laughing so hard that they are leaning on each other for support. It reminds me of when Anna and I first started going to bars in our early twenties. We used to joke that we needed to tie a rope around our waists, connecting us, so that on barhopping drunken nights we would always be able to find each other. As we got older, we said we needed that rope to tether us together even more, as our busy lives took over and pulled us in different directions. In my heart, I knew the rope was not necessary. Anna was a part of me, and I could feel the rope binding us wherever she was, whenever she needed me. When Anna died, I thought that I would feel the rope snap and I would be left holding the frayed end, raw and directionless. Instead, I feel the pull of her rope relentlessly, like a mountain climber whose partner has slipped and is dangling off the face of the cliff, dragging me with her backward into the abyss.

CHAPTER 5

June 1999

By the time Anna and I arrived at the summer festival of music and art in Dilworth Park, it was already teeming with people. Market Street had been closed to traffic and craft merchants lined both sides of the street in rows of identical white tents, offering everything from handmade jewelry to colorful kites to handcrafted dog bowls. There were food trucks to accommodate any craving from tacos to sushi, their long lines twisting inward and crossing over each other. Power supply cords ran behind the trucks, forcing people off the sidewalks and funneling them into the melee of the middle concourse. The combined scent of food and sweat made the air sticky, adhering to our skin like plastic wrap.

Anna and I were taking our time walking through the festival, stopping to admire the crafts and sipping cups of tart lemonade.

I was browsing a rack of hand-dyed clothing when Anna said, "Oh, I've always wanted to try that!" I looked up to see that she was referring to a section of the street blocked off with orange traffic cones where a new vendor was offering trials of in-line skates. Anna checked her watch. "We shouldn't, though," she said. "I need to meet Paul at the main stage at twelve thirty; that's in a half hour. He'll be waiting."

"It looks like the line isn't that long. We should have plenty of time."

"Well," she said, debating for a moment. "Sure," she decided, and I returned the skirt that I had in my hand to the overstuffed rack, pushing aside the clothes to make room for the hanger to fit.

The line moved slowly, and we passed the time watching the people ahead of us attempt to skate, wobbling like bowling pins. Men in white shirts that read 'City In-Line Rentals' skated swiftly between the newbies, steadying them by holding them at the waist.

When it was our turn, we sat together on folding chairs, stuffing our feet into the stiff skates. As I bent over, I noticed the time on my watch. It was already twelve thirty. I realized that Anna had totally forgotten about meeting Paul. Selfishly, I decided not to remind her.

"Remember Star's Skate-A-Way?" I said rhetorically, knowing that Anna remembered it well as I did. We had spent many Saturdays there, playing games in the arcade and drinking soda from the snack bar. I would pretend not to be hurt when 'couples only' was announced and Anna was inevitably asked to skate, leaving me behind. I'd stare at the smooth floor of the rink, watching the pattern the lights made shining off the mirrored disco ball, circles trapped in squares, spinning endlessly round and round. "It can't be much harder than that, right?"

"Right!" Anna said as she stood up, waved her arms in comic circles, and promptly fell. I laughed unapologetically, and Anna gave me a smirk that said, 'So, you think you could do better?'

I stood, balanced proudly for a moment, my knees turning in. Then, I lifted my right foot to push off and fell next to Anna.

"Ow!" I winced, laughing even though it hurt and rubbed my hip.

"We can do this," she said confidently. Clumsily using each other for balance, we tried to stand. When we were finally upright, we managed to skate forward for a couple of feet, directly into one of the workers. He took each of us by the upper arm and skated expertly backward with us on either side. A few people cheered as we made it past the first traffic cone. Between the two of us, we were pulling his arms akimbo, but he took it in stride, just another couple of damsels in distress. When he let us go, we continued to skate awkwardly but with growing confidence. Anna circled the cones slightly ahead of me and returned to the seats. I joined her, using the chair next to her as a crash pad, knocking it back a good six inches and making a noise loud enough to make several of the workers look with alarm in my direction.

"I'm fine, everything's okay!" I yelled reassuringly and began unlacing the skates. Amused by our accomplishment, we returned our skates to the attendant, who gave us coupons for ten percent off our first rental. The look of satisfaction on Anna's face reminded me of us as girls, learning to skate on four wheels turned so tight they barely rolled. As we walked casually down the crowded fairway, I risked a glance at my watch. It was almost one.

"Do you think I can sue for personal injury? I think my butt is bruised." Anna said.

"No, we signed a waiver and besides, I'm not taking a picture of your black and blue butt as proof."

"But you are such a good photographer!" Anna teased. "You could make it cute." She pulled out the waist of her shorts and twisted around, trying unsuccessfully to look inside, like a dog chasing her tail. "C'mon, just look, do I have a bruise or not?"

"No! Ew!" I shrieked. "Stop."

"Geez, you'd never believe you're a nurse. Don't you look at butts for a living?"

"That's totally different. The butts at work are anonymous."

"Anonymous butts, just another job perk for you." Anna teased, nudging me with her elbow. Suddenly, Anna's smile disappeared as if it had been ripped from her face as she spotted someone ahead of us. Paul. He was standing in front of the main stage, staring at Anna. He pointed sharply to his watch without lowering his gaze.

"Shit! I have to go," she said.

"I totally forgot you were meeting Paul," I lied, trying to look remorseful. Goddamn Paul.

"No, it's fine, but let's just—" She paused, not knowing what else to say. "I'll call you." She gave my arm a quick squeeze, then hurried off, obviously not wanting me to follow. I stopped walking and watched her as she approached Paul, the apologetic look on her face doing nothing to appease his fuming glare. I watched them argue until Paul turned and walked away, Anna followed sheepishly behind him, her shoulders sagging. Worry and guilt tugged at my conscience as I watched her go.

• • •

A thin Asian hostess wearing a short black skirt and matching silk blouse greeted me at the door of the new Thai restaurant where I was meeting Anna for dinner. My eyes followed the perfect knot of black hair resting on the nape of her neck as she guided me to our table. The lights were flat rings that hung above the tables. The décor was a contemporary mix of midnight blue and stainless steel. A massive fish tank glowed in the center of the restaurant. I sat and opened the menu, furrowing my brow as I scanned the unfamiliar entrees. Anna loved trying new restaurants, but I always needed some coaxing.

"Sorry I'm late," Anna said as she approached the table. The pile of laundry that I left neglected in the dryer in order to get to the restaurant on time flashed in my mind, but I dismissed Anna's apology.

"No problem," I told her as she leaned down to give me a quick hug. Her purse caught my eye as she hooked the strap around the back of the chair. "Is that new?" I asked, gesturing to it.

"Yes, I got it from one of our advertisers." She handed it to me so that I could take a closer look. "God, I love my job," she said with a self-satisfied smile. Issues of the magazine had been piling up on my coffee table since Anna was hired, and I resolved again to read them over the weekend.

"Oh," I exclaimed, rubbing the soft leather wistfully between my fingers. "This is really beautiful."

"Isn't it?" She responded then, changing the subject she added, "Anyway, happy birthday to you, old lady!" The fact that Anna was younger than me by about a month was something she never let me forget.

"Thank you. By the way, I got your letter in the mail. The *actual* mail," I added for emphasis. "You're lucky I checked it. My mailbox is mostly for decoration." The letter, written in Anna's large loopy script, was wedged between the cable bill and a birthday card from my grandmother. I had ripped the envelope open immediately and sat on the inside staircase of my apartment building to read it.

Sweet Amy,

I've known you as long as I can remember. When I look at you, I can still see the little girl that sat next to me at lunch in kindergarten and gave me half of her cookie. You are the sister that I never had, the one person who is always there for me. I know that our lives are changing, sometimes too quickly, but I am so thankful that I have you to help me through it all.

All my love, Anna

Just thinking about the simple letter warmed my heart. I put it in a keepsake box littered with concert tickets and pressed flowers. Memories preserved in objects that could be called to mind with a touch.

"I wrote an article for the August issue of *BTB* about the therapeutic effects expressing your thoughts in writing. I was skeptical, but honestly, it makes you think more about what you want to say then just signing a card. And hopefully"—she smiled at me—"the recipient feels appreciated by the effort."

"I do. But you still brought me a cupcake, right?" I was referring to our long-held tradition of buying a single cupcake from Gigi's
for each other on our birthdays.

"Of course," Anna said, holding up the cupcake in its signature pink bag. "Oh, did I tell you that we hired a new editor? David
Garrison, he's fantastic. He wants to make the magazine more scien-
tifically based. It's still about keeping life simple, living in the moment
and all that, but he wants the articles to have research behind their
ideas to give them validity and separate us from the other self-help
magazines." I liked the way Anna talked about her work. She seemed
to have found her niche in a highly competitive market. I bragged
about her as if her successes were my own.

The waitress brought over the plate of spring rolls we'd ordered
as an appetizer. Anna reached for one, and as she did, the short sleeve
of her shirt pulled up slightly. I noticed an oval-shaped bruise on her
arm, just below her shoulder.

"What happened?" I asked, gesturing to the bruise, suspicion
edging into my voice.

"Oh," Anna said, tugging at her sleeve. "It looks terrible, right?
I was doing curls at the gym and I kind of lost control of the weight."
Anna spoke a little too quickly before dipping the roll in the sweet
basil sauce and taking a bite. The spring roll crumbled, and she
caught the flaking rice paper with her hand.

"Anna," I said gently and waited for her to respond.

"What?" She sounded a little annoyed, food still in her mouth.

I looked at the bruise again and my face tightened with con-
descension. "I'm a nurse. I know what a bruise from being grabbed

by someone looks like and that," I said, pointing, "is clearly a thumbprint."

"Okay, well. But it wasn't like that. Paul, he just doesn't know his own strength." Anna stammered, caught in her lie.

I could feel anger rising in me.

"Paul *hurt* you?" I asked, straining to keep my voice level.

Reluctantly, she began. "It's like this. He got home late; he'd been out with Evan and some of the other guys. I was mad because he didn't call to tell me where he was. I was getting worried. So, when he did finally get home, I started yelling at him, like, as soon as he opened the door. I shouldn't have been so quick to jump on him about it, though," she said quickly, wanting to make me believe that it was not a big deal. "I mean, time just got away from him, you know? And calling me slipped his mind. It's not like he was near a phone, anyway."

"Don't," I said.

"Don't what?"

"Don't defend him," I said. "It is never okay, and it is never your fault." I didn't mean to sound patronizing, but from my standpoint, the situation was simple.

"Oh, Amy," Anna said, giving me a look of frustration. "You just don't understand. You've never been married; you've never even had a long-term relationship." Her words surprised and stung me. "I'm sorry," she said immediately seeing the wounded look on my face. I wasn't expecting that. She had never rubbed the fact that I didn't have a boyfriend in my face before, and without thinking, I found myself blaming Paul for her unprecedented loss of etiquette. "It's just that, things happen. It was a one-time thing and Paul swore it would never happen again. He was so sorry. Really, he almost cried. Can we just drop it, please? I don't want to ruin your birthday."

I could tell by the look on Anna's face that her emotions were running high. On the surface, she was desperate to appear fine, everything in her life was still in order, as it had been moments ago. She was angry at me for bringing it to light, as if my not seeing the bruise belied its existence. But here I was, holding a mirror to her injured pride. This tactic was not going to work with Anna. I would have to find another way in.

"Okay," I relented. "Just know that I'm always here for you, whatever you need."

"I know, but there is no reason to worry." She took a deep breath and exhaled loudly, looking around for the waitress, who noticed and responded by coming quickly to the table. Anna ordered us a bottle of Moscato and put a fake smile on her face. For a moment, she looked just like her mom.

• • •

July 1999

The Independence Day Regatta was held each year at Boathouse Row. The race could be viewed from the walking path that winds along the Schuylkill River near Kelly Drive where the iconic boathouses of Philadelphia stand. The German-style structures, half-timbered with multiple triangular roofs, had always reminded me of ginger-bread houses lined up like ornaments along the river's bank.

I had recently joined a photography club at the suggestion of the owner of Expert Images, the print shop on Arch Street, where I took all my photos to be developed. Today, the club was meeting to photograph the race. I stepped out of my car and stretched, looking up at the cloudless sky, cerulean blue and endlessly high, feeling as if I could swim straight up and into the atmosphere. Sculling boats were lined up along the bank, appearing too narrow and delicate to stay aloft in the river's swift current. Teams gathered wearing their brightly colored uniforms, ready to propel themselves through the water with strokes so perfectly choreographed, they seemed effortless. I greeted a few familiar faces as the other members of the photography club gathered on the steps in front of the Fairmount Park Recreation Center. We stood in the blazing morning sun using our hands as visors, while the group leader explained how to take the best photos in the bright sunlight. She showed us how to use a fill flash to keep the subjects from being backlit before sending us off to take pictures. We were to meet back at the steps in two hours to talk about the session.

I started walking along the path, slightly ahead of the people in my group, taking a few test shots and adjusting my camera settings. Sunlight glinted off the waves in blinking crescent moons and I decided to stop and change lenses. It was at that moment that I noticed a couple picnicking along the bank. They sat together on a sand-colored blanket that looked itchy like it was woven from wool. They were surrounded by discarded breakfast sandwich wrappers and empty Styrofoam coffee cups as they settled in to watch the race. The man was leaning back on his hands with his knees bent and the woman was sitting between his legs with her back resting against his chest. He leaned down and moved her brown hair from her shoulder to kiss her neck. She pulled back and smiled, looking at him. Thinking it would make an interesting photograph, I centered them in the frame, intending to blur the couple in the foreground and focus on the racers in the river. But when I zoomed in, my hand froze on the dial as the man came into view and my breath caught. It was unmistakably Paul, but the woman in his arms was not Anna. He leaned deeply onto his left hand and pointed to a boat in the distance with his right, making his army tattoo clearly visible. I clicked the shutter, over and over, my heart pounding. When I was sure that I had indisputable pictures of him, I dropped the camera, letting it hang on its strap around my neck and stared at his back, still unbelieving. As if he felt my eyes on him, Paul looked over his shoulder without warning and I gasped; I didn't want him to see me. I turned my face away from the bank of the river and began walking quickly back to the recreation center, trying not to draw attention to myself.

By the time I got to the gravel parking lot, I was positive Paul had seen me and I began to run, my feet kicking up small stones that bit into the back of my shins. When I reached my car, I risked a glance behind me as I fumbled with the key in the lock, expecting to see Paul looming, but he wasn't there. I opened the car door and sat heavily in the driver's seat trying to calm my racing pulse before turning over the ignition. The fear I felt was slowly abating and being replaced with a heartsick sort of victory. Anna couldn't possibly stay with him now, but the road ahead of her would not be easy, nor would it be easy for me to tell her about what I had seen. Although I dreaded being the catalyst for the end of her marriage, I knew it was unavoidable—she needed to be told. I just didn't know how I was going to tell her.

I called my sister for advice when I got home. Anna was visiting her mom in Bell's Lake for the holiday weekend, so I had some time to think before I talked to Anna.

"Are you sure it was Paul? I mean, completely sure?" Sam asked me. I pictured her, a multitasking mom, walking around as she talked with the phone tucked between her neck and shoulder and my niece, Emily, balanced on her hip. She would be picking up toys and straightening the sofa cushions while listening to me.

"Yes, I stopped at an instant photo booth to get the photos developed on the way home. It's Paul, no doubt. You can even see his tattoo."

"Oh god, that's rough."

"I know. Sam, what do I do?" I pleaded.

"You need to tell her. Don't wait, just call her up and invite her over. Show her the photos. Do it tonight."

"I can't. Anna isn't here. She went to visit her mom. She genuinely sounded excited about seeing her. It was strange." I said, thinking that it was the first time in a long time that Anna had been eager to go back to Bell's Lake.

"Well, as soon as she gets home then."

"She'll be home tomorrow. What do you think she'll do, Sam? What would you do?"

"Ask the other woman if she changes diapers," Sam said jokingly, and I let out a small sigh, relieved to have the tensions broken for a moment.

"No, seriously, what would you do?"

Sam was silent for a minute. "You need to be prepared, Amy. She might forgive him."

"You're joking, right?"

"No," Sam said. "I've known Anna as long as you have. She always had a boyfriend and then this whirlwind marriage thing. It's like she has a hole to fill. She's been that way forever. I know losing her dad messed her up, but even before that, can you remember a time Anna wasn't dating someone or didn't have a group of admirers around her? And the two of you, you never stopped being best friends, even for a day. She clearly doesn't want to be alone."

"Yeah, I get that," my head nodded involuntarily as I answered.

"I hope she comes around and sees that this asshole isn't worth it, but…"—I heard Sam breathe out through pursed lips—"honestly…," she said, her voice strong again.

"Yeah?" I responded.

"I know you need to tell her about this. Just, when you do, make sure that you let her make her own decisions, back off, and give her space. And," she groped for the right words, "don't get too involved. You have your own life, you know." This was not new advice from Sam. Sam was the one person who called me out for wanting to be controlling of other people's lives, especially Anna's.

"I know," I told her absently and hung up the phone, ignoring her guidance about knowing my place, already rehearsing the words I would use when I showed Anna the pictures and worrying again that the backlash of telling her about her husband's cheating would fall on me.

• • •

Anna settled onto my sofa and crossed her arms. Although it was late afternoon on a Monday, today was the observed Fourth of July holiday, and like most people, she had the day off from work. Anna was still wearing the clothes that she had worn to the picnic her mother hosted in Bell's Lake earlier in the day, a light blue halter top and white shorts that set off her tanned skin. Her blonde hair was pulled into a French braid, making her look younger than twenty-three. I suddenly remembered that her birthday was only two weeks away.

"Okay, I'm here. What is it? You sounded so dire when you called, it scared me," Anna said with a nervous laugh. I knew she left the picnic earlier than she had planned. I hadn't meant to alarm her when I called her at her mom's house that morning. I wanted to casually invite her, over but keeping this to myself was killing me.

"Anna," I started the words I'd been repeating to myself for most of the day. "I was taking pictures at the regatta yesterday and I saw this couple sitting on the bank, and…." I wanted to say more to soften the blow, but I hadn't been able to think of anything to add that would help.

"And?"

"Well, I really hate to show you this, but… here." I handed her the photographs. Anna took the pictures I offered her, giving me a confused look with her lips tightly drawn. Her mouth dropped open as she looked at the pictures in her hand.

"That's... that's Paul?" she said and looked at me for confirmation. I nodded my head. She quickly flipped through the other photographs.

"I'm so sorry," I said. As always, these words felt inadequate, but I said them anyway.

"This can't be right," Anna said, astounded. "I mean, maybe it's just the angle of the photo. He has a lot of female friends, you know. I'm sure he's not cheating, I'm sure it's innocent." Anna was falling over her words, scrambling, clawing like she was looking for an exit in a locked closet, not even bothering to sound convincing. "Maybe it's not even him."

"Anna," I said, "I saw them. I couldn't look away, even after I took the pictures. It was him, and it wasn't innocent." We sat in silence for a beat.

I was waiting for anger, for tears, for any kind of reaction, but Anna just sat there, eerily quiet, looking at the most incriminating picture of Paul kissing the girl's neck. She put the pictures face down on top of a stack of magazines on the coffee table and began rubbing her bare arms with her hands as if she were suddenly cold, smoothing down bumps that covered her biceps.

"Here," I said, handing her a blanket and putting it around her even though it was close to ninety degrees outside. "I'll turn down the air." I stood up and adjusted the thermostat.

"Thanks," she said. I tried to stay calm and let Anna get her bearings, but she was beginning to look a little pale.

"I'll be right back," I mumbled and got her a glass of water from the kitchen. She said nothing as she absently raised the glass to her lips without taking a sip.

"What do you want to do?" I asked as gently as I could.

"I don't know," she said, giving me a vacant stare. She pulled the blanket more tightly around her. Worried about Anna's state, I offered her a cup of tea. She shook her head.

"I'm here for you, you know."

"I know," she said barely above a whisper.

"You can move in here," I told her, and she smiled weakly.

"I," she paused, "I'll talk to him. I need to hear what he has to say before I decide anything."

"You're not thinking of staying with him, right?" I asked her. Sam's voice warning me to let Anna decide echoed in my head, but I forcefully ignored it.

"I don't know, Amy," she said. "We're married. I don't want to just walk out on that. I can't. I need to at least talk to him first."

"But what could he possibly say? There is no excuse for this," I said. My voice rose in anger. "You are worth so much more than that. I hate how he treats you. You deserve better."

"Stop!" Anna yelled, giving me a harsh look filled with scorn. My fear of being the messenger rose to the surface. I started to speak, desperate to defend myself but Anna cut in, gentler this time. "Please, just stop. I can't think straight. I need time." She rubbed at her temples.

"All right," I relented. A few more minutes passed. The refrigerator hummed noisily in the silence.

"I… I'm going to go home now," she said flatly, standing and letting the blanket fall to the floor. She picked up the top photo and put it in her purse. A little of the color had returned to her face.

"Do you want me to take you?" I asked. "My car is close by."

"No, it's okay. I'll walk."

"Are you sure? Do you want me to come with you?"

"No, no, I'll be fine," she said. I got up and hugged her. She felt stiff in my arms. She started to pull away, but I squeezed her closer until her arms finally returned the embrace. I thought that she was going to start crying, but she didn't. She just pulled back and gave me an empty look, then walked out the door.

As I closed the door behind her, I realized that I couldn't let her go home alone. Paul scared me. I grabbed my sandals from my bedroom and slipped them hastily on my feet. Taking my keys from the hook near the front door, I hurried outside. Anna had already descended the stairs, and I followed her onto the sidewalk. I intended to call out to her, to run and catch up to her, but she was walking in a daze and the tears that she didn't want me to see were now running freely down her face. She wiped them away crudely, like she was swatting flies, and I stayed behind her. Strangers hurried past her, either oblivious to her crying or quickly looking away, not wanting to get involved.

I kept my distance without losing sight of her as we passed the shops on Washington Square West and turned right onto her narrow side street. Trees, their leaves heavy with summer, draped over the street in a canopy blocking out the sun. The sidewalk became uneven, broken by the roots that had pushed their way stubbornly through the concrete.

As Anna approached their building, her body language changed. Her slow, tortuous strides were gone. She snatched the picture out of her purse and stormed up the stairs, face flushed, fist clenched, nearly crushing the photo. Paul was coming out of the door, a basketball in his hand, as Anna reached the small square landing in front of the door to their building.

Oblivious to her anger, he greeted her with a smile at first, but seeing the look on her face, he stopped. Anna met him without breaking stride. She propelled herself forward and pushed Paul hard, putting both her hands flat on his wide chest, throwing him back into the common hallway. "Hey!" he yelled sharply, clearly surprised.

"You dick!" she shouted. "You fucking prick! Who is she?" The door to the old building was wedged open, and I could hear their voices from the street. I hurried up the stairs and stood in the doorway. Anna was shoving the picture in his face.

"What the fuck is wrong with you?" he shouted and took the picture from her hand. He angled it toward the doorway to look at it in the light. "Shit," he said under his breath and threw the basketball hard against the wall. It hit with a sound as sharp as a gunshot and echoed as it bounced down the hall. "Where did you get this?"

"It doesn't matter where I got it. Who is she?" Anna demanded.

"It *does* fucking matter where you got it," he said, "because I fucking *asked* you where you got it."

"Who is she?" Anna said, ignoring his question, each of them lost in the tempest of their own anger, whirling tornados about to collide. "Who are you with?" Anna repeated.

"I said—" He threw Anna against the row of metal mailboxes, jagged and misshapen from years without repair. She gasped at the sudden strike; caught off guard as her head clattered loudly against the metal. I stood frozen at the doorway, the surprise of his vicious attack rooting me to my spot. Anna looked like she was going to pass out from the impact, her eyes rolled back, and her eyelids fluttered. Her body sagged but Paul grabbed her by the shoulders and shook her hard.

"Where'd you get this?" he said, releasing one shoulder and brandishing the photo in front of her dazed eyes. Seeing her struggle to focus woke me from my stupor and I sprang toward them, yelling at him to stop. If Paul was surprised that I was there, he didn't show it. I tried to push Paul away from her, but it was like pushing against a boulder. I was as insignificant as a gnat to him. His face was inches from hers. He snarled. Anna's eyes started drooping again, and he roared, "Answer me!" spit landing on Anna's cheeks. With a sudden practiced move, Paul put his forearm across Anna's throat, pushing into her larynx, strangling her, the veins in his muscular arm pulsing. Without looking, he pushed me back with his other arm, and I fell on the floor. Fear replaced Anna's disorientation. She clawed at his arm violently, desperate for air, carving deep scratches in his skin. Blood from a cut on the back of her head flowed around her neck below Paul's arm and pooled on her shirt. The stain grew larger as she twisted and turned, tearing her scalp on an uneven metal corner of one of the mailboxes.

"Stop it! Paul, stop!" I yelled, jumping up and pulling desperately at his arm. "Stop! She can't breathe! She can't breathe!" I shrieked; my voice hysterical. Paul turned and shoved me out of the way again, this time releasing Anna. Anna rubbed her throat urgently, retching and coughing, bending at the waist. She sucked in raspy gulps of air, sounding like a wounded animal, trembling and gagging.

"You bitch." Paul glared at me as if I had just registered in his vision for the first time. The loathing in his voice was so intense that it unnerved me to my core. "What were you doing?" He took a step toward me. "Following me?" He came closer. "You heard me. Answer me. You were following me, weren't you?"

"No," I said, keeping watch on Anna, who was still heaving. Paul stood inches from my face. His stance was solid. His legs were straight and strong in a V formation, and his hands were clasped behind his back. Frightened, I stepped backward, and Paul moved even closer, towering over me.

"She'd be so much better off without you." He sneered the words at me. Behind him, Anna continued to cough and spit.

"Stop it, Paul," I said, forcing my voice to be calm. I moved to the side, but Paul mimicked my movement, blocking me from getting to Anna. He looked directly into my eyes; his pupils were dilated to an unnerving black. I could feel my heart drumming in my chest, and my mouth was completely dry. He seemed to sense that I was now frozen with fear, and he smiled wryly, as if enjoying the confrontation, which terrified me even more.

While Paul's eyes were locked on me, Anna grouped her way around to the open door, desperate for air. She clutched at the door jamb and tried to straighten up, her breath gradually coming under control. She looked up. "Paul," she said in a ragged breath, "leave her alone."

Without warning, Paul lunged at Anna.

"No!" I yelled as Paul pushed Anna hard through the doorway. I leapt past him, and I jammed my body between them, quivering but not backing down as we stood in a standoff on the outside landing.

"Move," Paul ordered as he pulled his right arm back, his hand in a closed fist. I squeezed my eyes tight and cringed, steeling myself for the feel of his punch.

"Paul, what the hell?" a voice called from the sidewalk.

Paul turned toward the voice and dropped his arm quickly, recognizing Drew in his basketball shorts and a sleeveless shirt.

"Hey, man," Paul said, as if nothing was happening, backing up, and relaxing his posture.

"Are you alright?" Drew threw the question in our direction. I looked at Drew gratefully and nodded. "Let's take a walk and cool off, Paul."

Paul bounded lightly down the stairs and started walking up the street with unnerving nonchalance. Drew looked back at us. "You're bleeding," he said to Anna, who turned her face away from him and scrunching her shoulders as if trying to hide. "I'll keep him out for a while," he said to me and then ran to catch up to Paul.

"Let me see that," I said, gesturing toward Anna's head after the men turned the corner. Anna's breathing had returned to normal. She leaned her head down and fumbled with her hair. Her hands shook as she pulled out the rubber band that was holding her braid and tenderly separated the strands. "It's not bad, but you are going to need stitches," I told her. I took her purse from her trembling grip and looked inside for her keys. "I'll be right back." Letting myself in her apartment, I grabbed a dish towel from the kitchen. When I got back outside, Anna was sitting on the cement stairs, her head in her hands. She was still shaking slightly, and tears ran between her fingers. I pressed the towel against the back of her head, and she took it from me, holding it in place.

"Thanks," she said quietly. I put my arm around her shoulder, and she leaned into me.

"We should get a taxi to the hospital," I said as I stood up. "Are you dizzy?" I asked her as I gently guided her to her feet. She carefully shook her head. I waited a minute to make sure that she was steady before we walked to the end of the block where traffic was heavier, and we would have a better chance of flagging a taxi down. I kept my arm tight around her shoulder, supporting her, as we walked. At the corner, I saw a taxi waiting for the light to change and signaled to the driver with an upraised arm, keeping my other arm around Anna. As the taxi pulled over to the curb, Anna doubled over in pain, grabbing at her stomach as she let out a small, weak moan.

"What's wrong?" I pulled away to look at her. I saw a bright red stain beginning to spread between her legs, ruining her white shorts.

"Oh no, you're… did you forget?" My words drifted away as I saw the pained expression in Anna's eyes and her arms wrapped protectively around her midsection. "Oh my god, are you pregnant?" I asked, the realization dawning on me. Anna nodded.

"But I think… I think something's happening… something bad," she whispered softly before she doubled over in pain again, her eyes pleading with me to understand. She pressed her legs together tightly to hide the blood as I flung the taxi door open and helped her inside.

"You okay?" the driver said to Anna, pointing to the bloody dish towel on her head, which thankfully was his only focus.

"Yes," I answered for her. "We're just going to have this looked at. Philadelphia Hospital, please."

"Don't get any blood on my seats," the driver warned, still looking at her head.

As we pulled away from the curb, Anna looked back over her shoulder and finally started to cry in earnest. I squeezed her hand.

"I'm here. I'm here," I repeated. She rested her head on my chest. "I'm always here for you," I whispered into her hair.

• • •

At the hospital, mercifully, the emergency room was almost completely empty, a respite from the Fourth of July accidents that overwhelmed the hospital the day before. I mouthed the word 'miscarriage' to the receptionist, and she discreetly escorted us to a room with a sliding privacy curtain that wrapped around the triage table. She gave Anna a hospital gown and underwear that looked like a paper shower cap, along with a large sanitary pad, and told Anna to change in the bathroom and that someone would be with us shortly. Anna came back into the room, absently folding her shirt and shorts. She looked around for a trash can, and not seeing one, she threw her underwear on the floor, a bloody bundle, where it landed in a corner with a sickening sound. Wearily, she lay down in a fetal position on the table.

There was a wide red mark on Anna's throat that was already starting to bruise. Angry crimson scratches crisscrossed her delicate neck. The bleeding from her head had stopped from the pressure of the towel, but her light hair was matted, dyed with blood into a carmine spider web.

A woman in scrubs came into the room carrying a clipboard. She was sympathetic but detached. I didn't recognize any of the medical team on staff tonight, but that wasn't surprising for a hospital of this size. Anna struggled to sit upright on the table, but the woman told her she could lie back down while she answered basic questions about her name, address, and date of birth in a rote monotone. I handed the woman Anna's insurance card that I had taken from her wallet. It had been wedged behind her new driver's license with her married name. The woman tucked the insurance card under the clip and paused for a moment before she said, "Tell me what happened."

I could tell by the sudden change on Anna's face that she was going to lie. Her eyes darted away from the woman. Anna spoke quickly, looking at the ceiling.

"I fell down the steps at my apartment and hit my head," she feigned honesty, but the ineptness of her unrehearsed story clouded her words.

The woman stopped writing when I said, "Anna, no."

Anna looked at me utterly drained and hopeless, shrinking backward like a skittish kitten. She wanted to hide behind the lies that she had been telling for months, knowing that there was nowhere to go that the truth wouldn't follow once it was spoken out loud. These were the words she could never take back. Indecision darted behind her closed eyes.

"Listen, Anna." I took her soft hands in mine. I felt an urgency to make her stop protecting Paul. "There could be serious damage from what he did to you that we don't know about yet. You could have a concussion or—" I stopped myself from going on, thinking of all Paul could have done, slamming her into the wall and cutting off her air. The memory of Anna gasping for breath was too raw. "The doctors need to know everything and document everything, just in case. Anna, you don't have to press charges against him, but you have to say what happened, for your own sake, so they can treat you." The woman taking her information nodded in confirmation.

Anna seemed relieved that she didn't have to decide about Paul right now. Assured in the confidentiality of her story for the time being, she managed to tell it to the woman who wrote down notes without expression.

Anna and I had been sitting together in silence for about half an hour when the ER doctor came into the room. She introduced herself as Dr. Allen. She looked to be in her early forties, with a slender build. Her hair was pulled back into a tight, high bun, and her carefully applied makeup looked like a mask. She examined Anna gently, pulling out the bottom lid of Anna's eyes and shining a small flashlight into the crevice. Anna winced at the light. She asked Anna some questions, and Anna's voice sounded hoarse. Dr. Allen told us that she was going to order a CT scan and a swallow study. She looked at the cut on Anna's head. When she was finished, she patted

Anna on the knee and told her that the nurse would be back in to take pictures and to clean the area around her cut.

"I'll be back after that to stitch it up," Dr. Allen said and began to collect her things.

The miscarriage was the least of Anna's worries medically, but it was her heart's greatest concern. She stopped the doctor. "I think, I might—" she paused, catching her breath. "I'm bleeding." She looked down mournfully.

"Yes. It appears that you are having a miscarriage. I can check your cervix to confirm, but from the amount of blood and the cramps, I don't think that is necessary," Dr. Allen said. "Do you know how many weeks pregnant you were?"

Were. The word hung in the air with unspoken finality.

"About seven," Anna said, then to me, "I was going to tell you. I just told my mom yesterday." The memory brought a flood of new tears that made my chest ache. I stood and went to Anna's side.

"Shh, shh," I cooed, leaning over the table and pushing Anna's hair back from her forehead as if she were my child. The doctor told Anna that she might be able to prescribe medicine to help the miscarriage along but that they needed to do the other tests first.

"Let the nurse know if the bleeding becomes extreme or if the pain feels unmanageable," Dr. Allen said and left with a smile that was meant to be comforting but looked too contrived, her heavy foundation cracking in the creases around her eyes.

The nurse came back in and shaved a small spot around the cut, cleaning the wound and rubbing the area with lidocaine. She took pictures of Anna's neck and head, standing back when Dr. Allen returned to sew it closed with a deft hand. After the doctor left, the nurse bandaged the site.

"Let's get you to a room. They want to keep you overnight," the nurse said as she helped Anna into a wheelchair as I followed behind. Anna lifted herself onto the bed, her thin legs poking out from beneath the hospital gown. Seeing her naked fragility made my face sting with sadness. How easy it had been for Paul to break her.

"I'm going to call your mom and ask her to come. Is that okay?"

Anna nodded. She was lying on her side, staring out the window with a hollow expression. The view was another bland hospital building blocking what would have been the sunset. Rows of uniform gray windows set in bricks stared back at us, like a hundred unblinking eyes, mirroring the overcast sky as the day turned seamlessly to night. I didn't want Anna to have to listen to the conversation, so I left her room and used the phone in the waiting area, dialing the number of Anna's childhood home, which I still knew by heart.

"Ms. Kildare?" I said when she picked up the phone. "It's Amy. Sheppard," I added unnecessarily.

"Amy," Renée said pleasantly, and I could hear the smile in her voice. "How are you?" In the background, I heard the teapot whistle. "Hold on a minute, I was just making tea." She took a few moments to fix her cup and returned to the phone. "I'm back."

"Ms. Kildare," I started again. "I'm not sure how to tell you this. I'm at the hospital with Anna. She's going to be fine, but there was an accident… with Paul." Renée sighed in my ear. I quickly told her the story. Sadly, she seemed unsurprised, as if she knew this call would come someday.

"Let me pack some things, and I'll come right away. Can you stay with her until I get there?"

"Of course," I told her and hung up the phone. When I got back to the room, Anna was gone. The bed was creased where she had been lying, a small smear of blood left behind on the white sheet. I went to the nurses' station, and they told me Anna had been taken for tests. I went back in her room to wait. The events of the day started to replay in my mind, and I turned on the TV to block them out. It was almost two hours later when Anna was wheeled back in the room. The speech pathologist followed her to go over the results of the swallow study. Anna was cleared to drink liquids, but it was recommended that she stick to a diet of soft solids until the soreness went away. When Anna asked for a drink of water, her voice still sounded as if it were full of holes, and I poured her a cup from the plastic pitcher on her tray table. Anna winced as she swallowed but didn't cough. She laid her head back on the pillow and stared at the ceiling. There was nothing to say. The television filled in the background with nonsense noise and flickering lights.

I was still sitting in a small, cramped chair when Renée arrived. Anna had finally given into mental exhaustion and fallen asleep. Renée stopped in the doorway, momentarily stunned by the sight of her bruised and battered daughter. I was glad that Anna couldn't see the pain on her mother's face, but Renée quickly regained composure. She carried a bag of clothing and toiletries that Anna kept at her mom's house.

"Is it safe for her to sleep?" Renée asked, concerned, since I had told her there was the possibility of a concussion. I nodded. Renée cupped her hand lovingly on Anna's cheek. At her mother's touch, Anna woke slightly.

"Mom," Anna said weakly, closing her eyes and drifting off again.

"Oh, sweetheart, it's okay, go back to sleep," Renée told her softly. She waited until Anna's breathing became rhythmic again; then she turned to me, shaking her head and whispering, "Bastard."

Renée and I went to the waiting room to talk. She smoothed her skirt before sitting down on the hard sofa. "So." She sighed, wringing her hand while gaining her composure. "When Anna is well enough to leave, I think she should come home with me for a little while."

"I agree. Maybe you could call the magazine, get her a leave of absence or whatever. I could help get her things from the apartment, and well, I've seen this kind of thing before at work. She needs to file for a PFA, a protection from abuse. I can get you the forms for her to sign. Once Paul is served, if he gets anywhere near her, the police can arrest him. Even if she doesn't want to press charges, he needs to stay away. Ms. Kildare, I don't want him around her. It's just not safe."

"I agree," Renée said, shaking her head. Tears built up in her eyes, and she dabbed at them with a tissue from her purse. "Well, then. I'm going to head back to her room. I'll call you."

"Okay," I said. We stood, and I hugged her goodbye.

• • •

"*Tell me what you remember,*" *said Melissa Riley, MD. Her cheap plastic pen was poised to take notes on her yellow legal pad. I stared at the cardboard back of the notepad.* So odd, *I thought, studying the cheap brown cardboard.* Shouldn't she have something more professional-looking? Something sturdier, stronger, to hold her notes when I tell her about that night? *Somehow, I know these thoughts are irrelevant, unimportant details, but I can't seem to focus.*

Dr. Riley prompted me again when I didn't answer her. "*Tell me about the night of your birthday.*"

"*My birthday,*" *I whispered. I cleared my throat.* "*There was an accident, a car accident.*" *It felt so long ago, but how long ago was it actually? I had no idea.* "*It was a week ago, I think.*"

"*Your birthday was June tenth, right?*" *I nodded.* "*Today is the fifteenth. It's been almost a week, yes.*" *She let this sink in. When Sam told me that she made an appointment with a psychiatrist for me, I told her that it was too soon. That I needed more time to grieve before I could even think about therapy. But Sam pleaded.*

"*Don't you see? Mom, Dad, Charlie, me... we don't have any idea how to help you right now. We're all upset, and we don't know what to do. Please, Amy, every day we wait feels like we are handling it wrong, and we need advice. For you and for us.*" *Sam said on the verge of tears. Sensing my sister's desperation, I agreed to go. So far, our family had been spared from sudden deaths and none of us were prepared to handle this.*

"*Where were you when it happened?*" *Dr. Riley asked, bringing me back to the present with her question.*

"We were on Kelly Drive. On the way home." I watched Dr. Riley write on her pad.

She looked up. "Home from where?"

"Dinner, at Caravella's."

"Amy, let's back up a little. Tell me what you did that day. Give me as many details as you can remember."

I thought about that day. I went to work as usual, then I did some shopping and came home around six. I gave her details about my day as each one came to me. The hours I worked, who was on shift with me, how I stopped for some groceries at the supermarket. "When I got home, my husband wasn't home yet. I got ready to go to dinner and then went to the lobby of our building to wait for him. The weather was getting bad. When he came in, Anna was with him. They work together at the magazine," I told her. "Worked," I amended.

I thought about how strange it felt to use the past tense. I was still grappling with the definiteness of the words. The present reduced to memory as easily as adding two letters. "Anna was my best friend," I explained to Dr. Riley. "She was the other one that was—" I couldn't finish.

"I understand," Dr. Riley said. "Please go on."

"Anyway." I sighed heavily and gathered my thoughts. "They were already pretty windblown and wet. I asked him if he wanted to change clothes, but he said no they would just get soaked again, so we headed to the restaurant. It's in Manayunk. We knew the Schuylkill Expressway would be backed up at that time of night, so we used Kelly Drive. Dinner was fine."

I lost myself in the memory. Caravella's was classy without being pretentious. Large windows overlooking the Schuylkill River meant that the restaurant didn't need much décor. The walls were a warm copper color scattered with small square impasto paintings of scenes from Italy: an open-air market, spices and fruit cascading down the vendors' stalls; Venice at night, the Rialto Bridge glowing with white lights. It was unfocused and easy art, the thick, colorful paint casting shadows on its canvas.

I realized that I had stopped talking, and Dr. Riley was patiently waiting for me to continue. "We drank some wine during dinner, and...." I trailed off again. I wasn't sure how much to tell her. Did it make a difference what we ate? What we talked about? My memory was hazy, and the details felt unimportant. I skipped ahead.

"We had dessert. They told the waiter that it was my birthday, and he put a candle in my cheesecake. The waiters sang a version of 'Happy Birthday' in Italian. Then we left the restaurant." In my mind, I could still see the three of us walking out of the restaurant, the golden glow of the pleasant evening surrounding us like an enchantment. Outside, the sky was inky black with night. We stood on the steps outside the restaurant. The rain had slowed to a drizzle, a steamy, temporary respite from the summer storm that was coming at us in bands. The wind was picking up in a way that felt threatening, blowing away our peacefulness like me extinguishing the flame of my birthday candle. Feeling that the worst of the storm was quickly approaching, we decided to try to stay ahead of it and hurried to the car.

"My husband asked me to drive. He didn't have his glasses with him, and he handed me the keys." I didn't mind. It had been a long night, and the effects of the wine had worn off with dessert and

cappuccino. "I... I decided to take the Kelly Drive again." The express-way would have been fine, no traffic heading into the city at that time of night, but I liked Kelly Drive better—the way it wound along the river, the slower pace.

"I didn't think anything of it. Anna was in the back seat; my husband was next to me." I remembered closing my car door just as the rain started in a solid burst of heavy droplets that pounded on the roof and obscured the windows. I turned the windshield wipers on as high as they would go and pulled onto the road, stiffening my back and leaning forward, concentrating on the short bits of clarity when the wiper blades slashed through the water and offered a brief unob-structed view of the road. I fumbled with the controls, trying in vain to turn the blades on higher and setting the defrost to clear the steam. The streetlights shone weakly, ringed with hazy, futile light.

"We drove through some deep water in the lower spots on the road, but there was no place to turn off, so I kept going." In my head, I was behind the wheel again, winding and winding. Oncoming head-lights blinded me. "I don't know, maybe I was more tired, or I drank more than I thought, and then, around one bend in the road, oh god, I could feel the car hydroplaning, my tires unable to get a grip, and that's when, oh, we started slipping, going sideways...."

I was sobbing now, uncontrollably. Dr. Riley told me to stop, in a soothing voice. She said that we would continue at another time. She told me that she was going to talk to Sam, who was waiting for me in the lobby. She handed me a box of tissues as she walked out of the room.

I lifted my eyes as Sam slowly opened the door to Dr. Riley's office. I clutched the ruined tissue tightly in my fist. It had grown dark outside, and this surprised me.

"Hey," Sam said softly, a whisper of a word. "Come on, honey, let's go home now." I had been crying so hard that my ears were ringing, muffling and distorting sounds, Sam's voice sounded as if it were part of a dream. My head ached with an excruciating pain, and I held it in my hands to keep it still as I stood. Sam took my arm and guided me out the door.

CHAPTER 6

July 1999

When I picked up the PFA form for Anna, it only took a glance at the information requested to make me realize how little I knew about Paul. Even though he had been married to my best friend, I didn't know his exact age or his birthday. I didn't know his middle name. I didn't know him. The forms asked for details of the most recent incident of abuse. The date, the time, the place. The incident. It pained me to know that Anna would have to call to mind these details, reliving that day on paper, giving the protective, hazy edges of the memory a permanency in ink. The form asked if the defendant was involved in previous criminal actions. Paul's story about how he was discharged from the army came to mind and I wondered if criminal charges were filed and how I could find that out for Anna. After some digging, I faxed a request for more information to the federal courthouse in Fayetteville, North Carolina, where Paul's trial was most likely held.

Charlie and my dad had agreed to help me get Anna's things from the apartment she shared with Paul. We blocked the street with my dad's station wagon, hazard lights flashing, and carried empty boxes up to their place. I had spoken with Drew, and he agreed to keep Paul away until I called him later and told him we were finished.

The apartment looked the same as it did when I rushed in a week ago, but it felt like a year had passed since that day. As I walked around, I realized that I hadn't spent much time here. I knew that the outdated furniture belonged to Paul. Anna was waiting to redecorate until they bought a house, and so they had put Anna's larger belongings in storage. I showed the men to the bedroom and opened the sliding closet doors. They started packing Anna's clothes as I walked around the rest of the apartment, looking for signs of her. There were a few framed pictures on the wall, all from Paul's time in the army. Men posing in their beige and brown desert fatigues, sand coating their faces, making them grit their teeth and squint their eyes.

The tables in the apartment were bare, no candles or vases, just yawning, scratched wood surfaces. The single set of bookshelves in the living room was crowded with history books, none of which belonged to Anna. There were no blankets or throw pillows brightening the shabby brown sofa. I walked to the kitchen and looked for Anna's grandmother's flatware that had been passed down to Jack and given to Anna as a wedding present, but it wasn't there. I found a single coffee mug that I had given Anna for Christmas last year, yellow ceramic with a hand-painted daisy on the side. I absently passed the mug between my hands, feeling the weight of its emptiness.

In the bathroom closet, threadbare towels and bleached white sheets were stacked in precise rows. I collected Anna's toiletries, unplugging her lighted makeup mirror, and twisting the cord around the base while I wandered absently back to the living room. It felt like packing to leave from a hotel at the end of a short stay. There were only the bare necessities, no old bottles of face cream or samples of perfume. My dad called to me from the bedroom, startling me, and I flinched more than was warranted at the sound of his voice.

"I think we have all of Anna's things from in here," he said. "We pulled everything out of the closet. Shoes are in this box, and we emptied out the dresser drawers into here." He indicated three boxes sitting on the bed, which was tightly made, the blanket straining at the corners.

The absence of Anna's possessions was barely discernable as I closed and locked the apartment door. Outside, I saw the traces of blood on the cement steps, a part of Anna that was impossible to remove. I hoped Paul saw it too, every time he entered his empty apartment.

• • •

August 1999

"This looks promising," Anna said, double-checking her notebook to make sure that we had the correct address on South Twenty-Second Street between South and Lombard. A small red and black 'For Rent' sign was in the window with a telephone number written on it in black marker. The apartment was part of a group of four townhouses, each three stories high. The two end units were red brick, and the two middle units were gray stucco. Anna approached the end unit with an aqua-colored door and rang the bell. The landlord greeted her with a handshake and led us into a common hall.

"There are two more apartments upstairs." He pointed to the staircase while he fumbled with the keys to the downstairs apartment. "Both rented," he added.

He opened the door to what must have been the formal living room before the house was subdivided. It was a spacious room with a marble fireplace centered in the wall opposite the front door.

"Have a look around," he said. "I'll be in the hallway if you have any questions."

"Anna!" I said excitedly as the landlord shut the door. "Your furniture would look great in here!" I turned to see her smiling. We continued farther into the apartment. There was a small kitchen with open shelving and a miniscule bathroom. I laughed out loud at the size of the shower and teased Anna that if she gained any weight, she wouldn't be able to fit.

"It'll be great motivation to stay thin," she said as she peeked over my shoulder, trapping the two of us in the tiny space. Anna backed out of the bathroom and continued walking through the apartment, pausing to look at the fixtures and opening closet doors. In the back was a bedroom, barely wider than a queen-size bed, with an old wooden wardrobe attached to the wall. We wandered back to the stunning front room with the fireplace. Natural light streamed in from the street-side windows and the walls were painted an unusual sky blue.

"What do you think?" I asked.

"Oh, I'm done looking. This is *it*!" Anna said and turned to go in search of the landlord. I put my hand on her shoulder to stop her.

"Anna, this place is really nice," I paused. "But are you sure it fits in your price range?" The apartment was only slightly smaller than the one I rented with Gail and we both stretched our paychecks to afford it.

"Yes!" Anna said with exasperation. "I wouldn't have come to see it if it wasn't."

"If you're sure," I said, looking around again, feeling more than a little envious. I thought of the compromises I made in living with Gail. The zebra painting that Gail loved came to mind, hanging prominently in our living room. I hadn't been able to work up the nerve to ask her to take it down, even though it looked to me as if it were painted by a kindergartener. I imagined how Anna would decorate the place and without being able to visualize specifics, I knew it would be stunning. I also knew that she would spare no expense making the apartment alive with her style. Her disposable income often seemed endless to me.

Anna filled out the rental application and gave the landlord a check. Giving the agreement a cursory glance, he told her that as long as the check cleared, she could move in after the first of the month. We decided to explore the surrounding area. Anna eagerly pointed out a small grocery store on the corner of Twenty-Second and South Streets, an unbelievable convenience in downtown Philadelphia. We continued walking down Twenty Second Street, and as we did, the neighborhood quickly deteriorated. The continuous lines of townhouses shrunk from three stories to two. Iron bars appeared on first-floor windows and garbage filled the gutters, the runoff pooling into rank puddles.

"Let's head back the other way," Anna said. Crossing South Street again was like traversing an unmarked dividing line and Anna's new apartment was right on the edge. Unfazed, she walked along the sidewalk toward the more affluent neighborhoods in the direction of Spruce Street. We cut across Lombard and headed to my apartment near Rittenhouse Square, chatting amicably about Anna's new place.

"Do you want to get some dinner?" I asked.

"No, I want to get on the road back to Bell's Lake before the traffic gets too bad. I can't wait to tell Mom all about the apartment!" Anna said enthusiastically. We said our goodbyes, and Anna headed to the parking garage where she had left her car.

I walked inside the vestibule of my apartment building and stopped to open the mailbox. There was a large envelope amongst the flyers and junk mail. Inside, it contained a copy of the information I had requested about Paul.

One criminal court proceeding, *Jeffery Walters v. Paul Callaghan*. Paul was found guilty of third-degree aggravated assault. He was given a dishonorable discharge from the army, fined, and had served four months in prison. Most surprising was the description of the injuries sustained by the plaintiff. Massive concussion, loss of consciousness. I thought back to the day I first met Paul and he admitted to a bar fight that got him kicked out of the army. Jeffrey Walters wasn't over-reacting as Paul had said. I wondered if Anna knew the real story. At first, I thought that Anna couldn't have known, but what part of me hated to admit was Paul may have told Anna about the prison time he'd served, and she hid it from me. I could hear him explaining it away, saying it was a misunderstanding, that he got a raw deal, but he served his time anyway and now he was better for it. Anna would be all too eager to accept the downplayed version of events. I knew Anna well enough to know that she'd believe anything, do anything, when she was in love.

· · ·

September 1999

The judge assigned a hearing date of September fourteenth for the Protection from Abuse case. It was three days after what would have been their first wedding anniversary.

The last time I visited Anna at her mom's house, I shared what I had found out about Paul. By then, I had convinced myself that Anna couldn't have known, so I was expecting her to be appalled and upset when I showed her the paperwork, and she was, but not because of Paul's history, of which she was aware, but with me.

"How did you even get this?" she asked, looking at the copy of the court proceedings.

"It's public record. I requested it."

"But, why?" Her voice told me I did something wrong. That I had crossed a line into a part of her life she didn't want me to see, which felt absurd. To me, our friendship had always been as transparent as a window.

"Why would you do that?" she asked again, shaking her head with disbelief.

"I was… trying to protect you."

"Oh, Ames, that is a little over the top, don't you think?"

"But he almost *killed* you." I countered and we sat in silence for a moment, flashbacks of Paul pressing Anna against the wall in a chokehold replayed in both our minds, the image unstoppable. I waited a little longer before admitting, "I was afraid you were going to stay with him, okay? And I couldn't take the thought of you giving him another chance."

"No. I know I can't stay with him. If I couldn't protect our baby before it was even born, then…." Her eyes circled around the kitchen, seemingly not wanting to look at the papers or at me. She stood and examined the leaves of an ivy plant that sat on the windowsill. She ran her hand along the long, trailing stems, pinching off the brown and yellow leaves with her fingers. She lay the dead leaves on the counter and rearranged the remaining vines to cover the holes left behind. I started to speak, to question her reasons for staying with Paul for as long as she had, but she interrupted me.

"I thought I could give us a fresh start," she explained.

"So, you knew when you married him that he'd been in *jail*?"

Anna took her time answering. "No," she sighed as if admitting defeat. "He told me when I wanted to start looking at houses. Somehow, he thought it might come up as part of the mortgage application. Well, that is what he said at the time, but I think he just wanted an excuse to tell me." She stood facing the window, her eyes roaming over the trees in the backyard.

"If you knew, why didn't you tell me?" I asked.

Anna turned around. "I didn't want you to hate him even more." I started to protest, but she gave me a look and said, "Please don't. I know how you felt about him. But you have to understand, Amy, *I* loved him." She picked up the dead leaves and threw them in the garbage can next to the refrigerator, as if throwing away the past. Noticing that the refrigerator was covered with pictures, she paused in front of it and started pulling off the ones of her and Paul, collecting them in her hand. I wanted her to dump them in the trash can as well, but I knew she wouldn't.

"It was my problem. I brought him into my life. I married him. I felt like if I told you, told my mom, told anyone, then it would always be there. You would always *know*. And so, I didn't. And"—she paused, gathering her thoughts—"Paul *was* trying."

But it wasn't enough, I silently filled in for her.

The day of the hearing, we stood outside the courthouse. Although we couldn't see it, I knew the statue of William Penn stood sentinel from atop the building, anchoring the center of the city.

"Are you okay?" I asked before opening the door.

Anna gave me an almost imperceptible nod. "Do you think he'll be here?" she added in a small voice. The pain in her eyes was equal parts dread and hope, but I didn't notice.

"I don't know, but it's better if he isn't." I said pragmatically. A no-show by Paul would mean an automatic judgment in favor of Anna. "And besides, you don't actually want to see him, right?" She didn't answer me. I sighed inwardly and opened the heavy door.

In the end, Paul didn't come to the hearing, and the petition was granted for Anna. We paused outside the courthouse, standing at the top of the stairs to say our goodbyes before we went our separate ways, when someone across the street caught my eye. It was Paul, standing at attention, facing us. When Anna's gaze followed mine, she grabbed my shoulder, alarmed. But the man who looked back at us wasn't the man she had once loved or the man that attacked her. He was just a man who had been broken long before he crossed our paths. He didn't wave or gesture. He didn't indicate that he has seen us in any way. He just stared in our direction for a moment, backlit by the afternoon sun, and then turned on his heels and walked away, mixing into the lunch crowd. It was as close to an apology as Paul could manage.

CHAPTER 7

November 1999

Anna and I sat at my kitchen table drinking tea. We had a few minutes to spare before the nine o'clock drop-in yoga class at Grow, the yoga center on Twentieth Street near the Museum of Natural Science. Anna wanted to detox from drinking at the *BTB* costume party the night before.

"So," Anna said, "I wore a red devil costume, not a 'sexy red devil,' because it was still a work thing, even it if was a party, you know, but I thought I looked good." I nodded in agreement, confident that Anna had looked fantastic. At first, Anna had been indifferent about going to the party, but I was glad when she decided to go. She seemed to slowly be returning to her old self as her time with Paul faded into memory.

"Anyway, holy shit, some of the women at the party really didn't get the memo, because it was cleavage central!" She squished her boobs together and leaned forward, making kissing sounds. I chuckled and pushed her backward. "And David, the hot new editor, he certainly didn't seem to mind. I saw him leaving with Tonya from accounting. She was dressed as a sexy secretary, which to be honest, is kind of how she dresses anyway, so it wasn't much of a costume. She just added nerd glasses." Anna paused and raised the mug to her lips, softly blowing a column of steam toward me that smelled of oranges and cinnamon before taking a sip. "At least David was trying to be discreet. He didn't say goodbye to anyone, but Tonya was smiling ear to ear."

"And who did *you* go home with?" I asked, opening my eyes wide in a fake accusation.

"Just little ol' me," Anna said. Born and raised in Pennsylvania, Anna didn't have her dad's accent, but she could really sound like a Southern belle when she wanted to. "How were things in Bell's Lake?" Anna caught me off guard with the question, asking just as I took a sip of my tea.

"Mmm!" I said, swallowing fast and putting my mug down, spilling a few drops on the table. "Big news, Sam is pregnant again!" I grabbed a paper napkin and wiped up the spill.

"That's great. When is she due?" Distracted, I missed the strain in Anna's voice.

"Late June," I told her, concentrating on cleaning up the tea before it became yet another stain on the table. I crumpled up the napkin and put it in the trash, spying an envelope of pictures sitting on top of my phone book. "Oh, you have to see this picture," I said as I flipped through them until I found an unbelievably sweet picture that I had taken of Emily, my niece, next to a jack-o'-lantern so large, they were nearly the same size. "I just got these developed yesterday. Isn't she adorable?" I squealed. Anna took the picture, holding it gingerly as if wanting to drop it, and I immediately regretted showing it to her.

"Oh no, I'm sorry," I said. I quickly took the picture from her hand, but this seemed to make it worse.

"It's fine." Anna countered. But I knew since the miscarriage, her life had become a tedious walk through a field of landmines. Babies were everywhere. I watched her turn the other way when a woman with a baby stroller passed us on the street or quickly change the channel when there was a newborn on TV. "Actually, I think I am going to skip class today."

"No, please come. I'll—" I started to say, but I didn't even know what I *could* do.

"It's not that, honestly, I'm just starting to feel a little queasy. I think the hangover has finally caught up to me."

"Are you sure?" I asked, knowing she was lying.

"Yeah, but you better get going if you don't want to be late." Anna was already walking to the kitchen, and she poured the remainder of her tea down the drain. She slung her yoga mat in its bag over her shoulder and smiled as she said goodbye. But my callousness followed me for the rest of the day like a shadow, as I feared I had pushed my friend back down the hole she was emerging from.

• • •

December 1999

It took all my strength to climb the last fight of steps to my apartment and unlock the door. Once inside, I collapsed on the faux leather chair in the living room without taking off my coat. I was so exhausted from the twelve-hour shift that started at 6:00 p.m. that I could barely see straight. Babies may have been everywhere for Anna, but for me, lately it seemed I was being haunted by untimely death. In the newspaper, I'd read stories about young women being fatally shot by a lover or going missing while on an afternoon run, later turning up in a ditch on the side of the road. At work, there were things beyond medical help, a tumor found too late, a mental illness uncovered after a suicide.

A few months ago, I had been transferred from ambulatory care to a medical unit. On one of my first night shifts in the new unit, I met a patient named Carmen who was diagnosed with sclero-derma, a rare autoimmune disease of the connective tissue. A disease she'd never heard of, a word she could barely pronounce, would now become the center of her existence. Eventually, she would learn about calcinosis and sclerodactyly, words that would twist them-selves into her vocabulary, a second language that only a few people could speak, and no one learned willingly. The night Carmen was admitted was a quiet night on my floor, although I wouldn't dare say this out loud, not wanting to chance a widely held superstition among medical personnel. But since I had the extra time, I attempted to distract Carmen by making small talk while flipping channels on the TV that hung from ceiling in her room. We landed on a cooking show, and I learned that Carmen was a chef at Havana, a trendy new restaurant on Rittenhouse Square near my apartment.

"Have you eaten there?" Carmen asked, her voice lilting, her accent a charm dangling off the bracelet of her words.

"No," I admitted.

"Oh, you must come! The best time is Saturday night when we have live music at the bar. Mention my name and they will hook you up with reservations. I plan to go back to work as soon as they let me out of here."

The next weekend, I insisted that Anna and I have dinner at Havana. I was excited to introduce Carmen to Anna, feeling that I could show off my status as a friend of the chef. Anna always seemed to know the most interesting people, the owner of a consignment store that put aside the name brand clothing in Anna's size or the guy at the farmer's market who greeted her by name, adding items to her bag after he weighed it. But tonight, it was my turn. We were having drinks in the lounge downstairs when I eagerly caught sight of Carmen coming out of the kitchen to greet an older gentleman who was holding court in the corner, trapping a waitress and a busboy who listened to him with polite smiles on their faces.

"Carmen, hello!" I said, addressing her with a loud familiarity. She returned my greeting, saying 'hey there' with a questionable look, smiling politely but obviously not recognizing me. I quickly glanced at Anna, whose face bore a tinge of embarrassment for me. "It's Amy." I explained. "From the hospital." I added.

"Amy, of course," Carmen said, coming to us, her outstretched arms pulling at the sleeves of her white chef's coat in a welcoming gesture. She covered her initial confusion with utter composure, making it tricky to know whether she truly remembered me or not. Carmen looked good from a distance, deceivingly healthy. However, as she got closer, I could see that her eyes, hidden in the shadow of the toque that covered her hair, were ringed in dark circles. With all that she had going on, I could not fault her for forgetting me. I just wish I hadn't talked up my new friendship so much to Anna.

"We're happy to be here," I said and made quick introductions.

"Do me a favor," Carmen said. "Tell that old man that you hear the *moros y cristianos* is the best dish here," she said, indicating her father with a tilt of her chin. "He thinks his is better," she added in a stage whisper.

"I can hear you, Carmi," he said to our table in a gravelly, thickly accented voice that made me think of a lifetime smoking thick cigars. "I may be old, but I am not deaf. Order it and take your chances," he said to us, lips covering his yellowed teeth, hiding a smile.

"Cooking may be my passion, but getting you fired up, Papi, it is a close second." When she looked at him, they seemed to embrace each other with their eyes, until the old man looked away and sniffed softly. He pulled a cloth handkerchief from his pocket and wiped his nose. Carmen turned her attention back to us. "I must go," she said. "Nice to meet you, Anna, and good to see you, Amy. Enjoy your meals." She touched my shoulder affectionately as she hurried past.

I can't believe that was only a few weeks ago. Last night, I found out through the hospital grapevine that Carmen had been brought to the emergency room feeling that she couldn't breathe. She didn't survive. It all happened so quickly; she didn't even get the minimal three years she was promised. Not even close. Now, sitting in the soft chair with my coat still on, I was overcome with the heartbreaking indifference of death.

As tired as I felt, the urge to leave the apartment was stronger, anguish moving the walls inward, suffocating me. I dug my camera out of my bedroom closet and walked to Rittenhouse Square. The sun had recently risen, allowing the rest of the world to start the day without significance, going through their normal routines.

In the square, a man had set up his bongo drums next to a breakfast cart, hoping to catch spare change from the early morning commuters stopping for coffee and egg sandwiches. His head was bowed covered with an oversized knit hat with yellow, green, and red triangles meeting at the center, a waterfall of dreadlocks pouring out the sides. He tapped the drum lightly, sliding his hands across the animal skin, to a soft, somber beat. The unlit sign for Havana was just above his head on the restaurant's brick wall facing the street. The curtainless windows exposed the dark, empty inside.

Anger at death overcame me. Its reckless and indiscriminatory pickings. I photographed the outside of the restaurant from every angle, catching the dirty snow left piled in the corners, the leafless trees around the entrance, as if I were writing the ending of a story that I didn't want to be a part of anymore. I felt some satisfaction with the familiar feel of the camera in my hand, clicking the shutter until I ran out of film. The art of photography taking me out of the world, keeping me out of the frame.

• • •

January 2000

The food court inside the Gallery Market East was swarming with the lunchtime crowd. When I had first moved to the city, I found the multi-level shopping mall in the heart of Center City overwhelming. I stood in the concourse and stared up at the four stories, mouth gaping like a tourist, and longed for the simple shopping mall of my youth, where I would meet my friends at the central fountain on Saturday mornings. But like the rest of the city, the mall seemed to shrink with time and familiarity.

I looked around the food court and didn't see Anna. I ordered us our typical fast-food lunch and walked to an empty table juggling the bag and two sodas. Anna came striding in, looking for all the world as if she owned the place. Her black swing coat spun around her like a superhero cape, and the high heels of her calf-length leather boots made her three inches taller, taking her from 5'9" to a full six feet. Businessmen looked her up and down appreciatively as she walked by. She greeted me with an air kiss on both cheeks that stunned me slightly.

"What's going on with you?" I asked slowly, perplexed by her entrance. Although a grand place to shop, the food court was hardly worthy of a European greeting.

"I'll let you see for yourself," she said and handed me a copy of the magazine as she settled into a plastic chair. "It's an advanced copy." I looked at the cover, still questioning why Anna was show-ing it to me. She made an exasperated noise and took the magazine back, opened to the masthead, and pointed to her name listed under assistant editor. "I am the youngest person on that list!" she beamed. "And I've been there less than two years. David Garrison took over as editor-in-chief because Alexandra retired. He came to my cubicle and told me about the promotion personally. He even hinted that I could make another jump to full editor if this works out. We've got a small circulation now, but we are growing, and oh, I'm just so excited!"

"That's wonderful! I'm happy for you!"

"It was quite a surprise, I thought it would go to Felicia; she's been there longer." I knew from past conversations that Felicia sat in the cubicle next to Anna and drove her slightly crazy.

"You are just better than her, and your smart bosses realize that."

"Is this the kind of ass-kissing I can expect now that I have people reporting to me?"

"Absolutely. How did Felicia take it anyway?"

"Oh my god, she was so nasty! She said sarcastically that I 'really worked hard to get it.'" The tone of Anna's voice implied the air quotes that she was too cultured to make. "Like I was sleeping with David to get the promotion or something." Anger pulled at her face as she remembered the remark.

"Are you sure she wasn't being serious?" I asked. I knew better than to defend Felicia, but I also knew that Anna could be oversensitive when she thought someone assumed that she had used her looks to get something. It was a side effect of having a mom who came of age during the women's movement of the 1960s. Renée drilled into Anna that being pretty wasn't an accomplishment nor did it warrant a reward. "You *did* work hard. I mean, I barely saw you over the holidays! I swear, you've been living and breathing the magazine since Halloween."

"Oh, it was absolutely sarcastic," Anna said. "That bitch. I could ruin her, you know. Half the time she's on the phone with her boyfriend. I could just mention that to David, and she'd be gone."

"Forget about her," I quickly interjected, not wanting to spoil her mood. "She doesn't know what she is talking about. You've been working all the time; we didn't even go out for New Year's Eve because you were so exhausted. You deserve this promotion. Here," I said, quickly unwrapping a straw and jamming it in the lid of my cup. "To your new position at *BTB*; they are lucky to have you. You'll be the best assistant editor they ever had!" I held my cup up and Anna touched her cup to mine, smiling again, her good mood restored.

"That is definitely my plan." Anna's eyes were suddenly hard with ambition, like hail forming from a spring rain in a way that made me inexplicably anxious.

I opened the paper bag of food that had been sitting on the table and handed Anna a burger wrapped in wax paper. As we ate, we discussed her new responsibilities. When she hinted at a generous raise in her pay, I felt a prickle of envy, but I pushed it down. Anna left before I did, hurrying to catch the light rail that rattled beneath us, and I watched her disappear down the escalator. The *BTB* office was close enough that she could have walked, but the January weather made it preferable to stay inside. The mall's large grandfather-style clock assured me that I had plenty of time before work, and I decided to get a coffee from the street vendor outside the mall to take with me on the ride home.

The icy air hit me with a gust, and I hastily pulled a pair of old knit gloves from my purse. As expected, there were a few people in line, shuffling and stomping their feet to keep warm. This vendor was relatively new, but its reputation for coffee that was always hot and strong was worth the wait. A man got in line behind me. I smiled reflexively at him when our eyes met. Smiling reflexively at strangers was something I was warned about when I first moved to the city. "You can't do that anymore," my friend who had been living downtown for a year scolded me when she caught me smiling and nodding to a person as we passed on the street. "You have to look tough. Always. This is Philly."

"Tough? Have you met *me*? The closest I can get is 'pouty.'" I quipped and was rewarded with an eye roll and a stern warning to up my game.

This guy, however, smiled back, and I was immediately attracted to him in a way that made me wrack my brain for a way to talk to him. Maybe it was how his dark hair curled or the funny way he squinted at the handwritten white board on the side of the truck, wrinkling his nose. He looked at his watch and gave the man behind the small serving window a frustrated look. As we inched our way forward, I could feel his impatience growing.

When it was almost my turn, I said, "If you're in a hurry, you can jump in front of me."

"Really? Thanks." His dark eyes locked on mine for the slightest moment before he moved forward as I stepped aside. He ordered a well-practiced version of something complicated involving soy milk. I had assumed that he'd forgotten about me when he added, "Keep the change for hers; she's a lifesaver. Thanks again," he grabbed his cup and winked at me. "I won't make it through the afternoon without this."

"Anytime," I said wishing I could think of more to say, but he was already walking away. I shrugged off the interaction. He was probably out of my league anyway.

• • •

May 2000

Traffic was heavy on the Atlantic City Expressway, but that was nothing compared to the bumper-to-bumper stream of cars approaching Ocean City and its oppressive forty-mile-per-hour speed limit.
Closer to the shore, we crawled along Central Avenue, keeping watch
for one, just one, open parking space. Anna and I thought we were
being smart, going to the beach on the Saturday before Memorial
Day weekend. But the combination of the unusually warm weather
and it being the last weekend before beach tags became mandatory
made it the destination for everyone desperate for summer in the
greater Philadelphia area. I nudged into a space that was just wide
enough for my car—there is a reason that cars have bumpers—and
we gathered the sunscreen, diet sodas, and towels that had spilled
out of our tote bags during the jolting starts and stops of the seemingly endless and stuffy drive.

We walked across the boardwalk—the ash-colored wood
bleached by the sun looked deceptively brittle—and walked down
the steps onto the beach. Kicking off our flip-flops, we hung them off
our fingers and I curled my toes into the refreshingly cool sand. We
found an open spot near the surf, both of us holding a corner of the
blanket, and spread it out as flat as possible, fighting the persistent
ocean breeze. I sat down quickly to keep the blanket in place.

"At last," Anna said with a sigh, pulling off her coverup and
sitting down next to me. She began the process of coating her fair
skin with SPF 30. I noticed that Anna's bikini was new and smaller
than the styles she'd worn in the past, but with her knockout body,
she completely pulled it off. I thought of Quinn comparing her to a
Barbie doll, and I had to admit, I could see why. I propped myself

up on my elbows, feeling dowdy in my one-piece swimsuit from last summer.

In front of me, navy blue and army green waves, the camouflage pattern of the North Atlantic waters, rolled to shore. I longed to swim, but I knew the water would be freezing. Later, we'd go in ankle deep and use our hands to splash ourselves with the cool water until our skin grew goosebumps.

"Help me think of a story idea that I can give to David," Anna said. She had learned that her new job included everything from reviewing and briefing David on freelance pitches to coming up with new story ideas when freelance options were running low. As she spoke, she wiped her hands on a towel and then dug in her bag and got out a pack of Marlboro Lights. She tapped the unopened pack against the inside of her wrist before peeling off the cellophane and stuffing it in the bag. Holding a cigarette in her mouth, she pulled the brim of her woven sunhat low around her face, turning away from the wind to light it. She sat back and blew a stream of blueish smoke into the air that quickly dissipated. Smoking was something that we had done off and on over the years. It started with juvenile curiosity in seventh grade. We stole her mom's cigarettes two at a time trying to figure out how to inhale until Renée caught us. Renée immediately quit smoking for good, cutting off our supply. In high school, Anna and I smoked occasionally, imitating the cool crowd with a desperation that was both obvious and ineffective. I mostly stopped smoking in college, never having fully embraced the habit when Anna wasn't around, but Anna's smoking had increased since her promotion at *BTB*. Many of her co-workers smoked, a breakroom bonding ritual that had insidiously seeped beyond working hours and into her daily life. Anna tilted the pack in my direction. I shook my head, but Anna gave me a look that said I should join her, so I took one and lit it, feeling unpleasantly lightheaded from the first inhale.

"David wants me to have ten pitches ready at all times," Anna said, tapping ashes into a small divot she dug in the sand next to the blanket. David's name came up so often on the drive that I wondered if he was in the backseat.

"It kinda sounds like you're into David. You talk about him *all* the time. Maybe you should ask him out. You guys sound perfect together." I took a drag on the cigarette and winced at the hefty taste of nicotine.

"Date my boss? No, thank you." Anna held up her hand.

"I'm serious! It could be okay. I bet your HR department has a policy for employee dating if you guys were upfront about it. What's the harm?"

"No. Absolutely not. No matter what HR said, you know how that would look. Any promotions that I got would be dismissed as a special treatment. Journalism is competitive enough without bringing that into the equation." Anna stopped talking to take another drag on the cigarette, making the end light up with orange embers.

"I guess. But plenty of people date at work. Look at your mom and Doctor Ben." I abandoned my half-smoked cigarette, burying it in the sand, hoping that Anna wouldn't notice.

"Ha! You really think that Doctor Ben is the boss in that office? He may have the title, but Mom runs the show. And not just at work," she added under her breath. "It *might* be okay on paper, but I know if I started dating David, I would be judged unfairly. There are already rumors about the two of us, but I shut those down fast. I am careful to be extra professional around him."

"So, you're putting your ambition first. I think your mom would be proud of you."

"Yeah, but Dad would be disappointed. Love was everything to him."

"Scopes guy," I said suddenly, nudging Anna and abruptly changing the subject. She reflexively ditched the cigarette and sucked in her already flat stomach. I tried to nonchalantly pull out my pony-tail and shake out my hair. Philadelphia heat made for frizz, but ocean air was my hair's best friend. The guy in the blue shorts with 'Scopes' written across the butt approached us, a collection of keychain tele-scopes with photos inside jingled from his hip. Scopes had been a New Jersey beach tradition for as long as anyone could remember and unfailingly, Scopes guys were the most attractive guys on the beach.

"Hi, ladies, smile for the camera?" he said as he approached. Anna and I arranged ourselves into optimum photo-readiness so quickly it made him laugh. "How is it that every girl knows exactly how she wants to look for the camera?" He began to click away.

"Isn't it a little early in the season for you guys?" I asked when he finished.

"Maybe, but I live here, so I never miss an opportunity." He looked directly at me when he said it and flashed a striking smile. He pulled a paper ticket from his clipboard and stopped to write on the back. "You know where to pick up the photos?" I nodded as he bent down and handed me the ticket, holding my gaze just a little longer than necessary. "Later," he said and walked away, the word 'Scopes' swaying from side to side as he did. Anna and I watched him walk, Anna pulling down her sunglasses as coquettishly as a pinup girl.

"What did he write?" Anna asked when he was out of earshot.

I tore my eyes away from his backside to look. "His phone number. Here, he probably meant this for you." I gave the paper to Anna, who handed it back to me.

"He gave that to you, silly."

"You think so?"

"Uh, yeah," she said, as if it were obvious. I sat up a little straighter as I put the ticket in my bag.

Hours later we left the beach, covered in sticky sea-salted sweat, the strap of my bag rubbing uncomfortably against the tender skin of my sunburnt shoulder. We settled into our seats in the sweltering car, putting down the windows to release the hot air, and joined the commotion of traffic heading to the city.

• • •

June 2000

Having to work on your birthday sucks. It feels childish to admit that, but it does. It didn't help that no one on my shift remembered it was my birthday until I reminded them and then I received a few half-hearted 'happy birthdays!' Some people asked me the lame question of 'so how old are you?' and that was just a reminder that I was not in my early twenties anymore. I was twenty-five, officially in my mid-twenties, which felt a lifetime older than twenty-four. To top it off, it was a busy day on our floor, no time for cake or songs—not that anyone had bought a cake. At least it was over.

When I got home, the empty lobby of my apartment building felt desolate; the sound of my footsteps echoed as I crossed it and unlocked my mailbox. There wouldn't be a card from my parents, but I knew my mom would have left me a message for me on the answering machine. She'd tell me that we would celebrate the next time I was in Bell's Lake, bribing me with a cake in exchange for visit home that would be overshadowed by a very pregnant Sam and Emily, who was almost two years old and the epitome of adorable. There was a fifty-fifty chance that Sam herself would remember. By the end of the day, it was confirmed that Sam had forgotten entirely.

The mailbox was overstuffed with pizza coupons and credit card offers. But among them, I found what I was looking for. I had been watching for it for days. Anna's letter was tucked between the advertisements, the bright orange envelope shining out like a ring buoy, floating among the detritus of the everyday. I waited until I was in the apartment to read it in a manner that was almost ceremonial.

Sweet Amy,

I can hardly believe that it is your birthday again. There were times this year when I felt like my life was unraveling. Paul. My miscarriage. My divorce. But I feel that I am getting my life back on track and I couldn't have gotten through the last year without you! Thank you for always being there for me.

All my love, Anna

I thought about the last year. Anna had been through so much and my life largely was the same. A peculiar emotion tingled under my skin as I reread the letter before placing it carefully in my keepsake box. Her life, with its myriad of ups and downs, held something that I found somehow enviable, like a ride at a pop-up carnival that I was too sensible to go on but watched from below as it spun above me, teasingly close to going out of control.

• • •

I walk the endless grid of city streets. My body is tired and sore, but my mind pushes me to continue. I won't stop until I am ready to collapse. My self-imposed treatment for insomnia. I see her likeness of everywhere. I never before noticed how closely human beings resemble each other in appearance and behavior, leading lives so mirrored that they are almost interchangeable. Strangers become images taken from my memory, replicas acting out insignificant and forgotten moments, played all around me on a life-size screen. I narrow my vision to block them out without success. Two women gossiping in a coffee shop; women laughing as they get into red Chevrolet. For a second, I think the car is mine until I remember. The car was totaled. There was no point trying to salvage it.

CHAPTER 8

September 2000

The bar was spinning in my vision. Anna had called me after her promotion party. It had been just over two years after she started at *BTB*, and she was named a full editor.

"Aw, please," she had begged on the phone. "Just come for one drink. Everyone is starting to leave and I'm not ready to go home yet. This is a big deal for me! It's still early, it's only ten! I'll have you home by eleven, eleven thirty at the latest. We are right around the corner from you at Ray's Tavern," her voice rising as she added this final enticement to her offer.

"Okay," I said reluctantly, "but I need to work in the morning. Only *one* drink. Seriously, I can't make it a late night."

I was too embarrassed to admit that I had already been asleep when Anna called and I really didn't feel like going out, but I didn't want to become the friend that she called last because I was always saying no. She seemed to be meeting new and interesting people daily. And lately, it seemed that I had to work whenever she invited me out.

I stood and walked into the bathroom, turning on all the lights to help wake myself up. Yawning at myself in the mirror, I pulled my hair into a sloppy ponytail. Loose ends that were not quite curls and not quite straight sprung from the elastic band. The black top with lace around the neckline, the one I thought of as 'old faithful' when it came to going out on short notice, was thankfully clean. I paired it with jeans and lots of black mascara that I hoped would emphasize the whites of my eyes and not the dark circles underneath. Outside, the cool September air had me fully awake by the time I walked into Ray's and looked around.

Ray's Tavern was a typical Philly bar with dark leather-covered booths and a full menu of fried bar food. It wasn't a large place, and I could see immediately that Anna wasn't there. Seeing my confused look, a bartender I didn't recognize called to me.

"Are you Amy?" he asked. I nodded.

"Your friends left about ten minutes ago, but they wanted me to give you the message that they are at Hooligans. I'm warning you, they are pretty tanked."

"Um, all right, thanks." I debated going home, but I knew Anna would be looking for me, so I walked outside and signaled for a taxi.

"Hooligans," I told the driver.

"Which one?" he asked.

"There's more than one?" I had no idea. Going home and back to bed was sounding better and better to me. "Uh, the one near the waterfront? It has a big pineapple on the sign." The driver mumbled something about next time knowing the address, not giving directions with friggin' pineapples, and I giggled unconcerned.

When I arrived, I gave the bouncer my ID and walked inside the club. The air was hazy, and I could feel the pulsing of the throwback seventies disco in my chest. The lights on the dance floor rotated flashes of red, green, yellow, and blue across my vision as my eyes adjusted to the dark interior. Anna was sitting at the bar with a girl I didn't know. I approached them, tapping Anna on the shoulder.

"Amy!" Anna turned and greeted me far too loudly. "You made it!" She glided off the barstool and hugged me sloppily, teetering on stiletto heels. She added, "I gotta pee," in the universal language of drunk people who feel the need to overshare and took off for the ladies' room. Anna was wearing a magenta dress with an open back that made her waist look impossibly small.

"Hi," I said to the girl who was left. "I'm Amy, Anna's friend."

"Jasmine," she said, offering me a limp hand. "I'm Anna's new assistant." Jasmine was young with pale skin and jet-black hair that framed her face in a bob with a solid line of bangs. Her lips were painted a shocking red that would have perfectly completed the Russian spy look if it weren't smeared in the corners. She wore a tiny black sleeveless dress and delicate-looking kitten heels. I felt unexpectedly odd and heavy in my jeans and boots that had looked fine to me when I left the apartment. But it was officially fall and my sleeveless things had been packed away with my swimsuits and shorts.

"Congratulations," I said, "on your new position, working with Anna." Jasmine gave me an odd look.

"Wish me luck is more like it," she said, slipping a little off her barstool and catching herself on the bar. "Sorry," she added, straightening up. "Please don't tell Anna I said that."

"Oh, I won't," I said, figuring that she was just nervous. This was probably her first job. She looked to be fresh out of college. "But don't worry about it. Anna will be a great boss. I bet you'll learn a lot working with her."

"*For* her. Felicia was the last person to make that mistake, and look where it got her," Jasmine said, assuming I was privy to the office gossip. I wasn't sure what to say next, so I leaned forward and got the bartender's attention.

"Coors Light," I said. The bartender nodded and tilted a beer mug under the spout, filling it quickly as I handed him my credit card. He took the card from my hand without making eye contact and silently handed me the receipt, pointing to where I should sign.

"Chatty guy," I said and turned back to Jasmine just as Anna came stumbling back to the bar.

"Well," said Jasmine, glancing at the clock behind the bar. "I really need to call it a night. See you in the morning, Anna." Before Anna could protest, Jasmine headed unsteadily to the door without a coat, her shiny black shoes sliding on the slick floor. She stopped in the doorway and fumbled in her small black purse.

"She's not looking for car keys, is she?" I asked.

"Cab fare," Anna said dismissively. She stared at Jasmine's back for a few seconds with glassy eyes and then looked at me. "Shots!" she yelled. "We need shots. You're too sober, Amy. You need to catch up."

"Anna, no, I need to work tomorrow," I protested, but Anna ignored me and banged on the bar.

"Hey," she yelled needlessly, as the bartender was already heading back in our direction. "We need a couple of shots. What do you recommend?" Anna looked at him coyly from under her eyelashes. "Something sweet." The bartender disappeared wordlessly and returned with two shot glasses and a bottle of Southern Comfort. He poured the dark liquid into shot glasses and slid them in front of us.

"Cheers!" Anna said, handing me one.

"To your promotion," I added, and we downed them. I could feel the liquid burning the back of my throat, but the sweet aftertaste helped me relax as I sipped my beer. "So," I leaned toward Anna. "What happened to Felicia?" Anna paused to light a cigarette, waving the initial burst of smoke away as if it were an unintended consequence. She pointed the pack in my direction. I shook my head and was glad she didn't pressure me into taking one.

"Oh, I fired her. I never thought she was a good team player, and her work was never up to my standards."

I was shocked by her coldness. "You can fire people?"

"Well, *I* didn't fire her exactly. After they offered me the promotion, I just suggested that we needed to make some changes and her name came up." She blew a plume of smoke out the side of her mouth and tapped her ashes in an ashtray on the bar. It would be years until Philadelphia adopted the smoking ban in the city. "How did you know about Felicia?"

"You started to tell me about it on the phone." I lied instinctively to protect Jasmine, hoping that Anna was too incoherent to remember.

"I did?"

"Yeah," I said vaguely. "Come on, let's dance." I hopped off my barstool.

"First, more shots," Anna said. I rolled my eyes as she signaled the bartender and pointing to the empty shot glasses. Anna was all business this time, aware that her earlier attempt to flirt had gone unreciprocated. We clicked shot glasses and downed the drinks. Anna ground her cigarette out before strutting her way onto the dancefloor, hips swaying to the beat, and I followed. Anna danced with a controlled grace, raising her arms above her head, and letting them slowly drop, keeping time with the rhythm of the music. I found myself imitating her moves, but I always seemed to be half a beat behind. Soon, we were engulfed by the repetitive thumping of the music and the small, gyrating crowd. Anna left and returned with beers in plastic cups. Getting caught up in the mood, I bought more shots in brightly colored beakers from a waitress in a low-cut shirt who approached us with a phony smile. Guys drifted into our dance space, mostly facing Anna, leaning over to speak directly into her ear to be heard above the shatteringly loud music. Someone surprised me from behind by yelling in my ear, "Is your friend seeing anyone?" I nodded my head yes, not sure why I fibbed. Around midnight, I started gathering my things.

"I need to go," I said, slurring my words more than I expected.

"No, the night just got fun. One more dance, just one more, I promise." Anna's words ran together. She took my purse and tried to hide it on the barstool under her coat. It kept falling to the floor, which we both found hysterically funny. Anna took my arm and pulled me onto the dance floor that was slowly emptying. After a few more songs, I gave Anna a look, and she pouted before I could even tell her I wanted to leave. I walked off the dance floor, and Anna followed me.

"Wait, Amy," she said, "those guys are coming over." Anna smiled brightly at them. It was the same guy that had asked me if Anna was available earlier. This time, he had a friend and four beaker shots. "They're so cute. You gotta stay," she begged.

I groaned.

After a quick introduction, the guys offered us the beakers. I shook my head, but then I saw Anna's reproachful look. I thought *what the hell*, and I drank the colorful liquid remembering the last one I bought was mostly mixer.

"Let me ask you a question," the taller guy said looking at Anna, who matched his height with the help of her high heels. "She said you were taken, but you look pretty available to me."

"Amy!" Anna scolded. I shrugged. "I'm *not* seeing anyone," she clarified, and he moved a little closer to her. As the conversation continued, my thoughts drifted into worry about my shift in the morning, but I pushed my concerns away. Somehow, I would just have to make it work. At Anna's insistence, we moved as a foursome onto the dance floor again. The guys awkwardly kept the beat by moving side to side, their hands balled into fists. They bought us more beer, and by the time the house lights came on, the night was a blurry mess, and the room was spinning.

Our small group stood outside, starting to exchange goodbyes when Anna suggested we go to an after-hours club.

"No, Anna, please! I have to work tomorrow. I mean today. I mean, in a few hours," I said laughing off my panic as I tried to focus on the numbers on my watch.

"Please come with us," Anna pleaded in my ear. "I think I really like this guy."

"You can still come," he said, putting an arm around Anna. I didn't like the idea of Anna going alone.

"I'm only going if Amy comes," Anna said resolutely, picking up on the guy's possessive and suddenly intimidating vibe.

"But I—"

"Whatever." Anna cut off my weak attempt to protest and stomped over to a waiting taxi, slamming the door after getting in. I didn't look back at the guys as I got in a second taxi, surprised at Anna's forceful exit and her unspoken refusal to share a ride. It didn't matter. All I could think about was going to sleep. Finally at home, I turned on my alarm and fell into bed without undressing.

What seemed like minutes later, the shrill beeping of my alarm clock sent an electric shock through my ears. "Oh god," I groaned and lifted my aching head. I blinked at the dark mascara prints left on my pillowcase and slowly got out of bed, my stomach rolling with every movement.

• • •

Carrying my black coffee, I walked to the nurses' station and hid my purse in a drawer. I had taken a hot shower but worried that the smell of alcohol was seeping out my pores. My turnover nurse, Donna, gave me the rundown as she put on her coat.

"Busy night, Amy, we have a full ward. Charts are up to date. The guy in 326 is going to need meds at about ten. Broken knee cap. He is allergic to morphine, so Dr. Campbell prescribed hydromorphone."

"Got it." I sat in a chair. Outside had been brisk and cool, but now I was feeling overheated and nauseous as I struggled to get out of my coat. "Is anyone else hot? What's the thermostat set to?" I asked, not directing my question to anyone in particular. I stood and turned my back to Donna, studying the thermostat on the wall. I could feel my skin flushing and the taste of Southern Comfort rising in my throat.

"Are you listening, Amy?"

"Yeah, hydromorphone. I'm assuming he doesn't get a full dose?" We stored hydromorphone in two-milligram vials, but since it was rare for physicians to order that strong a dose, we would administer one milligram and discard the rest. Due to the rise in opioid abuse, there was a new protocol in place that another staff member would verify that the administering nurse had disposed of the extra drug properly.

"Yes, just one milligram," Donna said. "But Amy, this guy has had a lot of sports injuries. He asked me what was being prescribed and then asked if I thought it would be strong enough. Maybe he's just cautious because of his allergy, but I don't know, he might be a substance abuser. Something didn't seem quite right to me."

"Thanks, Donna," I said distractedly. "I'll watch him." My tongue stuck to the roof of my mouth like it was held there with dry paste. Ice cold water. That's what I needed and was suddenly all I could think about.

"All right, have a good one," Donna said as she walked away and pressed the button for the elevator, giving me a quick wave.

I walked down the hall to the basic kitchenette and pulled a Styrofoam cup from a plastic sleeve. I filled it with ice and tap water and quickly drank it down. When I was sure no one was looking, I picked out a piece of ice with my fingers and rubbed it across my aching forehead.

The minutes passed slowly, and my hangover seemed to be getting worse. I bought some stale crackers from the vending machine, peeled off the cheese spread and quickly threw it away, gagging slightly at its slimy feel, before nibbling the edge of the cracker. I was so tired, my eyelids felt like sandpaper scratching my eyes with every blink. Back at the desk at the nurses' station, the paperwork I had been filling out blurred in front of me, and I felt myself falling asleep. I decided to walk around the unit to get my energy up, which helped slightly.

"You're awfully quiet today," Kate said as I returned to the desk.

"Mmm," I answered noncommittally. "Just a little tired." I knew that I shouldn't be at work, and I felt guilty. I would not have qualified under the 'fitness for duty' regulations with all the alcohol still in my system making my thoughts fuzzy and my stomach churn, but I had taken too many days off to help Sam out with the new baby and didn't have any more vacation or sick time accrued. Calling out just wasn't an option. I wanted to get away before Kate could ask me anything else. I checked my watch.

Noticing that it was almost ten o'clock, I stood up and said, "I'm going to give meds to room 326." I unlocked the door to the storage room and took out the med cart. I pulled the cart outside the room and knocked on the open door before entering. A man sat in the bed, his back braced on several pillows, his face contorted with pain. His left leg rested on a pillow outside the covers, white bandages stabilizing his knee.

"Hi, I'm Amy. I'm here to give you something for the pain."

"Finally," he said, his voice tight.

I took the prefilled syringe and pushed the needle into the port on the mini bag that I would attach to his IV. Remembering that he would only get half the dose, I pressed the plunger down halfway and removed the needle. After I attached the bag to his IV, the drug flowed into his system, and his face relaxed. He smiled slightly as his body slumped deeper into the pillows. One of the pillows was pushed out from under his head by the sudden shift in weight and slid to the floor. Without thinking, I bent over to pick up the pillow, but the action of leaning my head down quickly made me sick to my stomach. I stayed down for a couple of seconds, my ears buzzing loudly, willing myself to gain control and swallowing the sticky, hot vomit that pooled in my mouth. When I straightened back up, everything had a sickish, yellow hue. I blinked to clear my vision, and that's when I saw it. The empty syringe.

"I'm sorry," he said. "I'm sorry," he whispered as he leaned back into the pillows again, a satisfied grin spreading across his face.

"Oh shit," I said without thinking just as Kate appeared in the doorway. The look on my face told her something was terribly wrong.

"What happened?" Kate asked.

"He…," I started and then stopped. "I, oh, Kate, oh no, oh shit." My hands started shaking. The patient groaned quietly and looked up at the ceiling, letting his head roll carelessly from side to side.

Kate walked into the room and closed the door. "What's going on?" she demanded. She pushed me to the corner and we lowered our voices so the patient couldn't hear.

I took a deep breath. "I was administering hydromorphone, one milligram, and I bent over to pick up a pillow and he grabbed the needle and injected the rest."

"Damn it," Kate whispered with clenched teeth, shaking her head.

"It's my fault. It's my fault." I was to close tears. Kate grabbed both my hands in hers.

"No, Amy, no. How could you possibly know that he would try that? People don't just go injecting themselves. It is not your fault."

"But Donna tried to warn me, she thought he might be a—" I stumbled over the next word, I didn't want to say it in front of him. "She thought he might have problems; she made it clear." In my extreme agitation, I felt all traces of the hangover leave my body. "And," I began again slowly, "and, Kate, I left the syringe where he could grab it. I practically handed it to him. Oh god, what am I going to do?"

The patient shut his eyes; a smug, satisfied smile stuck on his face. He started snoring heavily. Kate looked at him for a long moment.

"Nothing," she said finally. "Listen, Amy, you are a great nurse. You're off your game today, for whatever reason, but that doesn't matter, and I *don't* want to know. He's sleeping it off. If you really want, put something in his chart about him trying to grab the syringe and we'll make it clear to the other nurses that they need to be careful, but that is it. I'll verify that the rest of the hydromorphone was disposed of properly. We'll watch him, just in case, and go on with our night. He's going to be fine, and you need to forget it ever happened."

"I can't," I said.

"You can and you will," Kate countered. "This is not worth a disciplinary hearing. We are short-staffed as it is, Amy; think about it like that. We need you, and this guy is to blame for what happened. Anything else is just a waste of everyone's time."

"Okay," I agreed weakly. I looked at the patient and bit my nail.

"He's fine," Kate said.

"What if he tells someone?" I asked.

"He won't. He knows that if he does, he'll be watched like a hawk by everyone, not just us. His mom and dad were in earlier to see him. He's not the type to own up to this, I know it. Just let it go. It will be fine." She picked up the empty syringe and opened the door. She put the needle in the plastic biohazard bin on the cart and initialed the chart next to my name, looking back at me over her shoulder. "It's over," she mouthed, and I followed her to the nurses' station.

• • •

I parked my car in the driveway at Sam's house and picked my way over the toys strewn across the front lawn. I passed the plastic baby pool still half-filled from the last days of summer, floating toys and grass cuttings bobbing on the tepid water. I righted a bottle of bubbles that had spilled and made an iridescent puddle on the concrete porch. Unlocking the door with the key Sam gave me, I called, "It's me," and walked inside.

When Sam found out that she was having a second baby, they moved to a bigger house in a neighborhood of new homes. Sam quit her job and became a stay-at-home mom. Although she was nervous about putting her career on hold, she found that she liked planning play dates and nights out to play Bunco with "the girls." She planned to return to work when the kids started school. The new home was still close to the metro and bus lines, which made for an easy commute for Charlie.

The foyer was large, two stories high with a staircase leading to the second floor, blocked on the top and bottom with white plastic baby gates, which made going up and down the stairs an Olympic qualifying event.

"In here," Sam yelled from the family room. The only piece of furniture in it was Sam and Charlie's old sofa from their first apartment. It was completely dwarfed in the spacious room, and its sleek square design looked out of place. They had given away their glass and steel coffee table after Emily fell and hit her head on the corner, needing a few stiches on her formerly pristine forehead. I walked down the hallway toward the sound of Sam's voice. The family room was adjacent to a spacious kitchen with an island and breakfast area.

Large bay windows faced the backyard, but a thick plastic play set with a short slide took up most of the view.

Sam was lying on her side on the floor, her body forming a protective wall around my nephew, Robbie, the newest member of the family. He was lying on a baby blanket, staring contentedly at the ceiling fan. Next to him, Emily was arranging heart-shaped stickers on a sheet of pink construction paper. Her small, chubby fingers were bending the paper to peel the stickers off, and her tongue popped in and out of the corner of her mouth in concentration. I kissed her on the top of her head, her curly hair so much like Sam's.

"Oh, I can't believe how much he changed already! He gets bigger every time I see him," I said, scooping Robbie into my arms, cradling the back of his head. Sam stretched and rolled to her back, reaching her arms overhead.

"It's what they do," she said, yawning. "He just had his three-month wellness visit. Everything looks great."

"Sammy, why don't you go lie down for a little while?" I said, "I've got the kids."

"Are you sure?"

"Yes, yes, I am," I said in a high-pitched voice, answering Sam but talking to Robbie.

Sam gave a quiet 'thanks' and stumbled in the direction of the master bedroom.

I found the BabyBjörn and awkwardly strapped Robbie in, bending his arms at unnatural angles and pulling his legs through the holes. I wasn't as graceful as Sam, but I finally got it on and secure.

"Are you hungry?" I asked Emily, who nodded. "C'mon, sweet pea, let's see what's around for lunch."

We ate looking out the window and watching the birds at the birdfeeder in the backyard as Robbie slept contentedly in the carrier. Just as Emily began rubbing her eyes, Robbie began squirming and rooting. I washed Emily's face and hands with a warm washcloth and took Robbie to Sam, who was sleeping soundly. She sat up when she heard her baby, who was just beginning to cry in earnest.

"I think he's ready to eat," I said and unsnapped the baby carrier. I laid Robbie on the bed next to Sam, and she moved closer to the baby with a tired smile.

"It's okay, baby. Mommy's here," she cooed. "What time is it?"

"One thirty. Emily had lunch. I can put her down for a nap."

"Thanks, Ames, that'd be great." Sam said inside a yawn as she sat up and took Robbie in her arms. In Emily's room, we read a chubby board book about farm animals, and then I put her in her toddler bed, kissing the soft baby fat of her cheek. By the time I went back into the living room, Sam was making instant decaf, her spoon clanging against the mug as she mixed the hot water and coffee crystals. Robbie was strapped in a bouncy seat, staring at the built-in mobile, kicking his feet cheerfully and cooing.

"So, how's work?" Sam asked, sitting down and handing me a coffee. The question was innocent enough, but I immediately thought of the patient who took the drug from me. I debated telling Sam the whole story. It was the reason that I had come to visit; I wanted to tell someone, a confession of sorts. With her absolution, I might be able to let it go, but looking at Sam now, I knew I couldn't do it. She would blame Anna for keeping me out and me for not putting my work first. I used to tell Sam everything, but she was never quite the sympathetic ear I wanted. Sam had a way of bulldozing over my problems with curt solutions. She was blunt by nature. It wasn't that she didn't care about other people's feelings, or how oversimplified and condescending her advice might sound, she just never understood how I could care so much. Still, it felt weirdly dishonest not to talk about it.

"It's same as always," I said without enthusiasm. We chatted lightly about the kids and shared stories about our parents, relating in the way only siblings can, using the shorthand of family-speak. I came close to telling her again when she commented that I looked distracted, but I didn't. I couldn't. I realized that the person I needed to talk to about this was Anna.

• • •

I thought about what I would say as I drove home from my sister's house. Once I was inside my apartment, I walked straight into my bedroom before I lost my nerve. I pushed the door tightly shut until I heard it click in place. I didn't want to risk Gail overhearing the conversation. My stomach flipped as I dialed Anna's number.

"Hey, what's up?" Anna said; her voice was light and airy.

Anxiously, I walked around the room, holding the phone tight against my ear.

"Listen, I have to tell you something. You know how we were out really late at your promotion party?"

"Yeah, that was so much fun!"

"Well, I had to work the next day and—"

"Oh man, I called work and told them I was going to be late, but David had heard about the party, and he told me to just stay home. He said that he already had as many hungover people at the office as he could handle." She laughed heartily.

"Anyway, *I* had to work."

"Why didn't you just call in sick?" She said, taking advantage of my long pause while I reorganized my thoughts. The conversation wasn't going as I planned.

"I couldn't. I told you that. I don't have any more personal time to use."

"Did you tell me? Wow, I don't remember that. The whole night is a blur." I could hear the smile in her voice, and it made my chest tighten further.

"Anna, listen to me! There was an incident at the hospital. One of my patients. He was only supposed to get one milligram of hydromorphone, which is half a dose. I wasn't paying attention and he injected himself with the rest. I—"

"Oh, no. Was it fatal?"

"What? No, of course not. Hydromorphone is an opioid. I think the patient was a drug abuser. But—"

"Well, that's good."

I stopped pacing. My blood pounded in my ears. Nothing about this was good. "You're not getting it. I could have gotten in serious trouble!"

"You? Why? He was a drug abuser; you can't be expected to control that."

"Yes, in fact, I *am* supposed to control that. A good nurse doesn't show up for work unless she is able to do her job and that morning, I was in no condition to be there! I was tired and hungover. We were out way too late, and I drank so much. I shouldn't have done that." The guilt I felt was overwhelming, crushing me like an avalanche. I needed Anna to take her share, or it would flatten me. After all, I had stayed out for her. Why didn't she see that?

"Did you get in trouble?"

"No, I didn't get in trouble. Kate covered for me."

"That's a relief. What about the patient?"

"He's fine, he slept it off." My words were uneven with frustration. Just because there were no consequences didn't mean it was okay.

"So, why are you still this upset?"

I let this question hang in the air. It made me feel small and petty.

"I just am," I said meekly.

"Well, quit worrying about it, then. It's all in the past and you got away with it. No big deal."

I hung up feeling dissatisfied, the words 'got away with it' and 'no big deal' echoing in my head. I didn't want to 'get away' with anything at my job. I was proud of my work, normally. And I wondered what would qualify as a 'big deal' to Anna and if something in *my* life ever could.

CHAPTER 9

December 2000

When I arrived at work, Gail was at the nurses' station, putting on her coat and getting her purse from under the desk.

"Hey, are you heading home?" I asked her.

"No," she said, looking a little exasperated. Her hair had turned slightly frizzy from the long shift. "I have exactly two hours and twenty minutes to go to Macy's downtown, pick up my dress that was on backorder, and look fabulous for Quinn's office holiday party tonight, remember?"

"Isn't it a little early to be having a holiday party? It's still November."

"Flip your calendar, sweets. It's December. They always have the party early in December because they want to have it before employees leave for the holidays." Quinn worked downtown as a legal aid at a law firm known for its extravagant parties and fundraising events. Gail began digging in her purse, looking for her keys. "I wish—" She stopped for a moment, resting her hands on top of her purse, the fake leather creasing under their weight. "I wish that Quinn would understand how difficult it is to have a normal life with our jobs. I mean, everything happens on the weekends. I like my job, but the crazy hours, the twenty-four-seven on-call status, no one else gets it."

I nodded in agreement. We'd had this conversation before.

"I know," I said. "Anna's magazine party is on the sixteenth." *BTB* had reserved a hotel conference room for their holiday party that was mistakenly double-booked. It would be impossible to find another venue at such a late date, so Anna stepped up and offered to host the party at her apartment. She had invited me ostensibly for moral support, but I couldn't shake the feeling that she wanted someone there who would refill the hors d'oeuvre without being asked. "No one else at the party will be getting up at 5:00 a.m. on Sunday to work, yet they all complain about how stressed they are. Like a typo is going to end the world. Also, I have no idea what the hell I'm going to wear. It's a magazine, for God's sake! You should see the outfits they wear to work. I can't even imagine what their party attire will be like. They all know how to dress, and we just, well, don't. No offense," I said gesturing to the two of us, laughing at the state of my wrinkled and stained scrubs. "We live in sneakers."

"No offense taken," Kate said, joining our group. "It's the same for me. My neighbors are having a party. The email said, 'Bring an appetizer *to share.*' Like I'd bring an appetizer and eat it in a corner yelling, 'Hands off, it's mine!'"

"I've seen you eat Doritos," I said. "You might."

"Shut up." She pushed me teasingly on the shoulder.

"What are you going to make?" Gail asked Kate.

"Make? Ha! Who has that kind of time? I'll just bring whatever the supermarket has in the bakery section and put it on one of my plates."

"We should have a party that caters to our lives," I said. "You know, a party where everyone dresses down."

"Wears their eyeglasses and no makeup," Kate said.

"Hair in ponytails," Gail said, grabbing a handful of curls and lifting them off her neck.

"And we could have it on a Tuesday… in January," I added. "We could call it the Holiday Smackdown!"

"The Smackdown!" Gail and Kate repeated. They attempted to give each other a high five but missed. I awkwardly pretended not to notice.

"We could host it." I looked questioningly at Gail. "Are we really doing this?"

"Hell yeah!" She affirmed.

"I'm in," Kate said, and the Holiday Smackdown was born.

• • •

"I've never done this before," I said nervously as I was led past rows of mirrors behind spinning black chairs. The long and narrow room was flooded with natural light from windows that reached from the floor to ceiling, illuminating a view of the city that extended across the entire side of the salon. The wall opposite the windows was exposed brick with mortar pushing between the bricks like frosting. Mirrors hung on thick metal wires attached to the ceiling. This building used to be a garment factory. Now it was a day spa, fashionably named 'A Cut Above,' and the hair salon occupied the top floor.

"You've mentioned that." Sean, the hair stylist that Anna booked for me, told me with a smile. "Anna is already here. Would you like some wine before we get started?"

"Absolutely," I said gratefully.

Sean turned the black chair to face me and raised it by pumping the foot pedal and I took a seat. He put a thin paper strip around my neck, holding it in place while surrounding me with a billowing black cape. After securing the cape, he excused himself to get the wine.

Anna appeared from around a fabric room divider with a red and white Oriental print. "You came! I was afraid that you would devise some fake emergency and cancel at the last minute."

"I've never colored my hair," I said instead of 'hello.'

Anna laughed.

Sean returned and held a glass out to me filled with a Chardonnay so clear, the glass almost looked empty. I took a big sip.

"I know, Amy. Believe me, I know," Anna said. "I'm well familiar with your hair. I remember giving you a home perm in ninth grade. Remember when we thought a perm would tame your curls?"

Sean raised an eyebrow. "How did that go?"

"Let's just say there is a reason *you* have a license and *I'm* in journalism," Anna answered. "Anyway," she turned back to me, "Sean will take good care of you."

"But—"

"Relax," she ordered. "You asked for a makeover, and this is where it starts."

A few days before, Anna and I had met for lunch. When I arrived, Anna was already seated, looking effortlessly beautiful in a cream-colored cowl neck sweater, skinny jeans, and tall brown boots. I, on the other hand, had gotten caught in the rain, without an umbrella of course, and my brown hair had responded by frizzing out of control. I could feel that the small amount of drugstore mascara that I had worn was now somewhere around my cheekbones. When Anna asked me what I wanted for Christmas that year, I spontaneously said, "A completely new look," and Anna smiled broadly, self-satisfied and mysterious, at the suggestion I had given her. Anna's extravagance when it came to her spending was a benefit when it came to being her friend.

Sean began picking up and moving sections of my hair, tousling it back and forth and making noises that I couldn't decipher as good or bad.

"Nothing too complicated," I warned him. "And I need to be able to put it in a ponytail." Sean looked dramatically up at the ceiling as if willing God to intervene and sighed.

"Told you," Anna said, conspiring with him. "Just work your magic. Don't pay any attention to her." Anna flicked her hand in my direction.

"But—" I said again sounding small and helpless.

This time, Anna picked up the wine glass and handed it to me. "Drink," she said with finality.

"Anna, will you hand me the clippers?" Sean said, and although I knew he was joking, I sat a little straighter in my chair.

"Not. Funny." I said, but I sank back in the plush chair, giving in. I saw that Anna's hair was freshly cut and colored. She inspected it in the mirror above my head and smiled, clearly pleased.

For well over an hour, Sean separated my hair with foil and applied color to the sections with a brush. It was the longest I had ever sat in a salon chair. Anna went across the street to buy us coffee while Sean and I kept up a pleasant conversation. Sean stopped to give his arms a break, resting his elbows on his hips and keeping his hands aloft like a surgeon that had just scrubbed.

"Still going?" Anna asked, having just returned, carrying three cups of coffee in a cardboard tray. The fourth hole was filled with oversized cookies wrapped in plastic.

"Almost there," Sean replied, and I wiped at a bit of color that had dripped and was tickling the top of my ear.

Sean insisted on drying and straightening my hair while keeping me facing away from the mirror. After what seemed like days, he finally spun me around for the big reveal. The chair stopped spinning with a dramatic 'ta-da!' and jazz hands from Sean.

I stared at my reflection. I had stylish long bangs that fell forward, dusting the top of my left eye as they swooped to the side. It was a simple cut, falling just to my shoulders. My normally frizzy curls were tamed to a sleek, straight line that moved back and forth like venetian blinds when I turned my head. While I was still a brunette, the color had been lightened considerably, and glinting gold highlights gave the overall effect of blonde. My eyes appeared more vivid, a richer, deeper blue, and my face, which I had always faulted for being too full, looked slender, my features defined.

"Gorgeous!" Anna squealed. "I can hardly wait to get you downstairs." She had planned the whole day for us: eyebrow waxing and makeup on the fourth floor, and manicures and pedicures on the third floor after that. "What do you think?" she asked me.

"I love it," I said, a little breathless.

Anna leaned her head just above mine, and my face was briefly covered by her shadow. "I'm so glad," she said, smiling at our images in the mirror.

"Oh, beautiful!" another stylist exclaimed, flashing us a brilliant smile as she walked past. "Are you sisters having a spa day?"

"Yes," I answered, not bothering to correct her.

• • •

I took a deep breath while standing outside Anna's apartment door. The day before, I stood in the dressing room at Nordstrom with a pile of dresses and empty hangers strewn on top of my jeans and T-shirt, feeling desperate. I slipped a violet dress covered in sequins over my head, thinking that I was going to hate it on me, but I was running out of options. The dress was daringly short, well above my knees, and held up at the top with thin spaghetti straps. I closed my eyes and took a breath before looking in the mirror. But when I saw my reflection, I smiled. A lot. I turned and looked over my shoulder. The dress hugged my lower back perfectly and fit snugly on my waist. From the front, I looked longer, taller, with just enough curves. Normally, I wouldn't even think of putting on a dress that wasn't black, but with my new hair color, the shade of the dress was flattering. I felt lighter.

When the salesgirl rang the sequined dress up, I nearly choked at the 'on sale' price but swiped my credit card anyway. She hung the dress on a tall metal pole and pulled a plastic garment bag over it, knotting it at the bottom.

Earlier tonight, at my apartment, I carefully applied Anna's spa day makeup to complete the look. Gail gasped when she saw me, and Quinn gave me a low wolf whistle. But now, about to enter a party with *BTB*'s stylish cast of people, my confidence was crashing fast. I tugged at the bottom of the dress, stretching it downward, wishing it were longer or that I hadn't left my totally unglamorous but highly functional coat in the car.

I could hear the murmur of the party through Anna's front door. I opened it a crack and peeked into her living room. The party decorations made her apartment look like it was straight out of one of the magazine's issues. Rows of tiny white lights were strung across her ceiling, and dangling off the strings were gold and silver balloons. The balloons, filled with air, not helium, were hung so that they fell to random heights, all high enough to be above the guests' heads. Anna had opted for a gold and silver theme instead of the traditional red and green, something that wouldn't have occurred to me, but added an elegant air to the party and complemented her unusual pale blue walls. She'd placed candles around the room and dimmed the lights. Appetizers in ornate serving trays filled a long table under the windows facing the street. The table was decorated with pinecones colored silver with spray paint. I had helped Anna paint the pinecones a few days ago outside her building, a suggestion from *BTB* that sounded much easier than it was. We nearly asphyxiated from the fumes, and although we covered the ground with newspapers held down by rocks, we still managed to paint the alley behind her place silver.

"Call 911," Anna had said loudly, crumpling up the used newspapers and throwing them in the dumpster. "The Tin Man has been murdered!"

"We're totally screwed," I said, laughing with her and showing her my spray paint–covered hands. "Evidence."

With a quick breath, I smoothed my dress one last time, opened the door fully, and walked in. People were standing and talking in groups. I didn't see Anna yet, but I saw my salvation in the kitchen. The bar. Set up in the space where Anna's kitchen table would normally be, the bar was complete with a bartender, hired for the party, dressed in a white shirt with a black vest and a crisp black bow tie. I gave the bartender a smile and headed toward him.

"Sorry," a man said as he accidently bumped my arm.

"No problem," I said, stopping and smiling politely at him.

"I'm David," he said, transferring his drink to his left hand to shake mine. "Garrison," he added as an afterthought, although I had him pegged as the infamous 'David' as soon as I saw him. He was about five foot ten, but he had the commanding presence of a taller man. His dark hair was cut short to control its curly nature. He had a strong jawline and a five o'clock shadow peeking from under his skin that could *almost* pass as unintentional. In an odd way, he looked familiar. I was almost certain that I had met him before, but

I couldn't place where I'd met him. I let the thought go and extended my hand.

"Amy." I said, "Sheppard." His hand was cold and wet from the drink.

"Wait," he said. "Not *the* Amy." He gave me a wide, suspicious smile.

"Probably," I said with a pretend sigh. "It depends on what you've heard."

"I've heard," he said, leaning toward me and talking out of the side of his mouth, "that you enjoy spray-painting in dark alleys."

I laughed. "That would be me," I said, thinking that meeting this man made coming here worthwhile. Even if it did require makeup and bare shoulders.

"Anna's hands were silver for a week. No one at the office will let her live it down."

"She was so panicked, I told her the paint was water-soluble to get her to relax. How long did it take her to figure out I lied?"

"I think she got suspicious after the second bottle of nail polish remover."

"Amy, you made it! And you look fantastic!" Anna exclaimed, interrupting us as she approached and gave me a stiff, brief hug. I was embarrassed by her compliment and could feel my cheeks start to flush. I had almost forgotten about the dress I was wearing and now it was *all* I could think about. So much exposed skin. "*This* dress I may have to borrow," she said in a way that made me think this dress was the only thing I owned that Anna would wear. "Did you just get here?" I started to answer, but she interrupted me. "I see you met David." She put her hand possessively on his upper arm and smiled at me.

"Yes," I said, then struggled to think of more to say. She had thrown me too many half-conversation starters without letting me reply.

"Oh, you need a drink," she said, indicating my empty hands. "And you have to try the brie and smoked salmon."

"Sounds delicious." I said praying my stomach wouldn't growl at the mention of food. I hadn't eaten since breakfast to make sure the dress would zipper.

"It is. David, that reminds me, I want to talk to the caterer I used tonight about a possible article. She offers a cooking class on how to make appetizers. I think it would dovetail nicely with our articles about hosting parties after the holidays. Remember the 'keeping the holiday spirit alive all year' theme?"

"Oh, like the Smackdown," I interjected.

"Not exactly," Anna said at the same time that David asked, "What's a 'smackdown'?" Amusement snuck in his voice.

"Oh, it is just a party that my roommate and I are having after the holidays. We are both nurses and we don't always get a break over the holidays, so we're having a party in January to celebrate surviving and keeping our jobs. We want it to be very casual, though, a come-as-you-are kind of thing. The fun of a party without the stress."

"Could we use that idea in the magazine?" David asked leaning toward me.

"Sure." I looked into David's dark eyes. David started to ask another question when Anna spoke up.

"Great idea, we should definitely add that to the issue," she said, causing David and I to break eye contact. "I can do the research first-hand." She winked at me.

"You're welcome to come, too," I said to David.

"Sounds interesting," he answered noncommittally.

"Hi, David, Anna," another woman said as she joined our group. The conversation turned to work, as most office parties eventually do, and I excused myself and headed to the bar. I wondered if David was watching me as I walked away when without warning, my ankle turned slightly for an ungainly stumble. I quickly righted myself hoping that no one noticed when I saw the bartender grinning at me.

"Shit," I mouthed.

"I think you've had quite enough, young lady," he said when I got closer. He pretended to shield the bar with his hands.

"You wouldn't dare. I obviously need something strong to relax me so that I can walk in these stupid things, right?" I indicated my pumps. As short as I was, you'd think I got the hang of walking in high heels, but I hadn't.

"Yeah, I'm afraid alcohol has the opposite effect. But I *could* add more liquor to everyone else's drinks. You could be graceful by comparison. How does that sound?"

"Graceful by comparison to a bunch of drunk people, that sounds like it might be my best bet. In the meantime, I'll have a glass of… merlot?" My voice rose on the last word, drawing it out into a question.

"Or you could have a beer," he suggested. "I'll put it in a cut crystal tumbler. No one has to know."

"Thank you, that would be perfect."

I managed to survive the rest of the party with little incident. I saw a writer, Sarah, that I had met through Anna, and I approached her. We chatted comfortably with a few other writers in between drink refills and appetizers. I followed Sarah when she went outside to join a group of hard-core smokers huddled on Anna's back patio, shivering between drags, not smoking myself but also not wanting to lose Sarah's companionship for the night. Anna had quit smoking. She attributed it to David—he detested the smell and would wrinkle his nose in disgust whenever Anna had been in the breakroom. Since then, Anna had turned militantly anti-smoking and her co-workers knew better than to light up inside her apartment. I made sure to keep myself downwind, so David wouldn't smell smoke on me if I managed to talk to him again. I was already captivated by David. I found myself watching him as he so easily mingled, becoming the center of attention in each group be joined. His charisma was palatable; he was just as Anna described. Late in the night, our paths crossed again. I may have engineered it with a well-timed refill from the appetizer bar.

"I hear that you are an expert photographer as well as a spray paint artist." David said, continuing our conversation from earlier in the night with ease.

"Expert? Well, that's more than a slight exaggeration."

"No, Anna isn't known for being generous with her compliments and she talks highly of your photographs. I really would love to see your portfolio."

"If by 'portfolio' you mean 'disorganized pictures in a cardboard box,' I'd be happy to show you." I was surprised by my own suggestion. Aside from the few photographs that I'd framed, I hadn't shown my photographs to anyone except a few friends and my family.

"Great," David said. "Let me get your number." My heart skipped a beat. He put his drink on the mantle. The fireplace had not been serviceable in years, but Anna made it the focal point of the living room, filling it with large candles and a decorative garland that she changed to match the seasons. He reached inside his suit pocket for a pen. I dictated my phone number to him, wondering if he would really call or if this was just something that classy men did, like carrying a pen in their suit pocket to a party. He wrote it down on the dry section of his cocktail napkin.

Sarah joined us. "I think I'm going to head home," she said, noting that the crowd had thinned.

"Me too. I'll walk out with you." We said goodnight to David, and I followed Sarah to the bedroom to get her coat. When we got there, I confessed that I hadn't worn mine but quickly covered my embarrassment, saying that it was fine because I was parked close to the apartment, even though that wasn't true. We found Anna and thanked her as we said our goodbyes.

"You did a great job hosting tonight," I whispered in her ear as we hugged.

"It was a success, wasn't it? I'm so relieved." Anna pulled back. "Let's have lunch this week. I'll call you." She turned back to the remaining guests, and I braced myself for a frigid walk to my car.

• • •

"That'll be seventeen fifty, miss," the taxi driver told me, looking over his shoulder into the back seat. He turned on the dim overhead light as I struggled to see inside my purse, looking for my wallet. Fumbling in the semi-darkness, my fingers felt the edges of the envelope, the paper worn soft. My memento, my reminder. A fragile piece of my heart that could easily be ripped if I opened it too quickly or fade if I exposed to the light.

I found my wallet and handed the driver a twenty-dollar bill to cover his fare and a tip. Without speaking, I opened the door and stepped outside.

CHAPTER 10

December 2000

Halfway through my morning routine, the apartment phone rang. I hastily spit the foaming toothpaste in the bathroom sink and walked, still working the toothbrush in my mouth, intending to check the caller ID and call whoever it was back later. But when the caller ID read "D. Garrison," I froze mid-brush. Taking the toothbrush out of my mouth, I swallowed hard, grimacing, then I picked up the phone with my other hand, awkwardly pushed the 'talk' button, and said hello.

"Hi, is this Amy? This is David Garrison. We met at Anna's party."

"Hey, David, yeah, it's me." I wasn't sure what to say next, so I awkwardly waited for him to continue.

"I wanted to see if you would like to go with me to the Airess this Friday, the twenty-second. I know it's a little close to Christmas, but if you aren't busy, it's the last night for the photography exhibit featuring Mary Fireland."

I had never heard of the photographer, but he honestly could have said Big Bird and I would have said yes.

"Sure, I'd be happy to," I said, reviewing my work schedule in my head and confirming that I was off that night.

"Good. The gallery opens at nine. I was thinking we could go to dinner before the exhibit if you'd like?"

"Yes, that'd be great," I said, trying to sound casual, although mentally I was jumping up and down.

"Good, good," he said. "I'll make reservations. How does Marabella's sound?"

Completely unfamiliar to me, I thought, but I said, "Perfect."

"I'll probably be coming straight from the office, so is it okay if I meet you there at seven?"

"No problem, I'll see you then."

"I'm looking forward to it, Amy," he said.

"Me too."

I double-checked that the phone was disconnected before shouting, "Oh my god, Gail! Gail! You'll never believe who just asked me out!" My words ran together with excitement. I danced my way to Gail's bedroom and repeated the phone call word for word before I finished getting ready for work.

. . .

"Can you keep an eye on the call lights for my rooms, Kate? I'm going to take a break."

"Now? You've only been here an hour."

"I'm actually just going to make a phone call from the lobby phones."

"Not here?" Kate indicated the phone on the desk. "Who's the guy?"

"Tell you all about it when I come back," I said, rushing to the elevator before anyone could stop me.

In the hospital's main lobby, there was a small row of privacy phones set up at desks with partitions in between that made them look like voting booths. They were available for families to make local calls. Originally, the phones had long-distance capabilities, but after the first bill, the hospital quickly shut that down and made calling cards available in the gift shop.

I dialed Anna's number at work.

"Anna Kildare," Anna answered, sounding brusque and professional.

"You'll never guess who called and asked me out!" I said, knowing there was no need to say who was calling; she would recognize my voice.

"Who?" Her tone lost its professional edge immediately. "Was it someone from the party? I bet it was Miguel. He's part of the advertising staff; I saw he had his eye on you."

"No, it was David. Can you believe it? David Garrison asked me out!" I waited a beat, but Anna didn't say anything. "Are you still there?"

"Yes. Wow, Amy, that is great! I was just a little surprised." Anna recovered quickly. "When is your date?"

"Friday. He's taking me to dinner at Marabella's. Do you know it?"

"Yes, it's very nice."

"And then we are going to a photography exhibit at the Airess. Oh my god, I am so psyched! You have to come shopping with me before Friday." No one had style like Anna, and I was desperate for her help.

"That's only a few days away. I don't know if I can," Anna said vaguely.

"Anna, you know I'm terrible at this. I'll be a mess if you don't help me. Please?"

"Okay, sure. Wednesday night?"

"Yes, thank you! I have to get back to work, but I'll call you and we can set up a time. You're the best," I said and hung up the phone.

• • •

Marabella's was on Chestnut Street in the historic district. Although the night was cold, I had the taxi drop me off at the end of the block. I was early and decided to take a few minutes to calm my nerves before going inside. My inner monologue swirled with a few conversation starters. Ahead of me, I saw David getting out of a taxi, looking even more attractive than I remembered. He went inside without seeing me. I waited a beat, then walked into the restaurant and approached the hostess standing at her podium. The restaurant was small and upscale although it felt a little contrived, like it was striving to be featured in a romcom montage. It was dotted with small tables softly lit with tabletop lamps, each designed to fit two people, no more, leaving very little room for food.

David greeted me by standing and giving me a quick kiss on the cheek. I sat across from him and smiled, finding myself at a loss for words for the very first time. Ever. Literally since I learned to speak. All the preplanned conversations in my head ran away like frightened deer. I was surprised they didn't knock over the fragile-looking tables on their way out.

"So," David said, pulling the cloth napkin out of its silver ring, snapping it open, and placing it on his lap. I followed his lead and opened my napkin. "Anna tells me that you've been friends since you were five years old."

"Yes, since kindergarten," I said, relieved he had eased me in with a familiar topic. "We grew up in Bell's Lake together, right across the street from each other."

We talked briefly about my childhood, my parents, and sister. I started gushing when I described my niece and nephew, but I stopped short of pulling pictures out of my wallet like a grandmother. Anna warned me that when it came to Emily and Robbie, I acted one step away from having blue hair and feathered lipstick. She'd be proud of my restraint, I thought, and mentally patted myself on the back.

"So, where are you from?" I asked, turning the conversation back to David.

"Wyncote," he said, naming a prestigious suburb of Philadelphia. He continued to tell me about his family and his younger brother, William, who lived in Boston. David had attended Temple University and received a master's degree in journalism with a minor in graphic design.

After dinner, we stepped outside. The rush of cold wind felt as sharp as a knife in contrast to the pleasant warmth of the restaurant. My bare legs were dimpled from the chill, but Anna had threatened me within an inch of my life *not* to wear nylons.

"No one wears nylons anymore," she chided me while helping me shop for an outfit. "No. One."

"But—" I protested.

"Your mother doesn't count," she interrupted, and I conceded, mollified. With Anna's help, I had bought a black-and-white hound's-tooth wrap dress with a deep V-neckline. After much begging, Gail loaned me her black knee-high boots.

David hailed a taxi, and after a short ride to the Airess, he paid the driver. The gallery was on the first floor of an old department store that had been subdivided into shops. The front window was lit by recessed lights, and a large photograph—I assumed by Fireland—dominated the middle. It was a close-up of a person's eye, taken slightly off center. The photographer was reflected in the iris, a black figure surrounded by marbling shades of light green. The theme of the exhibit was 'Reflections of Virtue and Iniquity.' Once inside, I slipped off my heavy coat and draped it over my arm, intending to carry it through the exhibit. As I was readjusting my purse over my shoulder, I felt David gently pulling the coat from my arm. He walked back to the small coatroom that I had passed without noticing and exchanged our coats for a paper ticket that he put in the pocket of his suit jacket with all the confidence of a man who routinely attended art exhibits.

The front rooms were a collection of different photographers, an introduction to the main event. We walked slowly through the front, examining the art, noting the different styles and subject matters.

"I really would like to see your photographs," David said as we walked through a doorway leading to the main exhibit hall. The entrance was tight, and he brushed against me. I felt a rush of adrenaline as we touched.

"Oh," I said modestly, "I don't know, I'm just an amateur." David gave me a look that told me false modesty was something he didn't condone but I had been discounting myself for so long, I wasn't sure I could stop. Then something clicked inside of me. I *was* proud of my work, after all, so why not let him see it and judge for himself? "I'd be happy to show them to you." I said backpedaling.

"Then we'll be sure to do that." A flood of confidence washed over me, and I felt myself stand a little straighter.

The main room was subdivided down the middle with a temporary partition. On the left, the photographs were hung on dark walls with bright lighting to offset the dimness. On the opposite side, the photographs were hung on light-colored walls, and the lighting was muted. The overall effect was an equal distribution of light, masking the drastic differences in color.

David indicated with an extended hand that I should go first, and I started on the left side, exploring the photographs that encompassed the photographer's vision of iniquity. I expected to see black-and-white photographs of anguished faces and heinous acts that were considered art for their shock value, but Fireland's insight surprised me. She had captured iniquity in a subtler way. The photographs appeared to be unremarkable until you looked at them more closely. Each one had a reflection, a second image captured in water, in glass, in any reflective surface. It was in the reflections that the art was created, like the image of the photographer in the iris on the exhibit's premier photograph. A laughing person's sunglasses became the canvas for another image, an angry face making the laugh turn maniacal. A mirror in the background of an empty room holding the indistinct shadow of a person. David and I had settled into a natural museum pace, exploring the exhibit mostly on our own, but stopping and waiting for each other to catch up when we wanted to comment on a certain picture.

I turned the corner at the end of the exhibit, and David followed closely behind me. This was the lighter side, and again, Fireland used an unconventional take on the subject. 'Virtue' was not immediately apparent until I found the reflection. A desolate frozen lake reflecting a single flawless cloud, as perfect as a child's drawing. A bouquet of bright flowers reflected in the shiny surface of a granite tombstone.

A picture at the end of the room caught my attention, and my gaze returned to it several times as I wandered through the second half of the exhibit. It straddled the two sides of the room. It was hung across from the dividing wall, intended to be the final photograph of the collection. At last, I came to it and examined it without distraction. It was a photograph of two young girls. They were wearing school uniforms that minimized their differences, plaid skirts and crisp white tops with maroon bows tied at the neckline. The girls were young, about eight or nine years old. At first glance, both girls were smiling the kind of smile that girls have exclusively before their teenage years, when they still see themselves as capable of anything and their world has no limits. Virtue. I leaned closer to the photograph. The girls were looking into each other's eyes. The girl on the right appeared genuinely happy, but something in the expression of the girl on the left held something closer to anxiety. Her smile was forced, her teeth tight, and jaw clenched. I searched the image for a reflection but couldn't find one.

I felt David coming up behind me. He lightly placed his hand on the small of my back. I stiffened slightly from his unexpected touch, then I relaxed into it. He raised his hand slowly, tracing it up my back and gently laying it on my shoulder as he moved closer to me. I leaned back into him, aware of his breath enticingly close to my ear. My stomach tightened, and I was consumed with thoughts of kissing David. I broke my gaze from the photograph and turned my head over my shoulder, angling my chin up slightly so that our faces were inches apart. I felt myself smile as his eyes closed, and he leaned down, gently putting his lips on mine, a hummingbird taking flight in my stomach.

• • •

"Spill," Anna said to me.

I called her immediately after my date with David, climbing into bed with the phone to my ear, so I could wrap myself in a blanket while we talked, just like I had done when we were teenagers. "I didn't spend my evening helping you pick out that to-die-for dress to hear, 'We had a good time.' I want details."

"Okay," I said, jumping right to the good part. "He kissed me at the exhibit. And again when we were saying goodnight."

I tried to sound nonchalant, but Anna squealed. "Is he a good kisser?"

"Yes." My voice was as high and squeaky as hers. I nodded vigorously although she couldn't see me. Teenage girls at heart forever.

"So, what else? Did he say he'd call you? Any plans to see him again?" The questions rushed out of Anna's mouth.

"Well, he wants to see my pictures. Thank you, by the way; he said you really talked them up. I also re-invited him to the Smackdown, and he said he'd come, but I probably won't see him before that. He's leaving tomorrow, but you probably already knew that. He's going to spend the holidays skiing in Colorado with his brother and their parents. It's their holiday tradition. They own a small cabin in Woody Creek, near Aspen. Are you going home for Christmas? Your office is closed until after New Year's, right?"

"Yeah, I'll be heading to Bell's Lake." I knew from the deflated tone of Anna's voice that I had touched a nerve. It had been years since she lost her father, but the holidays would always be hard for her. I knew that spending Christmas with her mom and Doctor Ben felt to her like she was with the wrong family. As if she entered an alternate reality where her mom held her passion in check and loved a man who was safe and comfortable. Doctor Ben had proposed to Renée once—it was right after he moved into her house—but she politely declined. She said that she had been down that road before and there was no reason to do it again. But they continued to live together, and both seemed content. Renée liked that she could focus on her career. She turned Doctor Ben's one-man practice into a thriving business by adding doctors to their staff. Currently, she was deeply involved in a project to add in-house X-ray capabilities at their office.

"Stop by my mom's house; we'll all be there," I said, referring to Sam and her family.

"Maybe."

"Well, let's definitely plan something fun for New Year's Eve," I said, trying to rally her mood. "I hear that Slackers is having a ticket-only event. And then we could watch the fireworks on the waterfront."

"Okay. It's a date," she said with a little resignation in her voice that I forgave. I thought that despite her protests, she may have some feelings for David. But she had put her career first and, I reasoned to myself with newfound confidence, maybe it was time that she learned that she couldn't have everything.

• • •

January 2001

The morning of the Smackdown, I woke up early and stumbled into the kitchen in search of coffee. Our apartment didn't look ready for a party, I thought, remembering how beautifully Anna had decorated for the *BTB* holiday gathering. Gail was sitting on the living room sofa, coffee in hand. I poured myself a mug and joined her.

"We said, 'Come as you are,'" she said, sighing and looking around our very messy living space.

"We said we wouldn't clean," I agreed, looking around, feeling uncomfortable, like I was about to expose myself in a bikini with my skin still winter white.

"But maybe we could straighten up, just a little," Gail said with a pleading look.

"No one has to know that we aren't perpetually neat, right?" I said. "We can *pretend* we don't live like a couple of frat boys."

"Exactly." She picked up the newspaper from the living room coffee table and straightened the pages as she walked towards the recycling bin by the front door. I gathered my shoes that were strewn around the living room and began throwing them toward my bedroom. Suddenly, we had a lot to do, and time seemed short.

By the time the first guests arrived, the apartment had been miraculously cleaned and decorated with a random assortment of Hawaiian leis and Mardi Gras beads. Earlier in the week, we'd burned music mixes onto blank CDs, an eclectic mix of our favorite songs to keep the party going, Bob Marley followed by Paula Abdul with a little eighties' favorites like the Violent Femmes and Bon Jovi. There was a sign above the table with appetizers that read 'Nothing with Nutmeg' and a Crockpot bubbling with spicy Ethiopian chicken stew, Gail's family recipe. Greasy chicken wings from Ray's Tavern were being kept warm in a chafing dish. Assorted alcohol lined the kitchen counter, and Quinn, who had worked his way through college as a bartender, taped instructions with drink suggestions to the wall under a handmade sign that read 'Self-Service Bar.' Next to the counter was a cooler full of beer.

Guests started to arrive around eight. Gail and I took turns greeting people, most of whom were mutual friends from the hospital. Around eight fifteen, I opened the door to a foursome from the radiology department, all wearing flannel pajamas. I burst out laughing.

"You've set a whole new standard for casual attire. I am humbled," I said with a deep bow. Noticing their feet, I added, "The fuzzy slippers are a nice touch." I opened the door wider to let them in.

Anna arrived at eight thirty. She wore an oversized long sleeve black shirt over plaid leggings that somehow managed to look relaxed and stylish at the same time. An hour or so later, David arrived.

"You're a little overdressed for the Smackdown, aren't you?" I asked him, gesturing to his suit.

"I came straight from a dinner meeting. I didn't have time to dress properly, or underdress properly I guess would be more accurate." He took in my Bloomsburg University sweatshirt and Lycra leggings. His eyes stopped on the Hello Kitty barrette that I'd had since grade school, pinning back my bangs.

"David!" Anna exclaimed happily when she saw him. She abandoned her chair and walked over to us. "I know that you don't want to discuss work, but I have a quick idea to run past you." She touched his arm. "It'll only take a few minutes," she added apologetically to me.

"No worries," I said. "I'm sure there is an empty bowl of Cheetos that needs to be refilled around here somewhere." I left Anna and David and went to the kitchen. After checking on the snacks, I grabbed my camera and snapped pictures of the guests, who had moved the coffee table to make space for a makeshift dance floor.

The party started getting loud around midnight, and that is when David decided to leave.

"Amy," he said, tapping me lightly on the shoulder, "I'm going to call it a night. This was really fun."

"I'm glad you could make it."

"Do you think we could use some of the pictures you took to accompany the article? We'll get permission from your friends, of course."

"They would totally love that!" I said.

"I'll call you, and we can look at them once you get them developed."

I was wondering if that constituted a second date when David added, "And we could get dinner."

Score! I thought. It felt like our first date had been ages ago, and even though I knew he'd been traveling, I had assumed that David had lost interest. Calmly I said, "That sounds nice. Let me get your coat from the bedroom." We had thrown the guests' coats in a pile on my bed. David followed me into the room and shut the door behind him, drawing me into a passionate kiss that first startled me and then took my breath away.

"Nice?" he teased, pulling back to look at me. "Dinner sounds 'nice'?"

"Well, it does sound nice. I like food," I added coyly. David laughed and put his coat on. We left the bedroom, walking so close to one another that we bumped shoulders and giggled like we shared a secret.

"I'm heading out, too, Amy. Great time," Anna said.

"Aw, so soon?" I asked.

"Well, to use your line, I have to work in the morning."

"Good luck with that," I said, knowing that Anna would not be happy when her alarm went off. As I was heading back to the bedroom to grab her coat, I heard Anna ask David if he wanted to share a cab.

• • •

The following Saturday morning, I waited impatiently in Anna's living room while she finished getting ready to go step class with me at the Center City YMCA.

"C'mon," I mumbled under my breath, rolling my eyes. Anna had been acting strange all morning, distracted and disorganized.

"Sorry, sorry," she said without looking at me as she hurried into the room. "I can't find my running shoes," she said as she stooped to look under the sofa. I glanced at my watch; at this rate we were going to be late for our class. Anna's membership at her upscale gym near Chestnut Hill had expired and I suggested that Anna join the YMCA downtown, so we could work out together, but I was starting to regret it, as I hated being late. Anna seemed confident that we would still be on time or somehow the class would wait for her.

"Got 'em," she said, retrieving her sneakers from under the coffee table. "Let's go." She pulled the shoes over her feet and wiggled her ankles to get them in without untying the laces.

We walked quickly down Twenty-Second Street toward the YMCA, hunching our shoulders against the cold and dodging pedestrians as we went.

"Did you have fun at the party?" I asked, the warm moisture of my breath turning into a misty cloud.

"Yeah, sure, of course."

"You left kind of early; you missed the best part. Quinn brought out his beer bong from college. *No one* could do it anymore, but we tried. Gail and I will be finding sticky spots on the kitchen floor for a year," I said with a snicker. We stopped to let traffic cross in front of us on Walnut Street, and Anna repeatedly pushed the pedestrian crossing button on the stop light.

"Must have been a good time. Hey, are those new sneakers?" Anna asked, pointing to my feet.

"No. So anyway, it was hilarious. Jeff, the super tall guy, do you remember him? He decided that we needed to hold the funnel part higher, so he hopped on one of the kitchen chairs and it broke! Can you believe it? He landed flat on his back when he fell but didn't spill the beer!" I laughed, but Anna didn't join me.

After a beat, Anna said, "Well, if you are looking for sneakers, there is a great new place. Have you been to the new store near the mall in King of Prussia?" I shook my head, thinking that I really didn't care about shoes. Anna was obviously avoiding talking about the party. It was odd; she generally fit in with my friends from the hospital. I couldn't figure out why she was being so cagey. Normally, I would let this go, but I thought of Anna's promotion party and holiday party. We talked about those parties for days afterwards, the mandatory girlfriend recap that was almost as much fun as the party itself. I wanted to do the same thing now. It had been a big night for me.

"It *looked* like you were having a good time…," I said, letting the end of my sentence drift like bait on a fishing hook trying to lure Anna into telling me what was on her mind.

"I was, I swear!" she said, but something in her voice didn't ring true. "I was just sorry that I had to leave so early."

"Oh," I said, not quite buying her explanation but deciding to let it go. "You know, I could use some new sneakers. Maybe we could go shopping tomorrow? Do you have any plans?" I asked and Anna brightened.

"Nope! I'm free and you'll love this place; it has a great sales section in the back." She continued talking as the light changed and we crossed the street. I looked beyond Anna's profile at the red-brick townhomes with rounded archways encasing their doors, snow piled in frozen chunks along the freshly shoveled sidewalks. The endless pattern ahead of us was broken up by the occasional tree, barely surviving, just sticks and bare branches. The trees were planted by the city in the tiniest of squares where the sidewalk blocks had been removed. Unclaimed by cement, these sections provided just enough space for the trees to grow. I shivered and pulled my hood over my head as Anna continued talking.

• • •

February 2001

"Here," I said as I pulled the cardboard box of photographs out of my bedroom closet and dropped it on the bed where David was sitting, its weight causing the mattress to bounce. David sat with his back against the headboard and his legs stretched out in front of him, the twin creases of his khaki pants lined up perfectly, like railroad tracks. He wore a long-sleeve polo shirt in a shade of burgundy that looked expensive. I caught my reflection in my mirror. This morning, I had put on a jade green top that was a little faded but fit snugly around my waist and showed off the tiniest hint of cleavage. I had paired it with dark-washed jeans. I thought it was casually sexy, but against David's crisp appearance, it looked cheap and sloppy. I looked away from the mirror and returned my attention to the box, determined not to undermine my own confidence—I could hardly change clothes now. "This is it," I said dramatically as I unfolded the top of the box and pulled out a stack of photos, all in various sizes.

"Amy," David said with a disbelieving laugh, "you should organize these."

"It's on my list, right up there next to 'learn Spanish.'" David gave me a teasingly exasperated look. "Hey, at least it's before 'run a marathon,' so, you know, it's basically next in line." I flipped through the photographs in my hand and found the ones that I was looking for, a series of photographs of Swann Memorial on Logan Circle. I handed them to David, explaining, "I took these a few months ago. There are so many great subjects to photograph downtown. Every time I take my camera out, I find someplace new." When I had them developed, the clerk commented on how good he thought these particular images were.

"This is some quality work," David said with an unmasked hint of surprise as he looked at the first photograph, the archetypal view down Benjamin Franklin Parkway. "The play of the light on the outline of the museum in the background, that's what makes this photograph stand out." He held the photo at arm's length and nodded his head approvingly before laying it next to the box.

"Thank you." I stopped myself from adding any disparaging comment or qualifier about my work. I had learned that with David, a simple 'thank you' was enough.

We sifted through more photos of Philadelphia and then some family photos: Emily unwrapping a present under the Christmas tree smiling with delight, candid shots of family get-togethers, a picture of my newborn nephew, Robbie, sleeping peacefully, that I had enlarged and framed for Sam. While exploring the box, I realized that the pictures were organized by rolls of film, several still in their original envelopes, with the most recent photographs on top. Near the bottom were pictures of the Pocono Mountains I had taken on a breathtaking fall day in 1999. I had almost forgotten about those pictures. They were by far the most amateur, making me realize how much I had improved. David offered comments and suggestions, placing the photos in separate piles on the floor. I found myself abnormally quiet as he critiqued my work. He offered suggestions about composition that didn't make sense to me, but he backed off when I started asking him specific questions about the rule of thirds, something I had learned in one of my photography classes. It was a basic concept of photography that he didn't seem to know.

"Your scenic shots show potential, but there isn't much here. Do you have any that aren't local?"

"Not really. The Poconos are about as far as I've traveled. But I would love to do some serious traveling. Europe, Asia," I said wistfully.

"Well, what's stopping you?"

"Time, money, the usual. But mostly time; I never seem to have any extra." But then I thought about a trip to France with Anna that I had tried to coordinate years ago. It was surprisingly easy to get the vacation time with enough advance notice. Anna kept putting me off until she finally confessed that she didn't really want to go. She wanted to spend the money she'd saved for the trip on something else, something tangible that she could have forever, like this credenza she'd found at an antique shop on Pine Street. She told me how much she loved it and that she'd lose her deposit if she didn't pay it off. I remembered thinking I'd prefer experiences over objects and wondering why she put down a deposit in the first place if she didn't have the money, but at the time, I didn't push her about it and the trip was canceled. "Especially when you add in another person's schedule."

"If that is the case, why not travel alone?" David suggested.

The idea of a solo vacation had simply never occurred to me, and I dismissed the idea before letting it fully sink in. "Nah, I'd have more fun if I was with someone." I explained. Realizing that this might sound like I was hinting at a couple's vacation, I quickly added, "You could give Anna an extra week of vacation."

"Nope." He said abruptly, cutting me off. Although he was smiling, I got the impression that he found dating his employee's best friend awkward. "But you can take someone else," he added, steering the conversation back to me.

"Maybe, but it *is* hard to get away from work, and my sister certainly counts on me for babysitting," I said thinking of the number of times I had watched Emily and Robbie on short notice. But my excuses sounded lame, even to me.

"I'm sure they would all survive. You could make it work if it was something you genuinely wanted to do." His words triggered memories of when I first became interested in photography, looking through my grandfather's copies of *National Geographic*. I would sit mesmerized by pictures of African people, faces covered with painfully beautiful tribal scars or expanses of canyons, endlessly deep, bathed in golden light. The images in the magazine ranged from crowded city streets to single thatched-roof huts. I became fascinated by the life of the person who took the pictures, the person who linked the world's diversity by lining it up, side by side, negatives on a roll of film. When I told my grandfather that I wanted to be a photographer, he, always a pragmatic man, suggested that I pursue a profession that was more stable and keep photography as a hobby and see where it took me. "If you really want it, you'll find your way to it," he had said. He gave me my first camera when I was ten. The camera was small and square with manual focus and a built-in flash that didn't need to be replaced, which was the peak of technology at the time. I smiled remembering that my first picture was of him.

"When I was ten—" I started to tell this story to David, but he interrupted me.

"Some of these are pretty good," he concluded, having reached the bottom of the box. He looked at the stacks of photos. "But this box is a mess. I have an idea. Why don't you give them to me, and I'll have someone on our staff put together a portfolio for you. We'll organize it by category, one for scenery shots, one of family, like that. You have the negatives in the envelopes, so we'll print copies of the photos to use. We could crop some of the images to help with composition."

"Maybe, yeah, that sounds good," I said trying to ignore my proprietary feelings for my cardboard-box filing system. "It would be nice to have them organized, but I don't really need a portfolio." I said, a little worried about someone at *BTB* feeling put upon with this non-work project.

"Why not have a portfolio ready just in case you want to do this professionally someday? After all, you have already been published in a very prestigious magazine," he said, referring to the pictures in *BTB* of the Smackdown. Every one of my friends who had attended the party bought an issue that month.

"But I *have* a profession," I told him. "I'm a nurse, remember?"

"Yes, you say that," David answered, an enigmatic grin spreading slowly across his face, "but I've yet to see you in a uniform with white stockings…."

I hit him with a pillow. "Why do men *always* go there?" I said laughing.

"A little white cap," he added, ducking my next blow.

"Seriously?" I continued hitting him with the pillow. He grabbed me and kissed me. We fell back on the bed together, the photographs forgotten.

• • •

The next morning, I woke up to see David looking at me with a half-smile dancing on his lips, memories of our first night together floating near the surface.

"How long have you been awake?" I asked, blinking at the clock. It was already past 9:30 and I couldn't believe I slept so long with David in my bed.

"Not long—" David started to add something when my stomach let out a loud growl. "Was that your stomach?" He laughed with disbelief. Embarrassed, I nodded, and I pulled the covers over my head. David pulled them back down again.

"C'mon, honey, get up and I'll treat you to breakfast. I hear grizzly bears are mean when they are hungry." I groaned, tightening my face. "You are adorable when you blush," David said, making me smile. "That's better," he added, cupping my chin in his hand, and pulling me in for a quick morning kiss.

"Let me take a fast shower first," I said. I used one arm to hold up the sheet while I groped next to the bed until I found a long nightshirt and slipped it on before standing up. Even though we had just slept together, I wasn't quite ready for David to see me naked in full daylight.

After the shower, I put on my worn Yoga Experience T-shirt and zipped a soft gray hoodie over top. David got up and showered while I sat on my bed blow-drying my hair. He didn't seem self-conscious in the least, but I still wanted to give him privacy in the bathroom. David emerged wearing the clothes he had on yesterday that had somehow managed not to get wrinkled overnight. I had a vague memory of him getting up at one point, shaking them out, and draping them over the oversized chair in the corner of my bedroom.

"Where can we go that is close by?" he asked, sitting next to me on the bed and putting on his shoes.

"Um, there's The Tate on Fourteenth Street," I said. The Tate was the perfect place for Sunday brunch, if you wanted to read the newspaper in comfortable clothes while devouring fried eggs and greasy hash browns, which frequently fit my mood perfectly. In my mind, I had assumed that's where we'd go.

"Isn't that a diner?"

"Yes. They have *the* best hash browns," I said, missing the pretentiousness in his tone.

"Oh." He paused mid-tie and looked up at me. "Well, I was thinking of something a little more upscale. How about Houng Vi, near Center? That's not too far, is it? They have a weekend morning buffet that we might still have time to make," David squinted to see the time on my bedside clock to confirm this, and it tickled something in my memory. "It's an Asian fusion menu."

"Oh, okay." My stomach revolted slightly at the idea of Asian fusion for breakfast, whatever that was, but I decided to ignore it. If our choices in brunch were any indication, I realized, David wore the city like a Brooks Brothers shirt, whereas I was more of a concert tee.

"And they have delicious mimosas," he added for incentive.

Briefly, I thought about all the errands I needed to run that day. Morning alcohol was not on my list, and it would give me a headache by noon.

"Um, I can't really drink this morning, I have a lot of things I need to do later," I confessed.

"It's ok, they have amazing coffee too. It is one of the few restaurants that I can get soy milk in mine."

At the mention of soy milk, the memory became clear.

"Hey, I think we've met before," I said. David finished tying his shoes and looked at me, perplexed.

"Yes, I'm David. I woke up in your bed…," he said with a slightly confused but teasing cadence. I giggled.

"No, I mean before Anna's party. I think you bought me a coffee once, at the coffee vendor outside the Gallery East."

"No. I'm sure of it."

"I let you cut in line ahead of me," I led, hoping to jog his memory. He shook his head.

"How can you be so sure?" I asked, now positive it had been him.

"Because, if I had seen you, I would have asked you out on the spot." He walked over to me and gave me a long kiss. "You are unforgettable," he whispered, our faces still touching. I was about to say that I looked different then—my hair was darker—but stopped myself, although I wasn't sure why. David pulled back.

"Anyway, we need to leave now if we are going to make brunch." David's eyes traveled down my body as he took in what I was wearing. "You probably want to change. I'll wait in the living room." As he walked out of the bedroom, I was left staring at my closet, a knot forming in my stomach. I brushed my hand up a row of folded sweaters, mentally dismissing each one as if they belonged to another lifetime when I would wear something that was a little stretched out or pilling from over-washing without giving it a second thought. With a sigh, I pulled out a green cable knit sweater with the tag still on that I had been saving to wear on a date, if we went out again. *If this is appropriate for brunch, I'll be broke within a month*, I thought, biting off the tag with my teeth. I pulled it over my head and went to the bathroom to fix my hair, which had picked up the static from the sweater. I was becoming an expert with the flat iron. After applying a little makeup, something I usually didn't do on Sunday mornings, I quickly scanned my jewelry box for earrings, remembering Anna's advice that earrings are a must every day because they frame the face. She had mentioned it on our spa day and ever since, I noticed that she was never without them, no matter how casual the outing, and I found myself doing the same. I checked myself in the mirror a final time. The woman who looked back at me was completely put together. She was the kind of woman that David would date.

"That color looks nice on you," David said when I came out of the bedroom, and despite my grouching, I realized that I liked what I was wearing.

"Thank you," I said simply. David stood and held out my coat, pausing to hug me gently as I put it on.

• • •

Anna and I survived our first spinning class at the Y, but just barely. Although we were both in good shape, this class targeted endurance on a whole new level. When the instructor finally called for a slow coast on our stationary bikes, Anna looked at me with relief and dabbed at the perspiration on her neck with a gym towel. I stuck out my tongue and made panting noises. We wiped down our bikes and headed to the women's locker room. The steamy showers made it a struggle to get dressed, our clothes sticking to our damp skin. We kept up conversation about everything and nothing in our typical fashion, never running out of things to tell each other while we did our makeup and hair. When we finished, we headed down the street for a fruit smoothie.

At first, the air outside was refreshingly cold, but in the few minutes it took to walk down the street, I could feel the places where my hair hadn't completely dried becoming stiff and frozen, giving me an icy chill that rushed down my spine and into my feet. Snow was falling; weightless small flakes swirled in the air around us as if thrown from a window above like a ticker tape parade. We passed an abandoned house; the lawn was a green-brown field of weeds with snow accumulating in patches like white magnolia blossoms peeking out of the branches of the tree. I would have preferred to get a hot coffee, but Anna insisted that smoothies were a better, healthier choice.

Once inside, we ordered from the overwhelming choices listed on chalk board behind the cash registers and took our drinks to the table. Anna looked at me with a serious expression as we sat on opposite sides of the hard plastic booth. She took in a breath.

"How are things with David?" she asked, sipping her drink, straining to get the thick liquid through the straw, and raised her eyes to look at me, causing her brow to wrinkle ever so slightly.

"Oh, you wouldn't believe it," I exclaimed breathlessly, ignoring my drink. I had held off mentioning him, wanting to have Anna's undivided attention. "*I* can hardly believe it. He's incredible!" I was ready to talk nonstop about David, giving Anna every detail, but I saw her tense, the tiny creases between her eyebrows deepened slightly. "Yeah, things are going good," I said, backtracking with less enthusiasm. Anna looked past my shoulder out the storefront window. Anna's eyes unexpectedly filled with tears, and she began blinking rapidly, trying hard to keep the smile on her face. I couldn't let it go unacknowledged.

"I'm sorry, I know it's been hard for you since Paul, but you'll find someone. I know you will." I reached across the table and touched Anna's hand.

"Paul," Anna repeated as if she hadn't been thinking of him. "Yes, I still think about him, but—"

"Give yourself time; it hasn't been that long," I interrupted.

Anna let out a disgusted grunt. "It's been over a year, Amy. Well over a year and—"

"You will find someone," I interrupted her again. I glanced quickly at my watch and realized that it was later than I thought. "I hate to say this, but I need to go. I'm working three-to-eleven today. Do you want to walk out with me?"

"No, I think I'll sit here for a minute."

"Okay, call me later?"

Anna nodded as I stood and gave her a quick hug.

"You will," I said again reassuringly and hurried to the door.

"Amy," Anna called from her seat. I turned back to the table. "I did want to talk to you more about David. I know everything is great now, but just be careful. He's got a reputation around the office. He reminds me of my dad in that way, and I don't want to see you get hurt, okay?"

I wound a scarf around my neck, distracted by my lateness, wishing I had brought a hat.

"Okay," I said, mentally chiding myself for not paying attention to the time when Anna had suggested coming here. I internally debated whether it would be faster to take the bus or the metro to my apartment to change for work and drop off my gym bag.

"He's different than he comes across, and he's broken a lot of hearts. I wanted to tell you that he—"

"Oh, that's my route," I said cutting her off again as I saw number 12 bus approaching. If I could catch it, then I would make it back to the apartment in plenty of time. "I'm going to try to get that. Talk later?"

I heard Anna say 'sure' as I hurried out, the chimes above the door ringing as I left. I caught the bus which allowed me to relax a little as I sat with my gym bag on my lap thinking about our conversation. I had seen Anna's reflection in the glass door as I rushed out of the shop. Anna looked deeply sad and conflicted. And for a moment as the door opened fully, her image stretched, as if she were being pulled apart, until it broke in two. I knew Anna was still nursing her broken, divorced heart, and contrary to the words I used to reassure her, it *had* been a long time since she dated anyone seriously. But I couldn't allow her to color my feelings for David. I refused to let her dissuade me for falling for him. David may have been a player, but he was with me now and he was different. I was different. With David, I had shed the mousy image of myself. We were different together. I could feel it. I pushed Anna's misgivings from my mind and continued to go through my mental pre-work checklist, the familiar rattle of the bus windows filling my ears.

• • •

"Let's go through the events of that night again, starting with when you left the restaurant," Dr. Riley said.

I hesitated. It was painful to think, much less articulate. Dr. Riley waited seemingly unfazed, not pushing me or ignoring me, just waiting.

"It was starting to storm again," I said, "and I took the keys from my husband. He said that he still felt a little drunk from all the wine and he didn't want to drive, so—"

"Wait," Dr. Riley interrupted me, referring to her notepad. "Last session, you said that you drove because he forgot his glasses."

"No," I said, confused, "that's not right. He doesn't wear glasses." I thought of David squinting in his habitual way, endearingly conceited, not wanting to admit he might need corrective lenses.

"Oh." Dr. Riley paused, her pen poised but unmoving in her hand. "Amy, let's go back further. You worked that day, right?

I had to think. "Yes, I worked until three, and then I did some shopping. I got home around six."

"What did you do when you got home?"

"I, well, I got the mail. Anna always sends me a letter on my birthday. I mean, she did. It was a tradition. She'd tell me how much she appreciated our friendship. I've saved every letter." As I talked, I could taste the salt in my mouth, silent tears flowing down well-worn

paths on my cheeks. I fell quiet realizing that I would never get another letter from Anna.

"So, back to the night of the accident. What happened after you got the mail?"

"I took a shower and got dressed. Then I met them in the lobby. Like I told you last time, we went out to dinner. The accident happened on the way home." I clearly didn't have anything else to add.

Dr. Riley waited out the lull. Sensing that I was at a dead end, she changed tactics. "Let's talk about you. Your sister told me you are a nurse. That is a difficult career choice. Do you like it?"

"Yeah, I do. Nursing is good career for me."

"In what way?"

What did it matter? What did anything matter? It was so hard to follow her questions. Then I thought of Sam's pleading face. You need to do this, I told myself. Just answer her.

I took a moment to gather my thoughts. "Um, it suits me. I like being part of a team. I like that every day is different. I'm confident in my abilities when I'm at work." Dr. Riley scribbled a couple of notes that I couldn't see. She followed up with questions about why I preferred being part of a team, what it meant to feel confident, things of that nature. Then she asked me questions about my family. There wasn't much to tell her. My family was more average than felt honest, and there weren't any skeletons hiding in that closet. She pressed a little harder into my past.

"Let's talk about when you were growing up. Did you have many friends? Other interests? Did you play sports?"

What could I say? My childhood was great. Anna and I were together all the time.

"Anna was my best friend for as long as I can remember. I can't think about childhood and not think about her." And now I've lost her, I thought to myself. The small bit of lucidity I felt talking about work and my family was cut off, like the end of a television scene turning black for a split second before thrusting the viewer into a different but familiar place. I was falling back into my hazy fog. I started talking softly. "Anna was more than a friend. She was like a sister to me. She was…." My voice faltered.

"You were very close, I understand," Dr. Riley said in an attempt to quell the breakdown that was overpowering me. "I want you to be able to talk about her, and your husband, when you are here with me. Can you do that?" Dr. Riley looked at me, shaking her head ever so slightly up and down to encourage a positive response. She gave me a sympathetic smile and handed me a box of tissues that appeared out of nowhere. I took one and wiped my eyes.

"Let's pick up here next session," she said after glancing surreptitiously at the clock and standing to signal the end of our session. I felt as if the gears in my brain were grinding to a halt, getting clogged in old, dirty oil. Leaving the room, grief pressed on my shoulders as heavy as iron.

CHAPTER 11

March 2001

David and I were curled together in his bed, his arm draped across my shoulder. We were enjoying the gentle hush of morning that occurs just after waking together, the subtle sounds of the person next to you stirring, guiding both of you out of sleep. The sun peeked under the curtains in David's bedroom, giving me just enough light to admire his morning stubble and matted curls. I pulled the sheet up and moved closer to him.

"Morning," I said, infusing the word with the contentment I was feeling.

"Good morning," he replied as he lazily played with my hair, tucking my overgrown bangs behind my ear.

"Somebody needs a haircut," he said teasingly. I'd been a regular in Sean's chair at the salon every five weeks since December, but the upkeep was daunting. Between the time commitment and the outrageous expense, I was beginning to think that this hairstyle was more trouble than it was worth.

"I was thinking of letting it grow out and going back to my natural color," I said. But as soon as I said it, I knew it was a mistake.

"No," David said, quietly shaking his head, "this is the right color for you, Amy Sheppard." He paused, looking thoughtful. "What is your middle name?"

"Elizabeth," I told him, closing my eyes, and savoring the feeling of his hand, which had drifted to my cheek.

"Amy Elizabeth Sheppard," he confirmed as if he gave the name his approval. I nodded slightly, keeping my eyes closed as his hand traced my jawbone. He leaned closer and kissed me deeply. He traced his fingers down my sternum, reaching the hem of the nightshirt I slept in. He pulled it off and then tugged at his boxer shorts. We stayed in bed for a long time.

By ten o'clock, David was dozing again, but I was wide awake. I poked him a few times playfully, then stood and opened the curtains, with a dramatic flair, the grommets making a scraping noise against the curtain rod. David blinked at the sudden brightness and rubbed his face. "The weather is supposed to be in the high fifties today; it might even reach sixty. We could rent bikes and ride along the bike path in Wissahickon Park," I rushed the sentences out, anxious to get the day started. We both had the day off from work, and I had been thinking about it for the past hour while I waited for him to wake up. I was immersed in an overwhelming ache to feel the light touch of early spring on my skin.

"I guess we're getting up now." David shook off the vestiges of sleep, stretching lazily. "Bike ride? Well, it really isn't warm enough for that. Let's start with some breakfast and see where the day takes us."

David made omelets, carefully softening the vegetables in butter over a low heat while meticulously cooking the eggs into perfectly formed circles. By the time we finished breakfast it was nearly eleven thirty. I threw out a few more suggestions hoping to spur us into action. "We could drive to the shore. If we left soon, we could easily be there by two."

"What would we do at the shore?"

"I don't know. We could walk on the beach, maybe get seafood for dinner."

"Oh," David said reluctantly, "just for the day? We wouldn't have a hotel room or anything, so where would we wash off? I don't want to get sand in my car." David knew getting sand in *my* car wouldn't bother me in the slightest, but my car was in the shop. My frustration grew.

"Well, we could go to Atlantic City and walk the boardwalk to stay sand-free." My voice trailed off as I saw David's expression. "Or we could stay here and just walk around downtown. There's always something happening on days like this. We could go to South Street or Rittenhouse Square."

David sighed heavily, looking longingly around his condo.

"I've had such a long week. Honestly, I just want some downtime," he finally admitted. "I'll tell you what, I can teach you how to make a marinara sauce from scratch. The secret is to cook it slowly, simmer it for hours. Maybe we could rent a movie too."

"Okay," I said, deflated. Then, trying to rein in my disappointment, I added, "I'm just warning you, I'm really not good in the kitchen." The truth was I found cooking tedious, but I understood his need for downtime. "I am, however, really good at drinking wine and watching."

"We'll need to go to the market to get fresh garlic and tomatoes," David said hesitantly, obviously dreading leaving his condo.

"I'll go. Just make me a list. You can stay here."

He kissed my temple. "That would be wonderful. You're the best."

Pleased that I had packed an overnight bag, I quickly showered and changed, but I didn't bother with putting on makeup or blow-drying my hair. I didn't want to waste any more time before getting outside, but I would be sure to do all that as soon as I got back to his place.

"Be sure to buy Roma tomatoes and they should feel firm to the touch," David said, handing me the list he made while I showered. "Don't be gone long," he added as I unlocked the front door.

"I won't," I said over my shoulder as I practically hopped down the steps.

Closing the building's door behind me, I smiled into the sun, letting it wash over me like an embrace. I walked slowly, looking in storefronts, window-shopping the antiques that I would never buy. Passing Café Grind, I ordered a coffee and sat at one of the tables on the sidewalk, but nagging thoughts of David waiting for me lessened the enjoyment and I threw the cup away, half-full, rushing through the shopping list and returning as quickly as I could to the condo.

Of all the rooms in David's condo, his kitchen felt the most masculine. The stylish black cabinets gave a stark contrast to the gray and white marble countertops and state-of-the-art appliances. Two metal barstools fit snugly under his small island. The window above the sink was a compact square, just slightly larger than my face. It was usually covered with a pull-down blind, also black, but David had opened it to let the light in. The small patches of wall around the cabinets were painted a deep forest green. David had turned the radio on to a classical music station that made me feel like I was waiting to see my dentist, but I didn't say anything. He was contentedly organizing everything he would need to make the sauce. A large pot sat on the stove, and he had placed a wooden cutting board on the counter. He inspected the tomatoes and set them aside. He crushed a clove of garlic with a side of a cleaver and began peeling off the thin outer layers.

"Could you wash the tomatoes?" he asked as he began chopping the garlic with a thumping noise, like banging on a door. The strong smell immediately filled the kitchen in an overpowering and possessive manner.

"Sure," I said. I washed the tomatoes and gently dried them with a paper towel. Then, I settled myself on a barstool facing David.

"You want to chop the garlic as fine as possible," he said, demonstrating. Behind him, I could see out the window, the light spring breeze making the branches of a tree sway, like an outstretched arm, the new buds like fingers, beckoning to me.

• • •

The next morning, the alarm clock woke us with a jolt. David fumbled with the buttons, finally turning it off and lying back down.

"I can walk with you to the office," I said, stifling a yawn. "My shift doesn't start until three."

"Cool," David said, still groggy. He headed to the shower as I went to his kitchen to make coffee. I slid his expresso machine away from the wall to pour the water into the basin. It took David three tries to teach me how to successfully use this complicated apparatus, and I frequently reminded him that the only complicated part of my Mr. Coffee was remembering to buy filters.

David came into the room, his hair still wet and covered in a shiny gel to keep his curls in place. His suit looked crisp as he grabbed a bagel and stuck it in the toaster. I had already retrieved the newspaper from outside his door, and I was sitting at the table, drinking my coffee, and reading leisurely.

"Honey, you'll have to hurry if you want to walk in with me," he said. "I don't know how long it will take you to get ready." Normally, I'd walk home in my pajamas, which consisted of sweatpants and an old T-shirt, hair uncombed. But I got David's thinly veiled hint—I should get dressed properly if we were going to go by his office together, even if I would keep walking past it, so I abandoned the paper and headed for the bathroom.

David and I held hands as we walked to the *BTB* office. Like yesterday, the mellow taste of spring hung in the air like a sweet Riesling. Outside his office, we said goodbye, and he gave me a quick peck on the lips. Two women waited to enter the building behind us, and when David looked at them, recognition dawned.

"Elyse, Mia, hello, glad you could come in today," David said enthusiastically, pausing and holding the door with his back. He shook each of their hands as they passed.

"Hello, David," they greeted him as they moved into the building's large foyer.

David stayed in the doorway and turned to me, "Elyse and Mia are here to discuss advertising in *BTB*."

I smiled brightly at these impeccably dressed women as David introduced me, saying, "This is my girlfriend, Amy." It was the first time David called me that and my knees gave a little.

"Nice to meet you," they said automatically.

I shook both their hands in turn, my arm stretching across the threshold to reach theirs, a gesture that I remembered too late was considered bad luck in certain cultures. "Nice to meet you, too," I said.

"I'll call you later," David said to me and walked in with the women, letting the door swing shut, separating us and leaving me staring at my own reflection made taller by the polished brass door. At first, I mistook myself for someone else. Someone more like Anna with blonde hair and stylish clothes. But now I could see a resemblance between us that the woman at the salon who called us sisters must have seen, and I beamed with self-satisfaction. I was blending into David's world like a chameleon and the morning effort I begrudged suddenly seemed worthwhile.

• • •

April 2001

I arrived at David's condo around seven thirty after my evening shift at the hospital ended. We had been seeing each other whenever we could, working around our busy schedules. A quick lunch date, a late-night rendezvous, we even met once for his breakfast/my dinner after one of my weekend nightshifts. I had started a new position at the hospital that came with a raise, but a complicated swing-shift schedule.

My hands were full, so I used my elbow to ring his doorbell. David had given me a key, but it was buried in my purse, and I knew that he was home. I heard his footsteps as he approached and slid the cover off the peephole to see who was on the other side. He opened the door, looking slightly annoyed.

"Why didn't you use your key?" he asked. I lifted my arms to show him the overflowing reusable grocery bags with Green Fields stamped on the side. David took a bag from me and headed to his kitchen. I walked behind him and placed the rest of the bags on the counter.

"You look happy," he said, opening one of the bags. He pulled out a bunch of carrots.

"I am. I just found out that Green Fields is offering cooking classes. Anna has been dying to take a cooking class, so I signed us up."

"Really?" he said, frowning and sounding a little put off. "I thought you hated cooking?" I had to confess that cooking wasn't my thing when David's 'lessons' started to become a regular activity for us.

"But you love it. Maybe if I got a little better, I would enjoy it more and we could do it together." While that was true, it was only part of my motivation. Anna made everything more fun, and I knew we would have a blast. The actual cooking played a small part of the enticement.

"And you didn't think to take the class with me, not Anna?"

"Oh, be serious," I said, my voice like sugar. "You already know how to cook; you'd be bored. It is a beginner's class." This made him smile briefly, as I knew appealing to his vanity would, but after a moment, he frowned again.

"But what about your work schedule? When I suggested that we take that salsa dancing class, you told me that it wouldn't work because you couldn't guarantee having a certain night off every week."

"Yes, I know." My hospital schedule ran on a seven-week cycle, switching between three shifts and rotating days. I had to remind David of my schedule every time he made plans. He wasn't used to dating someone who wasn't guaranteed to be off on a Friday night or a Sunday morning. He was shocked that I didn't automatically have holidays off. I started marking my days off in red on David's desk calendar so that he could keep track. "This cooking class is offered every Tuesday for a year. You can buy a ten-class pass and show up for any class, it's like a class with a punch card."

"Well, maybe you'll make something interesting that we can bring to the *BTB* picnic on Saturday."

"This Saturday?"

"Yes, this Saturday," David repeated haltingly, as if he knew what was coming.

"Oh, David, I can't go. I have to work," I said.

"No, I checked the calendar, you're off," he countered.

"Well, I'm off during the day, but I start nightshift on Saturday night. I need to sleep."

"Can you just sleep in late in the morning, I mean later than you normally would when you switch shifts, and still come to the picnic in the afternoon?"

"Even if I did, I couldn't spend the day out in the sun. I'd never stay awake all night after a day like that."

He folded his arms across his chest. "Why does it seem that everything works when you want to do it, and nothing works when I plan it?"

"David, that's not true. I have no control over the schedule."

"But even when you aren't working, you always seem to have time for what you want, *especially* if it involves Anna, like this cooking class. And remember last week when I wanted to go to the movies, but you said you and Anna already had plans? And there was another time," he paused trying to place it, snapping his fingers. "Oh," he said, recalling and getting more agitated, "we were hanging out here and then Anna calls and, bam, you're out the door." He was speaking loudly, clearly frustrated, but not quite yelling. I remembered that day.

"But you turned on the Phillies game," I retorted.

"Yes, and it would have been nice if you watched it with me."

"Well, you didn't ask me, and besides, you know I'm not into baseball," I said thinking that at the time, he didn't seem bothered that I was leaving. I had told him I was going; it wasn't as if I left without saying goodbye.

"Well, sometimes I wonder if you are dating Anna or me," he said, drawing in a breath and expanding his chest ever so slightly.

"That's crazy."

"No, it's not."

"Yes, it is! Anna and I do see each other a lot, but you see your friends all the time, too. You always hang out at your brother's place when I work weekends."

"That's different," he said loudly, emphasizing his point by shaking his head.

"How?"

"Because that's not with Anna!" he yelled, his arms flying into the air. My mouth dropped. I was so shocked and confused, I couldn't even answer.

"What are you talking about?"

"She's just so demanding! She wants everything from everyone, and she won't stop until she gets it." His voice still raised, leaving me baffled as to why we were suddenly talking about Anna.

"So, you don't want me to see her because you don't like how she acts? I thought you got along with Anna." My voice was calm, trying to figure out where this was coming from.

"It's not that I don't like her. I do like her. That's not it. Just for-get it," he said. He was moving away from me, pedaling backwards with his words and his body, not looking me in the eye, but his voice had returned to a normal volume.

"No, I won't just forget it. I don't understand what you mean by that."

"What I mean is why should I give up all my free time to you, if you're not doing the same for me? Maybe *I* need more free time. Maybe I *should* start going out when other people ask," he said, looking at me again.

"I'd *never* tell you not to see your friends," I said, offended. Then something behind his words occurred to me—maybe he didn't mean going out with *friends*. "Are you saying you want to *date* other people?" I blurted out incredulously. He referred to me as his girlfriend, so I assumed that meant we were exclusive. The conversation paused.

"No, of course not," he said after the slightest hesitation, and I breathed out, relieved. "I just need to know that I mean more to you than anyone, and that includes Anna. I know she is your best friend, but I need to trust that you are putting me ahead of her because that is what I'm doing for you. I'm putting you ahead of everyone." His face looked anxious. My anger subsided at the rawness of his words.

"I am, honey," I said softly.

"Good," he answered. I started to go to him, wanting to hug him and put an end to this, but he stood stiffly, so I stopped.

"Let me make some calls and see if someone can take my shift for the picnic," I said wondering how this conversation got so far off track.

David stayed quiet and turned his attention back to unloading the rest of the groceries. I left him in the kitchen and used the phone in the bedroom so I could focus. After a few failed attempts, I found someone to cover, but it was going to mean working a long stretch of days starting on Sunday.

"I found someone to cover for me," I said in a quiet voice as I came back into the kitchen. David had started preparing dinner. His back was to me as he stirred broccoli and chopped steak in a wok. The air was filled with the smell of peanut oil and ginger. I came up behind him and tentatively put my arms around his waist. He turned and looked into my eyes.

"I'm sorry I yelled," he said, and I rushed to add, "I'm sorry too," although I barely raised my voice. David turned off the burner and set the bamboo tongs on a spoon rest. He took me in his arms.

"Did we just survive our first fight?"

"I think so."

"Do we get to have makeup sex now?" he asked mischievously.

"I think it's a rule," I said, circling my arms around his neck.

"Well, we wouldn't want to break the rules." He pulled me closer, kissing me, then nudging us toward his bedroom. The peculiar conversation that had sparked the argument shoved into a corner of my mind where it would sit, like an unfinished chore needing my attention.

• • •

The next day, I called Anna to ask her advice about what to wear to the picnic. I knew the dress code for *BTB* events was never casual but hitting the right note would be tricky. The last thing I wanted to be was overdressed and look like I was trying too hard. This was never an issue for Anna; it seemed like no matter what the occasion, Anna always styled herself with effortless perfection.

"David is bringing you? Wow, he must be getting serious. Showing up with a girlfriend will seriously hurt his player reputation at the office," Anna said.

"What?" I said, still sensitive about the fight I'd had with David.

"I'm just kidding," she said in a tone that didn't sound convincing, but she changed the subject too abruptly for me to ask again. "It's too bad we don't have time to go shopping before the picnic. Maybe you could wear the green shift dress with the square neckline, the one you bought to wear to Kate's baby shower?"

"That's a little dressy for a picnic, isn't it?" I asked still worried.

"Trust me, it's not."

"Won't that make it hard to play any games or anything?" I asked, thinking of Frisbee and touch football.

Anna laughed. "Amy, I'm sure there won't be any games. It's not like you're picturing. Think 'cocktail party with sunshine.'" She hesitated. "Are you planning to bring any food for the potluck?"

"Yes. I was going to make pasta salad. The kind with salad dressing and red kidney beans that you refrigerate overnight."

"Oh, Amy, don't," Anna said, not even trying to be delicate. "We publish a lot of recipes in the magazine, and the potluck can get kind of competitive. A lot of self-proclaimed foodies will be there. The food will be amazing, and trust me, you don't want to compete with that. Bring some wine," she suggested. "David can pick it out."

"If you think so," I said into the phone, feeling terribly uneasy about the event. "See you Saturday." I added before hanging up.

"Wouldn't miss it," Anna replied, and I wondered if I imagined her tone, somewhere between a warning and a dare.

• • •

When David and I pulled up to the picnic shelter, I could see that Anna was right and I was glad that I followed her advice about what to wear. It looked a little like a fashion shoot. David had smiled at me approvingly when he picked me up at my apartment, looking me up and down, although he suggested swapping the ballet flats for a wedge heel that he had bought for me. The wedges were the highest heels I had ever owned, and though my ability to walk in them was questionable, I adored the shoes. But I packed the flats, just in case. I had been back to Sean for a cut and color, and the Y membership with Anna was the push I needed to keep my muscles well-defined with my crazy new schedule.

Anna was standing inside the picnic shelter, holding a drink and chatting casually. Seeing us arrive, she excused herself and met us at the car.

"I'm so glad you're here!" she said to me and David as I swung my feet out of the car. Noting my shoes, she asked, "Why aren't you wearing the ballet flats with the buttons on the side? Your feet are going to be crying in an hour."

"I have them in the back seat. I'll change them, just give me a sec."

"No, don't. I like the wedge," David said.

"Change them," Anna repeated, gesturing to the back seat.

"Do I get a vote?" I asked.

"No!" David and Anna said in unison.

"We are talking about *my* feet, right?" I said, making Anna laugh. "You two must be *so* much fun to work with," I added sarcastically as David picked up the case of wine from the trunk and began walking to the picnic shelter.

"Come on," Anna said, taking my arm. "I'll introduce you to the poor folks who actually do have to work with us. We've added a lot of new staff since the holiday party." We walked together to the picnic shelter. Anna introduced me to the first group of people we encountered. David put the wine down and quickly joined us with his arm around my shoulder.

"I see you've met my girlfriend," he said to the group. I caught a few surprised looks, but everyone recovered quickly. The conversation touched on work lightly, something about a press release, and David began talking about his first job writing press releases for a small pharmaceutical company. He outlined his attempts to promote the drugs and yet somehow include all the possible side effects for legal reasons. The group burst out with laughter at David's anecdote about 'anal leakage,' and Anna slipped away to join another group.

I looked around. Anna was right: three-legged races were not going to happen with these people, but the food looked savory, and the alcohol was plentiful. I left David talking baseball with a group of guys, found my oversized handbag, and took out my camera.

"Do you think anyone will mind if I take their picture?" I asked Anna, who was refilling her wine glass with a bubbling prosecco, condensation making the bottle sparkle in the daylight. "David asked if I would take some candid pictures for the in-house newsletter."

"Mind? At a *BTB* event?" Her voice rose disbelievingly. "You'll have trouble fitting them all in the frame. Especially the photographers; they complain all the time about always being on the unglamorous side of the camera."

I started taking pictures trying not to call attention to myself. I wanted to capture people being natural and relaxed, but soon I was caught, and everyone began posing for the camera, the women with their hands on their hips, angling slightly to show off their trim waists, and the men flexing their arms and sucking in their stomachs. I took more pictures to appease them and then put my camera away. Someone set up a karaoke machine and the song book was being passed around. David took the microphone first to get the crowd going and sang "Sweet Caroline." What he lacked in his ability to sing on-key, he made up for with volume and enthusiasm as his voice echoed through the park. Watching him sing, a natural in the spotlight, I felt pleased. *He's mine*, I thought to myself, feeling oddly flattered and accomplished, like I had risen in stature just being here with him. In true party form, the crowd joined with the 'ba, dum, dum, dums' and cried out 'so good, so good, so good!' during the chorus. I saw Anna backing away from the crowd, looking melancholy. I went up to her.

"Are you okay?" I asked.

"It's nothing," she said. I gave her a look that said I didn't believe her.

"It's this song," she said. "Daddy used to sing it too."

"Oh, hon," I said, and I started to put my arm around her.

"No," she said harshly. Seeing the hurt on my face, she relented slightly. "Just… not here." She shrugged my arm away and moved closer to the crowd again. "It's all right, Amy. I'm fine." She wiped her eyes quickly and was smiling again when she tapped a co-worker on the shoulder and started a new conversation, her subtle way of reminding me that this was her turf.

David handed the microphone to the next person and came up to me, planting a big, happy kiss on my lips.

"What was that for?" I asked with a laugh.

"You just looked so pretty standing there, I had to," he said sweetly. "C'mon, let's have some fun." He took my hand and raised my arm, spinning me around to face the table that held the buffet and the wide assortment of alcohol. After refilling our glasses, he indicated with a tilt of his head that we should join the people seated at a picnic table near the makeshift bar. The long wooden tables under the shelters were worn and warped from years of exposure, but today they were covered with shiny paisley-printed table covers. The benches were also covered in fabric so no one would have to worry about splinters ruining their designer clothes. There was a gap between two women seated at the table, and I hitched up my skirt a little and swung my leg over the bench, holding my legs together as tightly as I could. At the same time, David tapped the man on the end of the bench facing me and he slid down easily on the silky fabric to make room for him. David grimaced somewhat as he watched me settling myself between the women. The woman on my right looked at me like I had just attempted to pole-vault in a mini skirt.

"David, she is a riot. Where did you find her?" the woman on my other side said with a laugh. I felt my skin getting hot as I blushed. I started to speak but was saved by David making an unrelated comment about the food. I shifted uncomfortably on the bench and took a long sip of my pinot grigio. On the table, I could see that they were in the middle of playing a drinking game using dice. A large jar filled with pennies sat at the end of the table. David reached in and took a handful and set them in front of me. Then, he helped himself to more pennies, declaring, "We're in."

"What are we playing?" I asked hesitantly. The game didn't look familiar to me, and I hoped that the rules of the game were easily explained. I didn't want to look dimwitted with such a sharp crowd.

"Left, Right, Center," the woman on my right said. She seemed intent on continuing the game. "Do you know how to play?"

"No," I admitted, shaking my head.

"It's not hard." She briefly explained the rules before slapping her palm on the table to get everyone's attention. "Come on, let's play!" She seemed perturbed by the interruption and the fact that I apparently had far more pennies in my start pile than were usually allotted, but no one was going to argue with David.

"Loosen up," the woman on my left said with a slight whine. "You forgot to tell her when to drink," she said as she leaned in and spoke around me to the other woman.

"Yeah, if you roll a 'C,' you have to do a Jell-O shot," she said. "That isn't an official rule." Her voice was clipped.

"Okay, thanks," I said. "I'm Amy, by the way."

"Leah," she said without offering to shake my hand. She pointed to the woman on my left and then went around the table naming people, skipping David. "This is Kirsten, Brody, and Jared." I nodded and smiled to each in turn. Kirsten had long blonde hair that reached down her back with the slightest hint of wavy curls. Leah had short dark hair cut out around her ears and bangs that fell into her eyes. Brody looked like a smaller version of David, from his close-cropped hair down to his beige chino shorts, and Jared had deep brown skin and dark eyes. His head was completely shaved. Together they looked like a Benetton ad.

"Looks like it's the boys against the girls," I said, referring to the fact that the men were seated on one side of the table and the women on the other.

"Yeah, we're not playing teams. You can't play this game in teams." Leah looked in my eyes and spoke slowly, her voice edging, like she was explaining something to a young, and very possibly annoying, child.

"Oh, I understood," I stammered. "I was just—"

"Whose turn is it?" Leah interrupted and then quickly added, "Never mind, just roll." She gave the dice to me.

I sighed under my breath. I looked at David, but he was unaware of my discomfort. His head was turned to Brody, engaged in conversation. I stared at him hard enough to get his attention, and he turned forward, saying, "Looks like we've started up again. C'mon, Amy. Start passing those pennies my way!" I got the hang of the game as we played, everyone making small talk until it started getting dark.

I was well past the giggly phase of drunkenness that held me through most of the game. There was a lot of good-natured jabbing, and even Leah seemed to lighten up, especially after she had a bad roll and did three Jell-O shots. Kirsten, being a recent transplant from LA, kept us entertained by using a different celebrity voice, most of whom she claimed to have met, during each of her turns. But now, I was beginning to feel a headache creeping up behind my eyes, the kind of headache that is unique to the beginning of a serious wine hangover. Anna and I nicknamed this headache the Curse of the Tannins. The sugar from the Jell-O wasn't helping. My mouth felt desperately dry. I could feel sticky white saliva unattractively pooling in the corners of my mouth when I tried to talk. I needed a cold drink, preferably non-alcoholic, immediately. My words slurred as I excused myself and politely motioned for Kirsten to slide off the bench so I could get up.

Before she did, she leaned toward me and put her hand conspiratorially on my knee. "You know, I wanted to tell you. I find it so refreshing"—she paused for effect and took a sip of her wine—"that you never got your nose fixed. It is so authentic. No one in LA would have the guts to keep it natural like that. It makes me wish I could care less about what I looked like."

Mortified, I just stared at her. Kirsten moved off the bench so I could get past, and when I stood, she sat back down, sliding close to Leah without another glance at me. *So much for understanding the rules*, I thought. David looked up at that moment and excused himself from the bench.

"Everything okay? You look upset."

"Oh, I'm fine, I just need some water, that's all."

"Sit, I'll get it."

I collapsed on a bench at an empty table, my confidence return-ing as I watched David navigating the tangle of people, hurrying to get back to me with a drink. "Here you go, beautiful," he said, handing me a cup. I took a sip and looked in his eyes. I still felt unsettled about the comment, but if David thought I was beautiful, maybe I was.

CHAPTER 12

April 2001

The forest was quiet except for the sounds of our footfalls on the trail. As we rounded the final bend, we came to the overlook, the pinnacle of our hike. The elevation was only about fifteen hundred feet, small by the world's standards, but the Pennsylvania countryside has a grandeur all its own. The rippling hills were budding with spring foliage that looked so soft, I had the urge to reach out my hand and rub along the landscape, like stroking a fleece blanket. In the distance, I could see the patchwork quilt of farmlands, neat squares dotted with red barns and weathered white houses.

"Wow." The word escaped from me in a whisper. David dropped his backpack and put his arm around my shoulder. We stood in comfortable silence, taking in the view.

"Ready for the best hoagie of your life?" he asked. He spread out a blanket and began unpacking the food. When David suggested bringing lunch, I was expecting his typical foodie fare, something involving porcini mushrooms, heirloom tomatoes, and perhaps, a fork. He surprised me by insisting instead that we stop at The Hoagie

Hut, a small sandwich shop near the trailhead. The Hoagie Hut was housed in an old log cabin with a faded wooden sign hanging from a pole in the parking lot that listed precariously to one side. Inside the cabin, huge ceiling fans circulated the smell of basil, parsley, and oregano that clung to my hair and clothes even hours later. David greeted the young man behind the counter by name, asking about his father while getting Cokes from the refrigerated case.

"Dad's still kicking," the man said. "Took the day off to go fishing. What can I get you?"

"We'll take two Italian hoagies." David looked back at me for my approval. I nodded. "Could you pack them to go? We are heading up to Steeple Mountain."

"Beautiful day for it," he said and turned from the counter to assemble layers of ham, capicola, salami, and provolone cheese on long, fat rolls with a crusty outer layer. David picked the trail near the small town of Carlisle because it was near his grandfather's house and one of his favorite places to come to as a child. The drive took us out of the city and after a few miles on Interstate 76, David abandoned the highway in favor of back roads. With David driving, I could appreciate the views out the window. We passed through coal mining towns so small that as you drove down the main street, you could see the end of town ahead of you and the edges of town if you looked left and right. Between the towns, the road dipped and climbed, twisted and turned like a ballet dancer. As the car wound its way through a valley between two mountains and I looked up at the trees, holding their ground with roots like claws digging into the steep hillside. David slowed the car to navigate the hairpin turns.

"Whoa, what is that?" I asked, pointing to an outcrop of rock jutting from the side of a hill. It looked like the profile of an American Indian's face, complete with a feathered headdress. Someone painted eyes and a mouth on the rock to further clarify the image nature had made. It could only be viewed properly for a few seconds before our car passed the optimum vantage point and the perspective shifted, making the rocks separate, pulling the features apart as the face disappeared back into the mountain. David smiled and told me about the unlikely legend behind the Indian face that I was fairly certain he made up as we drove along. He later confessed that making stories about the origin of the Indian was something he and his brother did whenever they drove on this road.

On the trail, we walked hand in hand at the beginning, which was mostly flat and ran along a small creek to the base of Steeple Mountain. The familiar ground prompted David to talk about his childhood, coming here with his family, back when his grandfather could still walk without a cane and his grandmother was alive. He talked about how he and his brother, William, would run ahead on the footpath and hide; then they would jump out from behind rocks, trying to startle the rest of the group.

The farther into the woods we hiked, the more David talked, as if this familiar patch of ground were suspended in the time before he moved to the city; before his career at *BTB*. He reminisced about funny family traditions, like the wooden elf that had been in his mom's family for generations that she would bring out at Christmas. It had evil eyes and a manic grin that he tried, and failed, to imitate for me. It scared him and William until they were old enough to use it for practical jokes, hiding it in each other's beds and hanging it from a hook in the shower. Lost in nostalgia, David appeared to relax.

His curly hair became matted with sweat, and he simply shrugged when I told him told he'd left a smudge of dirt under his eye after he'd swiped away a spider's web. I'd never seen him so unconcerned with appearances, and it suited him. He even seemed to listen more attentively to me as I countered with stories about my childhood. How as children Sam and I would meet on the landing of the stairs, tucked in our comfy spot where we felt invisible to the rest of the world. I felt uninhibited as I admitted to him how incredibly awful Sam had been as a teenager, a stage that lasted well into her twenties and at times, she reverted to even now. For a change, David didn't offer a solution to improve my relationship with her. He just listened.

On the way home, we stopped at his grandfather's house. David did simple chores for him, loading the dishwasher and tightening a loose screw on a cabinet door, distracting his grandfather with questions so that he wouldn't be able to protest until the chores were done. I saw the tenderness in the way David hugged his grandfather goodbye, and I realized I was falling in love.

• • •

May 2001

"Stop it," Anna called from her bedroom to me. I was waiting for her in her brightly lit kitchen. Anna had painted it a sunny yellow and replaced her bulky kitchen set with a two-person café table that opened up the tiny space. The table held a slim vase with two artificial daisies.

"Stop what?" I asked innocently.

"Stop worrying about what Kirsten said. There is absolutely nothing wrong with your nose."

"I know," I said defensively.

"Then why are you looking at your reflection in my toaster?" Anna said, fastening an earring in her ear as she walked into the kitchen, her ball gown making a swishing noise with her steps. Tonight, we were attending a gala at the Four Seasons. It was a fund-raiser for early childhood literacy, a pet cause of one of *BTB*'s biggest advertisers, who sponsored the event.

"Authentic, she called me 'authentic.' Who wants to be 'authentic'? No one. Big. That's what she meant. She meant big, Anna; I have a big nose."

"Your nose isn't big," Anna said for the hundredth time that night.

"I never used to think it was, but now…." I fretted and held the shiny surface of the toaster at an odd angle, trying to see my nose from the side.

"Honestly, she is just jealous because of David. All the girls at the magazine are. Hell, I'm jealous!" Anna admitted, and I froze. Anna had become increasingly depressed about being single, and sometimes it felt as if she blamed me for having someone. Although it was completely illogical, I understood this superstitious jealousy, the seesaw of our love lives, because I had been helplessly stuck on the ground for a long time until the balance shifted. I looked at Anna and was relieved to see she was still smiling, so I let the comment go. I was far too excited about tonight to worry about it.

I hadn't seen David in a week; he had flown to Chicago for a conference. With David gone, I took the opportunity to go on a juice cleanse to lose a few of the 'couple pounds' I had gained from all our meals together. David didn't say anything directly, but I was sure he noticed my weight gain. I saw him giving my thickening waist disapproving glances and he gently placed his hand on top of mine when I reached for a bread stick the last time we went out to restaurant. I wanted him to be knocked off his feet when he saw me tonight. David's plane was arriving late, just before the start of the event, so he had asked me to meet him there. I suggested to Anna that we get ready together at her place, the way we used to before high school dances. So far, it was like old times, the two of us fighting over the small bathroom mirror, complimenting each other's hair and dresses. I watched carefully as Anna applied her makeup and tried to mimic the way she did her eye shadow, slightly darker than she normally wore for daytime.

"Authentic," I scoffed, putting the toaster down on the counter. A few crumbs fell out, which I swept into my palm and dumped in her trash can. Dusting my hands together, I followed Anna across the living room to the door. "It would have been a compliment, maybe, if she was talking about my personality. But who wants to have an authentic-looking body part? Everyone knows the best body parts are manufactured. I mean, look at boobs! The good ones don't try to look real. They don't bounce; they just sit there in perky perfection." Anna waited patiently by the door, holding it open and waving me forward with her hand, as I kept mumbling nonsense about body parts and walked past her, so she could lock the door behind me.

"I'm sure she meant it as a compliment," Anna said cutting off my rant.

"No, it was code for 'Get that parrot beak of yours fixed,'" I said, and Anna laughed at my outrage, then stopped inside the shared hallway of her apartment.

"They are just trying to make you feel insecure. Those girls, they try so hard to be perfect, but the more they try, the more faults they see. But you are different. You're happy without perfection, and that makes you enviable," Anna said. She understood how deeply the comment from Kirsten had wounded me.

"If you say that I am full of natural beautiful on the inside, I'll bite you," I warned as we walked out the front door and onto her sidewalk.

"And you're funny too. Guys like that." Anna ducked as I swung my pearl-seeded clutch at her head. "With a nice personality," she said, dodging me easily again. The old, familiar teasing was like a soothing rain in the midst of unbearable summer heat. Anna had pre-pared preparty cocktails for us and the light, giddy feeling continued to return as we reached the corner where Anna signaled for a taxi.

"I'll prove it to you," Anna said as a taxi pulled up the curb and we settled in the backseat. "Sir," Anna said to the taxi driver after giving him the address, "do you find my friend attractive?"

"Anna!" I screamed and looked at her. The driver adjusted the rearview mirror, giving me a brief look and then moved the mirror back to its original position.

"I'd do her," he said, noncommittally shrugging his shoulders.

"Oh god," I said, looking out the window, trying to hide my face.

"See, Amy? This man is a Philadelphia authority on the fairer sex. He drives beautiful women around the city all day for a living, and he gave you an 'I'd do her,' which is his highest ranking, I believe."

The driver shrugged again with a thoughtful frown and nodded his head in solemn agreement. "I do know women," he said with a heavy South Philly accent as we drove past the LOVE statue. Sadly, I realized that this made me feel better.

As the taxi pulled under the Four Seasons' granite porte cochère, a nervous excitement flooded my chest. I had been here before, once, when it was rumored that Brad Pitt was staying at the hotel while discussing a sequel to *Twelve Monkeys* with Terry Gilliam. It was right after Gail and I had moved to the city. We were flat broke from paying first and last months' rent *and* the security deposit, but we came here for lunch anyway in hopes of seeing Brad Pitt in person. It was our first Philadelphia adventure. We ordered the cheapest thing on the menu, Caesar salads, and drank water, giggling and pointing at every glimpse of dirty blond hair. The check came quickly, and we left a fifteen percent tip. Now, the memory seemed like it had happened to someone else.

The doorman bent down to open my door, and I took his offered hand, standing firmly in my stiletto heels. I waited as he walked around the taxi to open the door for Anna. She came around the back of the taxi and grabbed my hand, excited, and for a moment, we stood outside the glass-enclosed lobby. Our reflections showed Anna looking stunning in a pale silver off-the-shoulder dress, whose drop waist showed off her narrow hips. My dress was an emerald velvet with a halter-shaped neckline that emphasized my shapely shoulders, and a sexy side slit in the skirt came to mid-thigh. I thought I should wear a necklace, but Anna suggested I pair it with only drop earrings. "You want all the focus on you," she said. "No distractions." Looking at us now, I could see she had been right. It looked perfect. And I felt something else, as we stood side by side, the unfamiliar feeling that we looked like equals.

"Ready?" she said, and we walked through the doors together.

The ballroom had been set with gold and white linens. Enormous vases of flowers towered in the center of each circular table. The glass crystals dangling from the multiple chandeliers showered the room in a soft twilit glow. I saw David standing near the dance floor, a drink in his hand. He turned to face me and smiled. He wore a black tuxedo and bow tie. He was completely in his element.

"You look gorgeous," he said, leaning over slightly to kiss my cheek.

"How did you beat us here?" I asked as he straightened back up.

"Carry-ons only," he said, "and I got lucky with the taxi. We should find our table."

BTB had purchased a table for an ungodly sum, and we were soon joined by Leah, another woman named Ashlea, and Brody, who had won the drawing at the office to come to the exclusive event. After a dinner of salt-crusted sea bass and a short slideshow about the anticipated new library programs that the gala would fund, the dance floor opened, and David led me to it. We danced to the first song, a cover of the old Bangles' song "Eternal Flame," the lead singer's silky voice lingering on the high notes. David left the dance floor when Madonna's "Vogue" was played, but I was quickly joined by

Anna and Leah. We danced together in a tight circle, mouthing the lyrics, taking me back to high school dances when Anna and I would spend the entire day together, primping and painting our nails. Back then, we'd sneak rum from Jack's liquor cabinet and drink it in the girls' bathroom. The band continued to cater to its audience, playing songs from the early nineties that had even Leah losing her inhibitions. The gala continued until after midnight, when the guests started leaving in groups of two and three.

David and I walked outside. The May night was breezy with a slight coolness in the air, Philadelphia's way of reminding us that summer hadn't quite started, and the pleasant spring weather could turn on a dime. This time of year, it was best to expect the unexpected. The night air ran down my exposed back and gave me a chill like seeing the morning frost out the window even though you were still surrounded by covers in a warm bed.

"Would you like this?" David said as he offered me his tuxedo jacket that he had slung over his shoulder.

"No, I'm fine," I assured him. I liked the way he looked at me all night in this dress and chose his admiration over warmth.

"Let's walk the city," David said. It was unusual for him. He usually didn't like to walk around Philadelphia after dark, but he knew it was one of my favorite things to do. As we passed under the restaurant deck of TGI Friday's, a group of people laughed loudly in unison, reacting to a comment from someone in their group, filling the night air with a sense of harmony and well-being. We crossed the street to Logan circle with the Swann Memorial Fountain dominating the center island. David stopped and put his arms around me. I turned into his embrace and looked up at him. He looked at me seriously. David looked older in the light of the fountain. I could see the shadows of fine lines beginning at the sides of his mouth and the corners of his eyes. I wondered if we would still be together when those lines etched into crevices and his dark hair lightened to gray. I realized that I wanted to be.

"I love you," he said softly.

"I love you, too," I said without hesitation. He kissed me just as the breeze blew water off the fountain and sprayed us with a mist that felt cold and ominous. My back arched and I pressed myself deep into David's arms, squealing. Over his shoulder, I could see a statue in the fountain of a young Native American woman lying down and holding a swan by the neck behind her. She was unconsciously naked, her bronzed skin hidden forever beneath a green patina. Her features were calm, her chin tucked slightly, almost resting on her chest, and her wide-open eyes had no detail etched into them. The coolness of the water on my back grew stronger as the statue started at me through blank, lifeless ovals. I pushed myself farther into David's arms.

"Let's go home," he whispered in my ear. I wondered if he realized that he referred to his condo as home, as if we both lived there. We ducked into a taxi and held each other in the back seat, sneaking kisses like teenagers. By the time we got to the condo, he was unzipping the low back of my dress.

Later, as David was snoring softly next to me, I replayed the evening and all its grandeur. David had said he loved me. I allowed the complete perfection of the moment to wash over me again and again, wishing it were possible to preserve feelings in photographs so that I could revisit them any time. I was in the spotlight of my life, so blinded by happiness that I couldn't see what was hiding in the shadows.

• • •

Late at night, even though I am sleeping in my sister's guest room, I can still hear whispers of my husband. With my eyes closed, lying still and flat on my back, I allow myself to believe I'm not in the tiny twin bed. I'm at our condo, and he's coming to bed. In my mind, I can hear the yawn of the bedroom door opening. The distinctive clink of metal on wood as he places his watch on the bedside table. The abrupt elimination of light seeping through my eyelids as he turns off the bedside lamp. The dry rustle of sheets. The scratch of his stubble as he kisses my cheek. I speak softly to him in the darkness.

"Why aren't you here with me? Now, when I have so much time for you."

CHAPTER 13

May 2001

The partners' yoga class started with introductions all around. First, the teachers, a couple that met in the '60s and had been together ever since. They reported this fact to the group as if that simple statement conveyed everything we needed to know about their relationship and in a way, it did. I knew the wife, Tessa, from her vinyasa class on Wednesday nights. I also knew better than to let her age fool me into thinking the class today would be easy. I had seen her drop into a full spilt and then rest her head on her knee without tensing her beatific smile. There were two other couples in the class. One couple looked like they did this all the time, stretching as they introduced themselves. The other couple was sort of a mismatch. The woman was obviously comfortable on her yoga mat, but her partner looked as if he'd be far more comfortable in the weight room than the yoga studio. David and I fell somewhere in the middle. I loved yoga and practiced whenever my schedule allowed. David told me how much he enjoyed it too.

We started sitting back to back, inhaling and exhaling on the teachers' count, using these calming breaths to center ourselves and focus on becoming one. Then we stood in unison, pressing into each other's backs to raise our bodies. *So far, so good,* I thought once we were standing, relieved. When I signed us up for the class after David agreed to go, I became a little apprehensive. I had no idea what level of yoga David practiced. *What if he was advanced and I embarrassed him?* I worried.

The teachers led us through some easy poses all the while making sure that we kept touch with our partner, hands held or legs entwined. One pose took us into a twist that brought our faces close enough to kiss, and I noticed that David was sweating and breathing hard, but he gave me a smile and squeezed my hand. In that moment, I felt a connection to him like a shared secret passing through the heat of our palms.

"Talk to your partner," the male teacher reminded us. "Ask them what they need. More pressure? Less?" He walked between the yoga mats, offering suggestions and adjusting the poses. At one point, the mismatched couple fell but laughed unselfconsciously, genuinely enjoying themselves. "And remember, if you are laughing, then you are doing it right, no matter what it looks like," the instructor said, loosening the rest of us up.

"Next, we're going to have one person lie on their stomach on the mat and your partner will straddle them." The teachers demonstrated the pose with Tessa on top. Following their lead, David lay down on the mat and I sat on top of him, my knees to either side of his waist. "Whichever one of you is on top, put your hands on your partner's shoulders and gently pull them back for cobra pose," Tessa cued, lifting her husband's shoulders off the mat into a gentle backbend. As I pulled David's shoulders off the mat, he let out an unreadable moan.

"Does that feel good? Do you need more?" I asked.

"No." David's voice sounded strangled. "Oh god."

"If your partner is calling out 'oh god,' that might be far enough," Tessa said teasingly. I straightened up immediately and let David go. His shoulders had been barely off the ground, and I noticed that his hands were too far forward for this pose. Like a novice.

"Hon," I whispered in his ear, "you've done this before, right?"

"Well, no. Not actually. I mean, I know how to stretch, but I've never done a class or anything." I kissed him on top of his head, vaguely relieved that I wouldn't need to try to keep up with him. I found his lie of omission endearing. After all, I'd never actually asked him if he'd done yoga before. The lie floated around my conscious-ness as harmlessly as a beach ball in a swimming pool, and I swatted it away without another thought.

"All right, pull your hands back and closer to your body, elbows in. Don't worry, I've got you," I continued to whisper to him, happy to be the expert for a change, and I felt his body relax underneath mine.

The class ended with Savasana, the final resting pose, typically done by lying flat on your back, completely giving in to the stillness of mind and body. It was always the hardest pose for me, denying myself the urge to move, fighting my natural inclination to mentally orga-nize the rest of the day. For this class, each of the couples held hands. I wanted to feel the connection between us as something bright and light and undeniable, but somehow, the thought of him dismissing yoga as 'stretching' crept into my thoughts with persistence. The way he'd led me to believe he practiced yoga was the beach ball racing back to me, caught on jet steam of water. My eyes refused to stay shut and I turned my head away from him and peeked sideways at our images in the mirror that made up the classroom's wall. On our backs, his body, while not huge, still overwhelmed mine, his reflection surrounding every part of me, his feet extended past mine, his head reached beyond my head, his torso higher. I lost myself in the image, staring until we blurred into one object, me inside him, no edges of my own. I turned my head to face the ceiling, forced my eyes shut, and tried to focus on the warmth of his hand, the connection I came here to find eventually pulsing through me again, as it had earlier.

We ended the class sitting cross-legged facing our partner, bowing to each other with our palms touching in prayer.

"Namaste," I said, *I bow to you*. Unsure of what to do, David nodded soundlessly back at me.

$$\bullet \; \bullet \; \bullet$$

"So that is when David called out 'oh god!' and I realized he'd never done yoga before!"

Gail and Anna burst out with laugher, a sound like balloons popping. Turning the story to an anecdote had helped with my feelings about David's duplicity. As my sister had pointed out when I told her, wasn't it a compliment that he wanted to impress me? I had to agree.

"What are you doing here anyway?" I asked Anna when the laughter subsided and Gail excused herself, leaving the room. Anna had knocked at our door while I had been telling Gail the story. Gail sat through the beginning again good-naturedly while I caught Anna up. I probably would have told Anna anyway, but maybe not. It felt a little like cheating on her; she had always been my go-to yoga buddy, although when she came to class, I envied the ease at which she bent and stretched, naturally flexible. Poses that I worked on for years came easily to her.

"I have something to show you!" Anna said. "It's outside."

"Okay…?" Curious, I slipped my feet into my sandals and followed Anna to the street.

"Here it is!" she said, gesturing to a silver BMW with her out-stretched arms. "My new baby! What do you think?"

"Oh my god, it's awesome! Can we go for a ride?"

"Yeah, jump in!"

I sat down in the passenger's seat, enjoying the new car smell of the interior. "Wow, it feels so modern. I wouldn't know what to do with half those buttons," I admitted looking at the complicated dashboard.

"Honestly, I'm still figuring it out myself," Anna said, sliding into the driver's seat. She pulled into the slow-moving traffic on the street, adjusting the rearview mirror as she motored forward. "That's better," she said as she pushed a button on the side of her seat and her seat moved back.

"Anna, you should put on your seatbelt."

She sighed but did as I requested, looking away from the road for a second to buckle it. Anna opened her window and stuck her arm out, waving it back and forth in the breeze, driving with one hand on the wheel. "Isn't this great?" she said, her voice ringing with delight.

"Yeah," I answered. Anna was driving close to the car in front of her. My foot automatically braked on the nonexistent pedal on the passenger side as we approached a red light.

"I've got it, Amy," Anna said, sounding annoyed. "The brake on my side is the only one we need." We drove a few more blocks in silence. Stopping at another light, Anna said, "Let's turn on the radio. Tell me when the light turns." She fumbled with the controls, her head down as she tried to decipher the dials.

"It's green," I said, and Anna impulsively jammed on the gas without giving the car in front of us time to move. The smashing noise was ear-splitting and unexpected. Our seatbelts held us in place as we were jolted forward and back.

"Shit!" Anna yelled when we came to a stop. "Shit, shit, shit!" She banged on the steering wheel. "Are you okay?" she asked as an afterthought. I nodded, stunned. Why had she gunned the gas so hard? She could have really hurt us, or someone else, but she didn't seem to care.

"I'm fine," I said, looking at the crushed hood of Anna's car. The car in front of us turned on its hazard lights, and a young boy stepped out. He barely looked old enough to have a driver's license. Anna got out of her side and approached the boy, yelling.

"Why the fuck were you still stopped? Didn't you see the light change?"

"I, uh, was about to go," the boy said, clearly shaken. He looked at his car. His car was an older model, built like a tank. The damage to his car was minimal, but the front of Anna's brand new Bimmer had folded like an accordion.

"I'll go call the police," I said, looking around for a store that might let me borrow a phone.

"No!" Anna said.

"Uh," the boy stammered, "don't we, uh, have to?" I nodded in agreement.

"Uh, uh," Anna said, imitating him in an ugly voice. "No, both cars are drivable. Let's handle this without getting insurance involved." She reached in her open window for her handbag. "Here," she said handing him a hastily written note on the back of an ATM receipt. "That's my address and telephone number. Give me yours," she ordered, handing him another scrap of paper. "I'll call you with an estimate for the damage."

"If you think so," the boy said sheepishly. The look of resignation on his young face was breaking my heart. I couldn't believe Anna was being so nasty. The accident was clearly her fault.

"Anna," I said, "you can't—"

"Stay out of it," she said. Shocked, I kept silent. The boy handed her the information and walked solemnly back in his car; his shoulders slouched somberly. My conscience gnawed at me. I knew calling the police was the right thing to do but I decided to let it go. She was the driver; it was her decision to make.

"Is there a garage around here?" Anna asked in the direction where a group of onlookers stopped to gawk at the crash. Most of the people shook their heads in answer, but one man spoke up, telling her about an auto repair shop a few blocks away.

"Do you want me to come with you to the garage, in case you have problems on the way?" I offered.

"No, I don't need any more of your help."

My jaw dropped. "My help? Are you blaming *me* for this?"

"You told me to go."

"No, I told you the light was green, like you asked me to. I assumed you saw the car sitting in front of you."

"Well, I didn't. I *assumed* you were telling me that I needed to go because the light was green, *and* the other car had moved."

"You just asked me to tell you when it changed. I did."

"Whatever. Can you walk home from here?"

"Of course, since you don't need me."

"I don't." Anna mumbled. She got in the car and drove noisily down the street. I watched her go, then turned and walked in the direction of my apartment. It was only a few blocks away, but I felt a tightness in my chest that caught with every inhale, feeling vulnerable and injured, although physically, I was fine. The intensity of the argument made the walk back to my apartment feel excruciatingly long. I replayed the moments before the crash in my mind like a loop of film. Had I told her to go too soon? No, I only told her that the light had turned green; *she* started moving without looking. The more I thought about it, the hurt feeling changed to anger. How could she blame me for this?

I was still fuming when I got to my apartment and told Gail what happened. Gail agreed that it wasn't my fault. I expected Anna to call me that night but when she didn't, I resisted the urge to call her, with support from Gail telling me not to give in this time, letting my righteous indignation fuel me like a fire.

To help me fight down the urge to call her, I told myself that I didn't need Anna, but I was unsure about that. My other friends seemed to be riding the wave of post-college life, where every new high was followed by the receding tide, taking them farther and farther from shore. Career advances moving them to other cities, serious relationships replacing Saturday nights out. It was getting harder to fill the gaps that was so easy to do in my early twenties. Sunday afternoons that used to be filled with shopping trips and matinees were now spent attending bridal and baby showers. Pretty celebrations dotted my calendar like clam-shaped shells left behind on the sand, but hollow and one-sided.

When I told David about the accident, he was noncommittal, saying he didn't want to get involved. I wondered what Anna would say about it at work when I wasn't around to defend myself and she had his ear all to herself. What if David thought she was in the right?

I resisted calling Anna for a full week, and with every day that passed the fire inside me shrank until it was only embers. I longed to see Anna; the plain truth was that I missed her. It was the biggest argument we had ever had, but I couldn't let this one thing ruin our long friendship. After checking my messages for the thousandth time that week and confirming that none were from Anna, I gave in and called her.

"It's me. Anna, I'm sorry," I said in a rush as soon as she picked up the phone.

"It's fine." Anna said, ending the discussion before it began. We talked for a few more tense minutes and then she abruptly said she had to go. I was so relieved to be talking to her again that it wasn't until later that I realized she never returned the apology.

CHAPTER 14

June 2001

"I know that your birthday is still a week away, but I wanted to give you your present early. I can't wait any longer," David said, his arm around my shoulder as we walked down the street, cocooned in the afterglow of the cozy dinner we had just shared at Bella Famiglia, a new Italian restaurant near David's condo.

"I won't say no to that," I answered, happily intrigued. It would make the ideal end to a wonderful evening. All through the meal, I entertained daydreams of the two of us eating at this restaurant often, becoming part of their 'beautiful family' as the restaurant's welcoming name implied, having no idea the restaurant would close a month later, before even the first set of candles on their tables had burned down.

David paused to unlock the gate to the common patio behind his building. I assumed the present was in the condo since his hands were empty, but he indicated for me to sit on the worn wooden bench across from the trickling fountain in the center of the patio. Behind the bench, dogwood trees blushed with pink blossoms; the bricks beneath the trees were littered with petals like confetti.

I sat down on the small bench and made room for him next to me. Nervously, he continued to stand. My mind jumped to the possibilities, the gift would have to be something that was easily hidden, could he have concert tickets in his pockets? *Plane tickets?* I thought, anticipation building.

"Amy, I know that we haven't been dating that long, but I love you and I can't imagine life without you." He cleared his throat. "Well, what I'm trying to say is"—David got down on one knee and my eyes flew wide with surprise—"will you marry me?" He reached in his pocket, pulled out a small velvet box, and opened it for me. My mouth fell open in shock as my eyes traveled slowly down to the solitaire diamond David was offering, feeling as if the moment wasn't quite real. Perfect as a romance novel, but somehow thin as a piece of paper.

"Oh my god… yes!" I answered, my voice just above a whisper. As I said the words, it was as if I could see the dialogue printed on the page. David slipped the ring on my finger and kissed me, as I knew he would.

"Do you like it?" he asked as he nestled his face close to mine and we both looked down at my finger. The round diamond was flawless and elegant, mounted on a plain silver band. It was perfect and I said so, unintentionally holding my breath as I moved my finger slightly side to side. We stayed like that for a moment, watching the diamond play hide and seek with the light. Gradually, I felt the haze begin to lift. This was real. David locked his fingers around mine and pulled me to my feet. As we strolled to the back door of his building,

I started breathing regularly again. David tapped in the code to open the door with his free hand, not wanting to let go of our entwined fingers. I squeezed his hand and squealed loudly.

"That's more like it," David said laughing.

By the time we got upstairs, it felt to me as if the engagement happened years ago. Even as I called my parents, it seemed as if I was retelling a story that I had memorized long before.

"Mom, I have good news. David proposed tonight. We are getting married!"

"Oh, sweetie, that is wonderful! John!" She called to my father, too excited to cover the mouthpiece, "John, it's Amy and she has some news." I could hear my mom walking as she talked. "Here he is." My mom handed over the phone and my dad's voice came on the line.

"Amy?"

"Hi, Dad," I said quickly. "David and I are getting married!"

"That's fantastic, I'm happy for you." I could hear my dad shifting in his recliner, its worn springs creaking under his weight. There was a lack of surprise in his voice, and I realized that David, ever the traditionalist, would have talked to him first.

"Dad," I said, drawing out the word suspiciously, "did you know David was going to propose?"

"David may have stopped by my office last week."

"You knew!" I heard my mom's voice filled with indignation in the background.

"Amy, I'm putting your mother back on. I may have to leave town for a while." My mom continued chiding him playfully as she took the phone back.

"That man," she said. "Anyway, when do you want to have the wedding?" I told her that we hadn't discussed it yet. Before hanging up, I promised to start thinking about a date and that we would get together soon to start planning.

"Love you, Mom," I said.

"I love you, too, sweetheart. And love to my soon-to-be son-in-law."

I smiled at the words and hung up the phone.

David called his parents, and I eavesdropped on the conversation. They must have already known about the proposal because David led by saying, "She said yes." He talked to his parents for a few minutes before handing me the phone.

"Welcome to the family, Amy," his mother said sweetly.

"Thank you," I said.

I had met David's parents a handful of times at their home in Wyncote. As I accepted congratulations from David's mother and father over the phone, I remembered an article I had read in an issue of *BTB* about how to have a successful marriage. It encouraged the reader to consider not just the person they were marrying but also the family they were marrying into. *This was going to be my family*, I thought. It was a strange feeling, not exactly unpleasant, but a little like signing a contract before reading it all the way through, assuming the small print and boilerplate language were inconsequential.

I didn't feel I knew his parents very well, but in that moment, I assumed David and I would have a lifetime together, so I shook the uncomfortable feeling off and dialed Sam's number.

Sam sounded as stunned as I was, but when she recovered, she asked how long she had to lose the baby weight before I stuffed her into a bridesmaid dress. "Everyone wants to know a date," I said, covering the receiver with my hand and yelling to David.

"Hey," he answered, "tell them I bought the ring and found the perfect proposal spot, if I do say so myself, so I am off the hook for making any decisions at least through the weekend."

"David said that he can't wait to make me his wife and we may elope tonight," I said into the phone, making Sam giggle.

"I thought you would have called Anna before Sam," David said after I hung up with my sister.

"I'm dying to tell her, but I have to think about how to do it. She's still upset about the accident," I said, although David was well aware of this fact. Even though Anna and I were ostensibly past any lingering animosity, we hadn't seen each other in weeks, which bothered me not only because it was unusual but because it also seemed purposeful. "She's so sensitive about relationships. I know she'll be happy for us, David, but I need to break it to her gently. Maybe I should do that in person."

"I don't know, Amy, it might be better to tell her on the phone. Let her get used to the idea before she sees you and before I start telling people at the office. I want her to be happy for you, and I know she will be eventually, but you know Anna. She doesn't really have a filter when it comes to her emotions."

"She used to," I said, confessing something that has been nagging at me for a while. Life hadn't been kind to Anna, and her trials had hardened her personality. David raised his eyebrows, unbelieving. "Seriously, she used to be kind of quiet and reserved. Paul really screwed her up. But you've got a good point. I'll call her with the news."

"But not tonight," David said, enveloping me in his arms.

"Not tonight," I agreed and breathed in the heady scent of David's aftershave, feeling happy despite Anna's continued distance. She'd come around. In the meantime, I was going to enjoy this perfect moment with my fiancé.

• • •

Anna's letter arrived on my birthday.

Sweet Amy,

I'm sorry I haven't been in touch since you called me with the news of your engagement. It came as quite a shock to me. David really is a great guy, and you deserve all the joy he can offer you. I'm excited to be a part of your wedding, and of course, I am thrilled to be your maid of honor. I'll see you at your birthday dinner, and we can start planning the big day.

I treasure you, and I would do anything for you. I hope you know that.

All my love, Anna

• • •

August 2001

I double-parked in front of Anna's apartment and honked the horn. I was still getting used to the new car, a red 2001 Chevrolet Cavalier, the first new car I had ever owned. I felt awkward when I admitted to Anna that David and I were buying it, cars being a sensitive subject between us, but she didn't make a big deal out of it. Anna had decided that she didn't need a car after all in the city, and after a few negotiations, she got a fair price without even bothering to get her Bimmer fixed from the crash.

Although the Chevy was registered in both our names, our first joint purchase as an engaged couple, I considered it my car because I made the down payment. David didn't understand why we needed another car, but I always kept one so that I could travel to Bell's Lake whenever I liked. My last car, a 1991 Ford Taurus, had died an honorable death. It had been a reliable eyesore that got me from A to B. This car, a two-door coupe, felt sleek in comparison. The shiny black faux leather interior was completely free of duct tape, and although I knew the pristine red paint would soon be filled with dings from life on the narrow downtown streets, I was trying to be careful where I parked it. I avoided high-risk situations, like parking next to something that looked like my old car or anything with children's car seats. David stressed that he wanted to keep it scratch-free for as long as possible, so I had to make a strong case for driving it to New York City.

"The train is so easy, and with traffic, it's probably faster," he pointed out.

"But Anna and I haven't taken a road trip in ages, and it just wouldn't be the same if we couldn't drink Diet Coke in Big Gulps and sing at the top of our lungs."

"Big Gulps? I thought we agreed that we weren't going to eat and drink in the car."

"Ha!" I said. "Oh, wait, you were serious about that?"

David looked at me unbelievingly; then he shook his head and smiled. "How can I resist you when you look so happy? Do what you like. It's all fine." He kissed me on the forehead, a beguiling smile playing on his lips.

I honked again, and Anna hurried out the door. She wore a tight black crop top that exposed her flat stomach. Her hair was piled sloppily on her head, held in place with a plastic clip. The overnight bag that hung over her shoulder was partially unzipped, and she shoved her keys into it as she walked. I smiled at how she managed to make complete disorganization look modish. I felt good in my light A-line dress that showed off my toned legs.

I hadn't seen much of Anna over the summer. As promised, we had gone out to dinner for my birthday. It was the first time I had seen her since I called her with the news of my engagement. She dutifully admired the ring and asked questions about our wedding plans. I turned the conversation back to her, asking about a recent date she had had with a guy she met at the gym. Slowly, the awkwardness faded. We kept the conversation to things unrelated to the wedding as we ate, but I didn't see her again until her birthday in July. She invited several friends to join us, turning our typical twosome dinner into a small party, but she had seemed in good spirits. Since then, the plans we made to see each other always seemed to get canceled at the last minute. That was until she called me with the idea of a weekend in New York. Her excitement was palatable, and the weekend quickly became a reality, though I had to cash in several favors to cover my hospital shift. It seemed the old Anna was back. Any begrudging feelings she had toward me were gone, and I wasn't going to miss out on the opportunity to spend time with her.

"You look NY fabulous," I said as she got in the car, launching her overnight bag over the front seat.

"So do you, darling," she said, giving me a dramatic air kiss and admiring the simple sleeveless dress I wore. My only jewelry was long dangling earrings and, of course, my engagement ring.

"Let's do it!" I said, putting the car into gear.

"To New York City!" Anna said, picking up the oversize soda that I bought for her from the cup holder and holding it in front of her, making a toast. "May this be the last nonalcoholic drink we have for forty-eight hours!"

"Yes!" I said, picking my cup up and tapping hers without looking, keeping my eyes on the road.

We arrived at the hotel, parked, and checked in. After several tries with the plastic keycard, the green circle finally lit up, and we walked inside our hotel room. The lobby had been refurbished and our room seemed remarkably dated by comparison. The carpet was worn down to fibers in spots and the bedspreads looked iffy. Anna turned on the light, which somehow made the room look even shabbier by surrounding us in a dim yellowish glow. I opened the heavy curtains, intending to let in the natural light, but the brick wall and rusted fire escape of the building next door stood inches away, blocking the sun.

Ignoring the disappointing room, Anna and I opened our suitcases and began reapplying makeup, talking nonstop as we did. I found an electrical outlet under the nightstand and unplugged the clock to plug in my flat iron. As it heated, Anna told me about a new bar that a co-worker had told her about called the Voodoo Lounge. We agreed it would be our first stop.

We took a taxi downtown, and at the address her friend had given her, we followed the signs to the Voodoo Lounge, which took us through a dark lobby and pointed to an ancient elevator. The elevator stopped on the eighteenth floor with a hair-raising bounce but opened onto a rooftop bar, which offered amazing views of the city. The Empire State Building with its triangle of lights stood proudly over the cluster of skyscrapers. The music was deafeningly loud on the lounge's small dance floor, and the insistent thump, thump, thump of the Euro music echoed in my chest as we walked past the DJ's mammoth amplifiers. At the other end of the dance floor was a doorway with a sign that read 'The Cauldron' in a spiky script. We pushed aside a curtain of black beads and followed the stairs down and back inside the building to a quieter bar, taking seats on the black leather barstools.

"What can I get you?" the young bartender asked, giving us a smile.

"What would you recommend?" Anna asked. "It's her pre-bachelorette party, kind of like a practice run."

"In that case, you better start building up your tolerance. How about a couple of lemon drops?"

"Sounds perfect," Anna said, and the bartender soon returned with glasses filled with lemonade-colored liquid and sugar coating on the rims.

"Here's to buying bridal magazines without guilt!" Anna said, raising her glass, surprising me as she had since we planned this trip with her sudden acceptance of the wedding.

"And trying on dresses," I clinked my glass against hers. "Wait, don't drink yet," I said, digging in my purse for my new digital camera given to me by my parents for my birthday.

"Excuse me," I said to the bartender, "could you please take a picture of us?" He nodded, and I handed him the camera across the bar.

"Say cheese," he said and pressed his finger on the shutter. He handed the camera back to me; it made a faint whirling noise when I turned it off and the lens cover closed.

"So," Anna said, looking around at the people in the bar. Her gaze stopped at a man sitting alone at a table. "He's cute," she said, tilting her chin in his direction.

"Mm-hmm," I agreed looking where Anna had indicated a man with blond hair, combed back over his ears. He had a trim build that was evident even in his business suit. His white shirt was unbuttoned at the top and his tie stuck out of his coat pocket. Feeling us looking at him, he lifted his drink in our direction. Anna and I laughed at being caught and turned back to face each other. I lifted my left hand to signal the bartender for another drink.

"Your ring is so beautiful," Anna said with a sigh. I looked down at the diamond, which caught the lights dangling above the bar.

"I'm still stunned it's mine," I said. I never thought I'd have a diamond this big.

"Let me try in on," Anna said, holding out her hand.

I tried to hide my concern. I just wasn't comfortable letting someone else wear my ring. It seemed inauspicious. "No, it's really hard to get off, and—"

"Oh, come on, Amy, please?" Her knee began bouncing under the bar with impatience. "This might be my last chance to wear one." She said, covering the worrying truth in her words with a laugh.

I wanted to protest more, but I reluctantly decided to let her try it on. It would only be for a minute, and I would get it right back. I twisted the ring and pulled it painstakingly over my knuckle. Anna slid the ring easily over her finger and held up her hand to admire it in the light.

"Wow," she breathed.

Just then, the blond man approached our table.

"You ladies look like you're having a good time. Mind if I join you?" He spoke with an English accent. Anna kicked me with her foot, knowing I was a sucker for a Brit.

"It's fate," she whispered discreetly in my ear before turning to the man, although I wasn't sure what she meant by that. "Of course we wouldn't mind. I'm Amy. Look," she said, holding out her left hand so he could see the ring, "we are celebrating my engagement! And this is my best friend and maid of honor, Anna." She put her hand on my back, pushing me slightly forward on my barstool. "Lucky for you, she's still available."

"Nice to meet you, Anna," the man said, shaking my hand before I could protest. "Celebrating, huh? Well, I guess I should buy you ladies a drink. Remember, Amy," he said looking at Anna, "nothing's final until you say, 'I do.'"

"Oh, I'm completely in love. I'm utterly taken," Anna said with an intentionally overdramatic air, crossing her hands over her chest so that her left hand was on top with my engagement ring sparkling and casting tiny triangles of light on the dark bar. "But" she paused flirtatiously, "I wouldn't say no to another lemon drop."

The man signaled for the bartender. "I'm Gilligan," he said, introducing himself.

"Gilligan, really?" Anna said.

Gilligan put up a hand. "Yes, really. And before you ask, no, my parents weren't shipwrecked after a three-hour tour, and no, the skipper's not with me, and no, I don't have any coconut cream pie. Bloody American comedy," he added under his breath.

"I guess you get that a lot," I said, smiling and starting to relax a little. Gilligan rolled his eyes in answer. It all happened so fast, but I was beginning to accept our little deception. Anna was just having fun. "I have to ask one thing, though." I looked at our new friend and he gave me a wary smile, waiting for my question. "If it bothers you, why don't you just go by Gill or something?"

"I do go by Gill, actually," he said, "but when I meet beautiful women, I like to find out right away if my name is a deal breaker."

"Smart man," Anna said. "I'd say your accent makes up for the name. Where are you from?"

"Outside of London, but then again, all us Brits say that. Don't we? What about you ladies? Are you girls local?"

This small bit of flattery did not go unnoticed. No one wanted to be a tourist in New York City.

"Visiting from Philadelphia," Anna said and looked at me. "It's a pre-bachelorette party. Anna is my oldest and dearest friend, and I wanted some time with my best girl before the big day." She lied with ease. It made me uncomfortable, but I didn't want to ruin her mood. She was obviously having fun playing the bride-to-be and I remembered that she missed out on this time with Paul.

Gill shuffled in his spot. "Why don't you have a seat," I said reluctantly. I pulled the empty barstool between me and Anna. Gill sat down and stretched his long legs out in front of him.

"I know what we need," he said as the bartender made his way back to us. A group of girls that barely looked twenty-one approached the bar, forcing him to move closer to us, the three of us forming a tight circle. "Can we get a Witches' Brew?"

"Coming up," the bartender said. He pulled a heavy wine glass the size of a cereal bowl on a thick stem out from under the bar. He began filling it with different bottles of alcohol, liberally pouring grenadine syrup and two different kinds of rum.

"You'll want to get your camera back out for this," the bartender said to me as he pushed the drink in front of us. He added a few pieces of dry ice with tongs, causing smoke to swirl upward from the glass as I took a picture. Anna looked at the drink and smiled playfully at me. The bartender topped it with cherries and three black bar straws. "Should I start a tab?" he asked, and Gill nodded, handing over his credit card. I set my camera on the bar.

"Shall we?" Gill said, and we all leaned forward to take a sip. Gill put an arm around each of us as we drank. We straightened back up, and Gill's hand lingered on my back for a few seconds longer. "So," he said, "what do Philadelphia girls like to do for fun?"

We launched easily into familiar remember-the-time-when stories that never failed to amuse us, and typically, people got caught up in our revelry as we reminisced, but Gill seemed antsy. He talked about partying in England and how different it was in the States. Another Witches' Brew appeared, and drinking it felt less awkward this time. I noticed that Gill was inching closer to me, asking me questions without excluding Anna from the conversation in a way that I found impressive.

We'd been talking and drinking for about an hour when I excused myself to use the ladies' room. I studied my reflection in the bathroom mirror and smiled at what I saw even though my eyeliner was smudged and my lipstick was a memory. As I applied a fresh coat, I thought about Gill. Obviously, nothing would happen between us, I was sure of it, but I felt like it could, even with the beautiful Anna next to me. It wasn't just that Anna was pretending to be engaged, I thought as I finger-combed my hair; it was me. Or the new me, as I had come to think of myself since David. I felt visible and confident. I was enjoying playing the role of Anna, and I felt that I was doing it flawlessly. "Sidekick no more!" I vowed out loud and laughed as the room spun slightly. Where had that come from?

I returned to the table to find Gill standing.

"Unfortunately, our new friend has to leave," Anna said, and Gill turned to me.

"I have an early flight in the morning, and I've already stayed too long. I'll regret this when the alarm goes off. It's a long way back to Heathrow," he said. "Congratulations, again, Amy. It was a pleasure to meet you," Gill said, bowing and kissing Anna's hand like Prince Charming, which made us laugh. Anna drunkenly ruffled his hair as he straightened back up. She stood quickly and surprised Gill by giving him a sloppy hug.

Gill put his hands on either side of her waist and set Anna back on her barstool, then he turned to me. "And you, too, Anna," he said, hugging me. He pulled back but didn't quite let me go.

"Go on, Anna, give him a kiss good night," Anna said loudly. Gill laughed at her brazenness and shrugged. Anna leaned forward and quickly whispered in my ear, "No one's watching. This could be your last chance, and he's British! Go ahead, I won't tell." Anna backed away from me and leaned on the bar for support. I looked up into Gill's eyes and swayed for a minute, tempted. He smiled, and his sexy dimples deepened. He leaned toward me, but at the last second, I turned my head.

"I'm sorry, I can't," I said quickly, just as I heard a faint whirring noise. I looked at Anna and saw that she was holding my camera. Her finger was pressing the 'on' button, and the lens cover was sliding open. Anna swiftly put the camera back on the bar, pressing the 'off' button and looking at me as if nothing had happened.

"No worries," Gill said and leaned over and kissed me on the forehead. As he looked over the top of my head, his body stiffened. "Oh shit, what is she doing here?" His voice sounded odd, and he practically pushed me back on the barstool. He hustled to the exit where a blonde girl stood, wide-eyed, her mouth set in a firm line. She turned and angrily shoved the door open with her palms. Gilligan following on her heels, saying her name, and starting a lame explanation.

"Did you see that?" Anna said.

I nodded, still stunned by her trick with the camera.

"Oh my god, what an asshole!" she said, unaware of how angry I was at her. "I wonder if anything he said was true. Did you notice? His accent disappeared!" She laughed and took a final sip of the Witches' Brew. It had turned a watery pink with a few ice cubes still floating about in it. "Let's go outside and dance!" she said, hopping off her barstool.

"Anna, wait. I need my ring back now."

"Oh yeah," she said nonchalantly, as if she had forgotten all about it. She slipped the ring off her finger and handed it to me. I put it back on and looked at it for a minute, reassuring myself that it was on securely and mentally swearing never to take it off again. When I looked back, Anna was already walking up the stairs to the outdoor bar. I hurried to catch up to her.

"That was a blast!" she called back to me.

"Wait," I said, putting my hand on her shoulder and making her stop. I turned her to face me. "Why did you do that?" As the words left my mouth, I didn't know if I was asking her about the ring or the camera or egging me on to kiss Gill. All of it, I supposed.

"I don't know, Amy." Her face betrayed some secret emotion I wasn't familiar with. "Sometimes I don't know why I do the things I do. It's not a big deal, it was just a joke. Don't be so serious. Nothing happened." She turned and continued up the steps.

Outside, the air was cooler, and it helped clear my head. Anna and I stepped onto the dance floor and began to move to the mindless beat. I looked around. Beyond the sparse crowd, the lights of the city dotted the darkness. Above us, the sky was black with no sign of stars, which made the view more vibrant, as if all the light in the world began with us and trickled downward and outward, covering the city. The twin towers of the World Trade Center lit the edge of the sky, standing together like best friends, seemingly indestructible. There was a slight breeze, and I felt myself giving in to the pure pleasure of dancing. Anna smiled at me, and I let the anger I had felt slip away.

CHAPTER 15

October 2001

I walked into the *BTB* offices, past the sleek white receptionist desk that was empty because of the late hour. The magazine's logo hung above the desk, a silver circle with 'BTB' in scripted letters that looked like a monogram. David and I were going out to dinner, and he had asked me to meet him here. I walked past the small cubicle farm, which was slightly less elegant than the reception area, but each workspace was decorated with individual touches: a square vase holding an orchid, a tapestry of chakras held to the wall with push pins, a tartan blanket over an office chair. 'Personalize Your Workspace'—I could almost see that as the title of a *BTB* article.

David's office was along the back wall, next to Anna's. I hadn't seen much of her since our New York trip. I had been busy with work, making up for the time off, but we had talked on the phone a few times. The door to David's office was open, and I saw that Anna was still here. She was sitting on David's desk facing him and looking down at the desktop to a magazine proof. Her legs were crossed, and her taupe skirt hugged her hips as she leaned to the side. David was sitting in his chair. Their heads were bent together familiarly, studying the layout for the next issue. I knocked on the open door, and they both jumped.

"Amy!" Anna exclaimed. "I didn't hear you come in. You startled me!" She hopped off the desk and turned away from me to get her shoes from the corner of the room.

"Hey. You guys were really deep in concentration," I said, covering the awkwardness with a laugh. "Ready to go?"

David nodded and stood up. "Yup," he said, stretching. "Anna, we'll finish up tomorrow, okay?"

"Sure," she said, looking at me over her shoulder as she bent to put on her shoes. "You kids have fun."

• • •

November 2001

David pulled the car into a narrow parking spot on the street in front of my parents' house. My mom had insisted that we come home to Bell's Lake for Thanksgiving because I would be joining David and his family for their annual Christmas ski trip to Aspen. David carefully retrieved two bottles of expensive wine from the back seat, and I carried the fall-inspired flower arrangement that he had ordered from the florist.

My mom came to greet us when she heard the front door open. "Oh, what is this?" Mom said, taking the flowers from my hands. She turned the basket to admire the flowers from all sides.

"David's idea. He wanted to give you this for the table," I said.

"They are lovely. Thank you, David." She leaned in to give him a quick kiss on the cheek. She kissed me as well and set the flowers down on the table in the foyer. "Here, let me take your coats."

"I got it, Mom," I said, folding David's coat on top of mine and walking to the hall closet. The closet was bursting with the winter clothing Sam and I had long outgrown but were kept 'just in case,' and I barely managed to shove our coats inside.

"I'll take these to the kitchen," David said, gesturing to the bottles he still carried.

"Yes, then you can grab a beer," my mom said, wrongly assuming David preferred beer but would suffer through the traditional glass of wine with dinner, like my dad. "Charlie and John are watching football in the den." David headed to the kitchen.

"Where are Sam and the kids?" I asked.

"Out back on the swing set."

"In this cold?"

"The kids needed to get their wiggles out. They were driving your father nuts, running in front of the TV, and blocking each play."

We walked to the kitchen, which was stuffy from the heat of the oven. The room was filled with the familiar scents of Thanksgiving, the mixture of roasting meat and candied sweet potatoes. David was opening a bottle of wine. "Where do you keep the wine glasses, Mary?" he asked.

"Up here." Mom opened the cabinet above the refrigerator and was standing on her tiptoes trying to reach a glass when David rescued her.

"I'll get down six," he said, "for dinner."

"Okay," she said. "I guess I should rinse them off. They're pretty dusty."

David put the wine glasses on the counter next to the sink. He rinsed a glass and dried it carefully with a paper towel. "Mind if I take this to the den?" he asked.

"Not at all," my mom said, and David poured himself a glass.

"I'll have a glass, too," I said, rinsing a wine glass and pouring from the open bottle. I started to place the cork back in the bottle, but David's hand stopped me.

"The wine needs to breathe. And I don't see a decanter," he added in a whisper. I moved the open bottle to the back of the counter so it would be out of the way. David walked out of the kitchen toward the den, where Dad and Charlie were yelling profanities at the Detroit Lion's defense.

"Mom, I'm going say hello to Sam and the kids, and then I'll help you in the kitchen," I said, heading out the back door.

"Take your time," she said. "I've got it under control. There really isn't a lot to do until the last half hour anyway." The door creaked loudly when I opened it. The screen door was jammed, as usual. I used my hip to push it open.

"I won't be long," I said, letting the screen door snap back behind me with a slam.

"Don't slam the screen door!" my mom and Sam yelled in unison, an old family joke. The spring on the ancient door was so tight that not slamming it wasn't an option, but my mom had yelled at us for years about it anyway.

"Wow, that was in surround sound." I walked toward Sam, shaking my head as if to clear it. "Did you guys practice that? Or is that what happens after baby number two? You officially have a 'mom voice.'"

"Yup, it's my 'mom voice,'" Sam said proudly. "Suddenly saying things like 'stop that or you'll put an eye out' just feels right."

I snickered and placed my wine glass on the picnic table next to the play set that had stood in the backyard since Sam and I were kids. Spying Robbie, I approached the plastic tunnel connecting the slide to the stairs. "I see you!" I said, sticking my head in a hole in the side of tunnel. I was rewarded with Robbie's cold hand pinching my nose.

"Yuck," I said, pulling my head back. "Why is his hand wet?"

"Do you really want to know?" Sam asked. I shook my head.

"I'm surprised this thing is still standing," I said.

"You know mom and dad," Sam said with a shrug, their pack rat status was legendary.

"Aumie!" Emily yelled, bursting through the bottom of the covered slide and hugging my legs. When Emily first tried to say my name, she couldn't quite separate 'Aunt' and 'Amy,' so 'Aumie' was the result. I sensed that this nickname was going to stick forever.

"Hello, cookie." I picked her up and gave her a big hug. "Wow, you are getting so big!" I put her down, and she ran to go up the ladder again. I retrieved my wine from the picnic table and took a sip.

"Oh no," Sam said, eying my wine glass warily. "We're not out of beer, are we?"

"Shut up. I drink wine," I said defensively.

"Mm-hmm."

"I do," I insisted, sitting on the picnic table and crossing my legs.

Sam gestured to my leather knee-highs with the top of her beer bottle.

"I like those boots," she said.

"Thanks, they're Steve Madden."

"Since when do you name-drop designers?" Sam said, taking a seat next to me.

"David's influence, I guess."

"He certainly has you dressing better, but you know this is a Sheppard party, right? The dress code is sloppy chic."

"David thinks there is a business casual dress code to go to the supermarket. He likes to say that 'it takes just as long to put on something nice as it does to put on something sloppy.'" I imitated his voice while giving my sister a sly smile that said I loved him anyway.

"I'd argue that buttons take longer than elastic," Sam said, jokingly snapping the waist band of her yoga pants. "These are maternity. Five seconds to put on, max."

I leaned against Sam and whispered, "Yeah, don't tell him, but I agree with you." I straightened up. "But," I added, "it *is* fun being a cool chick. You should try it," I teased.

"Hey!" Sam said. "If you remember, I was the queen of cool. I invented cool."

It was true. A person's ranking in the social hierarchy at Bell's Lake High was judged by how close you could sit to Sam at lunch. When people heard my last name, and I told them she was my sister, they unanimously responded with disbelief. "Really?" they would say. "You're Sam Sheppard's sister?" Even the teachers.

"Oh," Sam said abruptly like she just thought of something. "Can you babysit next Friday? Charlie and I are—"

"Sorry, I can't." I cut Sam off before she could finish, "David and I have tickets to a jazz concert with some of his friends."

"Since when do you listen to jazz?" Sam sounded annoyed. "Can't he go without you?"

"I guess he could, but I'm meeting these friends for the first time. I'd feel bad backing out now." Sam's lips pursed with annoyance, which I ignored, not wanting to discuss it further, worried I might give in. Putting my wine glass down again, I jumped off the picnic table, stretching my arms out wide and yelling "I'm gonna get you!" to the kids. Emily squealed delightedly and ran to the other side of the swing set as I chased her. Sam helped Robbie down, and he took off running after me as fast as his chubby legs could carry him, imitating his older sister's shouts.

• • •

As I carried Robbie into the house, I accidently kicked over my handbag, which had been left on the kitchen floor. I set Robbie down and he immediately toddled to the waiting, outstretched arms of his nana. When Sam walked in behind me, she stooped to pick up the scattered contents of my bag. Apparently, she left her irritation at me in the backyard, for which I was grateful.

"Are the pictures from the picnic in here?" She held up a thick envelope with the Expert Images logo. "I'm dying to see these people."

"Yes, along with an entire summer's worth of photos and ones from New York with Anna. I haven't had any extra time to get things done lately! Come on." I motioned for Sam to follow me to the stairs, knowing that I only had her attention for a few precious minutes before she would inevitably be needed by her children. We sat on the first step above the landing, where the stairs rounded a corner. This was our private spot, the one I had told David about. We had sat here many times as girls, feeling secluded from the rest of the house. We'd conspire about boys, our parents, our teachers. Our closest moments took place in our spot.

"Here we go," I said in a whisper, leaning close to Sam. "This is Leah, she's the one who turned the dice game into a competitive sport. And this is Tonya, the one who hooked up with David when he first started at *BTB*. Doesn't she look slutty? I mean, just look at how short that dress is."

"Oh my god, that's obscene!" Sam screeched.

"You should see it from the back! Let me see if I have another picture of her," I said, quickly thumbing through the rest of the photos. "Oh, I love this one of me and David." I handed her another photo. "And this girl is Erica. Doesn't she look like she walked straight out of the sixties in that flowy dress? I'm sure it cost a bundle."

"I think Mom has a dress like that in the attic," Sam said.

"And there is a reason it is in the attic. No one has small enough hips to pull off that print, especially not Erica." It was catty, I knew, but this was Sam. And we were in our spot. Anything said here stayed here. Our own little Vegas.

"Honey, are you in the house? I could use your help with the wine," David called from the bottom of the steps. Sam let out a loud, disbelieving laugh, and I covered her mouth with my hand to keep from being heard.

"How could he possibly need help with the wine?" Sam whispered. "That's gotta be code for a quickie in the bathroom, right? Don't go."

"It's code for 'I'm feeling out of place.' I'll come right back." I handed her the stack of photos. "Yup, I'm here, be down in a sec!" I yelled in the direction of the downstairs.

"Okay." David's voice was getting closer.

I started down the steps, and Sam continued to pick through the photos. Years later, I would find this pack of photos, abandoned in their envelope, the pictures never having been put into an album. Looking through them would give me pause. Sam was the last to look at these pictures and she had separated a picture from the set, putting it in front of the negatives. Finding it out of sequence, I would inspect it closely, looking beyond the men in the foreground, three smiling guys proudly holding their beers, and I would notice Anna in the background, sitting on a picnic table next to David. Anna looked directly at the camera, her arm wrapped possessively around David's shoulder. David's face was turned away, talking to another group of people. But Anna had the look in her eyes that I missed so many times until it was too late.

• • •

"Amy, how are you feeling today?" Dr. Riley said as I walked into her office.

"Fine," I answered. I sat down on the sofa and stiffly crossed my arms and legs. I didn't feel like being there. Not again. I was beginning to think these sessions were a waste of time.

"Let's start with the night of the accident," she said.

"I thought you were going to ask me more about Anna and David," I said.

"We'll get there, but I think it is good to have a common starting point. It lets me know where you are mentally—what you are thinking about and what you are focusing your energy on. By going back to the events of that night, I want you to be able to—"

"God! How many times do we have to go through this?" I asked, my voice rising with exasperation. These sessions were a Möbius strip of emotions, bringing me back time and time again to a night I would rather forget.

"As many times as we need to, Amy," she answered calmly. "It takes as long as it takes."

Feeling resigned, I mentally went back to the events surrounding the accident, the dinner, the storm. But this time thoughts flickered in my brain just beyond my consciousness. I started talking, hearing myself describe us going to the restaurant, but felt something pushing back inside my mind.

"It doesn't make sense anymore," I said, suddenly furious with Dr. Riley. "You've made me tell this story so many times that I can't think straight!" I started crying, hard and sudden, like the rainstorm on that tragic night. My thoughts turned to anguish. How could I lose them both? How could I have done this? I closed my eyes, giving in to the meltdown, my face contorting, tightening my jaw and neck while I sobbed a single word over and over. "Why?" I slouched over on the sofa. I'm not sure how long I lay there or how long Dr. Riley sat, unmoving, in her chair, but eventually, I found myself sitting up and telling the story of the night of the accident again, the drone of my voice echoing in my ears like the hum of tires on a road at the beginning of a long, tiresome journey.

CHAPTER 16

December 2001

"Maybe we could go to Asia. I hear that Thailand has some of the most beautiful beaches in the world," I said, turning my head from David's computer and rubbing my eyes. The whitish glow of the monitor was causing them to sting. I'd been staring at it too long, trying to find a spot for our honeymoon.

David was sitting in a leather chair, reading an issue of *The New Yorker*. "Amy, I hardly think we have time to plan for something like that. What about visas and vaccinations? Really, do you know anything about traveling to Asia? The summer will be here before we know it."

"I just thought maybe if we planned it together, we'd figure it out." I waited for him to look up. We had decided that after the wedding, we would spend the weekend at a luxury bed and breakfast in Lancaster, Pennsylvania, relaxing in Amish Country. We would postpone the 'real' honeymoon until the summer, when it would be easier for David to take time off. It would also give us more time to plan. When he didn't look up, I prompted him. "You were the one who was encouraging me to travel, remember? Get out of my comfort zone and see what real scenic photography would be like."

"Yes, of course," David said, recanting.

"Well, I'd like to start." I got up from the computer and sat on his lap. David shifted uncomfortably, and I stood up again. "I've been waiting for the opportunity, and our honeymoon would be a perfect time to try something new." I was thinking about David's remarks to me since we started dating, telling me that I needed to branch out more, to grow and to follow my passion. When David gave me the key to his condo, he put it in a card that quoted Maya Angelou saying, "Life is not measured by the number of breaths we take, but by the moments that take our breath away." I put the card in a silver frame and placed it on the end table in the living room. Now I was wondering if he had really meant it. I pushed the idea out of my mind. I was sure he had.

"Let's start smaller. Maybe the Caribbean? St. John is beautiful. And not too touristy. The restaurant at the resort I stayed at served authentic island cuisine," he said.

"You've been to St. John?" I asked.

"Yes, we had a conference there. The resort was outstanding. Let me see if I can find the information. That could be the perfect honeymoon spot," he said, standing and opening his file cabinet, the metal clanging as he flipped through his painstakingly organized folders.

"But you've already been there." I pouted. I walked up behind him and put my arms around his waist.

"Exactly," he said, oblivious to my disappointment. "This way, I know it will be nice." He leaned back and kissed me over his shoulder.

. . .

January 2002

I walked into my apartment and called out, "Gail, it's me!"

"Hey, stranger," she said, coming into the living room. "You know, technically you still live here. You don't have to tell me when you walk in the apartment."

"I know, but I feel like I haven't been here in so long, you might hear me moving around and call 911." I sat down on the sofa.

"You have a point. So, how are the wedding plans coming?" Gail asked, tucking her legs under her in a familiar move that made me realize just how much I missed her. Since David's proposal, she seemed to be distancing herself from me.

"Crazy," I said. "I have the invitations and the flowers. David's parents belong to a country club in West Chester with a wedding venue that was available in March. It has a beautiful ballroom and a cute little chapel for the ceremony. It's so pretty, Gail; I fell in love when I saw it. David wouldn't let me see the prices when we booked it. His parents are supposedly splitting the cost with my parents, but I think they are covering more than their share. Anyway, we're still on to look at bridesmaid dresses on Saturday, right?" She nodded. "I picked a few places that we can buy off the rack, since there isn't much time."

"What about your dress?"

I cringed. "I've tried on about a thousand. Still looking. Mom, Sam, and I are going to a place on Friday, so keep your fingers crossed."

"What style are you looking for?" Gail asked, and I realized that this was really the first time we had talked seriously about the wedding plans. It was all happening so fast. The date we set for the wedding, March twenty-third, was right around the corner. I also knew that it made Gail uncomfortable—she was still hoping for a ring from Quinn.

"That's part of the problem, I just don't know! When I look at the fitted mermaid style, I think 'Yes!' but then I look at some ballgowns and I love those too. And they look totally different on, so I feel like I have to try each one on to be sure. Seriously, I'm thinking of not bothering with clothes on Friday and just arriving in a strapless bra and thong because that is what I'll be wearing for most of the day." I sighed out my stress. Trying on dresses made me feel like an actor. Each dress was so different, it was like trying on different personalities. If I chose to be a princess, would I regret not being a vixen? And why didn't I know exactly what I wanted? "Oh god, enough wedding talk. Are we ready for the second annual Smackdown?"

"Got it all planned up here." Gail pointed to her head.

"So… nothing has been done."

"Exactly."

"Ah, the beauty of the Smackdown," I said. "No matter how little we plan, it looks intentional."

"Yup, so can I start telling people it's on the twenty-second?" Gail asked, picking a Tuesday night on purpose.

I pulled a small paper calendar out of my purse and turned to the first page. "Works for me. See? We're pretty much done."

"I'll invite the usual crowd. Is David coming? Do you want to ask some of his friends, maybe people from his work?"

"No, David can't be there," I fibbed.

In truth, David didn't even want me to have the party this year. I remembered our conversation. "We are getting married in three months. Don't you think that should be your priority?" he had said.

"It is." I'd told him, "But I enjoy the Smackdown. It's a good way to let loose. You had fun last year, right?" David gave me a half-smile but didn't answer. "Well, I did, and anyway, it's just one night; it won't interfere with the wedding, I promise." David nodded as if to say I better keep that promise.

"Well," Gail said, leaning back into the sofa, "that makes it easy, and I'm all about easy."

"Yeah, just wait until Quinn puts a ring on your finger. Easy will be over, girl. Enjoy it now." I said with a conspiratorial grin, but Gail didn't join in. When I caught the look on her face, I started to apologize, but she cut me off.

"Yeah," Gail said. "I guess this will be the last party we host together." Her words stung. As much as I would try to keep up with my single friends, I understood that this was ending of sorts. The closing of a door while still looking for the proverbial window, trusting it would be open.

• • •

February 2002

"Surprise!" everyone yelled in unison as I entered Anna's apartment. I tried my best to look stunned, but after the shouts subsided and Anna hugged me, she whispered in my ear, "You knew, didn't you?"

"No! Well, maybe a little, like when you insisted that we go to lunch at exactly noon, *and* you were on time. Then you kept checking your watch, and when we got here you put your key in the lock but told me to go in first. Besides, you don't exactly have a poker face. Who cares, thank you, sweetie, this is so great." I motioned to Anna's apartment, which was filled with familiar faces, ready to celebrate my bridal shower.

Gail handed me a pink drink in a huge glass that said 'Bride' and put a tiara on my head. "Bottoms up! You're the woman of the hour!"

I sipped the pink liquid. It was strawberry-flavored punch with a swift kick of vodka. A scoop of orange sherbet floated in the middle. "Wow, that's strong," I gasped.

"Sam was in charge of the punch," Gail said simply.

The party was off to a great start with people talking and *Father of the Bride* playing silently on the TV in the background. I mingled among the guests, which consisted solely of friends I had before I met David. I hadn't seen most of them in a while. Partially because my time was limited, but I had to admit, some of the friendships I had simply outgrown. I had been hanging out with David's circle of friends, a group of upwardly mobile twenty- and thirty-somethings of which Anna was a part. After the jazz concert, which seemed to go well, David started filling up our time introducing me to his circle, all of whom had jobs or hobbies that were unusual and interesting, making my old friends seem ordinary in comparison. I assumed that Anna had overseen the guest list for the bridal shower, and I wondered briefly why none of those people had been invited but was soon distracted as the party gained momentum.

The decorations had Anna's refined taste written all over them, down to the tiniest details. *The sherbet punch must be killing her*, I thought, but it was the recipe that was handed down in my family like an heirloom. I looked at the gift bags for the guests that formed a perfect circle around the presents that I would later open. Anna had appetizers spread around her living room on little stands that were bar height and covered in pink cloths. The stands were perfect to hold drinks and keep guests moving around.

"Did you find a dress yet?" Kate from the hospital asked. She popped a cube of cheese in her mouth as she waited for my answer.

"Yes!" I said, "I'm so relieved. Last wedding detail, checked!" I clinked glasses with her, surprised that the glasses were real and not plastic.

"Ooh, what is it like?"

"It's the same neckline as the bridesmaids' dresses. The saleswoman couldn't believe I decided on your dresses before picking out mine. Evidently that was a big blunder since the bridesmaids should complement the bride and not the other way around," I said, imitating the saleswoman with a wagging finger. "But when do I ever do anything in the correct order?"

"You're doing fine. And I see from the drink in your hand that you are not pregnant. With the wedding scheduled so quickly, I gotta tell you, there were rumors."

I let out a laugh. "Babies? I'm barely digesting the fact that I'll be married," I said just as Anna came up behind me, catching part of the conversation.

"Talking babies already?" she said, her voice tight.

"Oh no," I said reassuringly. "No, I'm not ready for that."

Looking relieved, Anna turned back to the party.

CHAPTER 17

March 2002

As my wedding day quickly approached, I was overwhelmed by the last-minute details. The florist couldn't get gardenia for the tables, could they substitute white freesia? The caterer needed a final head count. Did the venue have a highchair for Kate's little one? And through it all was the incessant worry about Anna. Everything had been all about the wedding, and me, for months. Anna dutifully listened as people asked me questions about cakes and dresses. She smiled as they admired my ring. She nodded her head as they gushed about David. But Anna's naturally dazzling personality was dulling like the stars in daylight. When she thought no one was looking, I saw her face fall and her mouth release its tightly held smile. Concern for Anna's feelings was always in the back of my mind, irritating the base of my skull like a worm digging into an apple.

David's brother was throwing a bachelor party for him, and he was spending the weekend with his friends in Center City. My bachelorette was scheduled for next Saturday and with the free time that had been in short supply for months, I decided to plan a weekend for just Anna and me. I considered scheduling a spa day or a weekend getaway, but with the wedding costs that seemed to increase at every turn, it just wasn't in my budget. I was wracking my brain for cheaper solutions when Sam suggested an at-home spa weekend consisting of homemade face masks, foot soaks, and movies rentals. It sounded like the perfect way to spend some downtime together. Sam had recently joined a new gym in Havertown that had all the best amenities, including a swimming pool and sauna, and she got us guest passes. I picked Anna up at her apartment and drove us to Sam's gym to kick off our weekend.

"Where's your engagement ring?" Anna asked, looking at my hand on the steering wheel.

"You're like the engagement ring police, you know that? It took you under a minute to notice I wasn't wearing it."

"So, where is it?"

"It's my stupid man hands. When we went to pick up our wedding bands, the jeweler asked me about it, and I had to fess up that it *did* feel a little too tight. It wasn't cutting off my circulation or anything, but it's hard to take it on and off and it left an indentation when I wasn't wearing it. The jeweler suggested I go up an eighth of an inch in size." Anna raised an eyebrow. "He promised to have it back before the wedding," I added.

"Wow, I can't believe you did that this close to the wedding; that's taking a chance." Anna's observation made me stew uncomfortably. Her antics in New York had left me paranoid any time I took off my ring, but the jeweler had made me feel like I didn't have a choice. "Anyway," Anna said, changing subjects, "there is still time to schedule facials at A Cut Above, if you want."

"No way, I already bought a ton of squishy, ripe avocados and something called extra virgin oil, although I'm not sure how to determine an olive's virginity."

"It's a complicated process involving a pimento, I think." Anna joked. "But… you could always make guacamole. My treat for the facials," she added as a final incentive.

"No, I can't let you do that, you've spent so much on this wedding already," I said, temporarily suspending my self-imposed 'no wedding talk' rule. "Besides, aren't you always publishing these 'at-home spa' ideas in your magazine?"

"Yes, which is why I go to Elizabeth. All the benefits of medical-grade products and none of the mess."

"Oh c'mon, it'll be fun. And we are staying at the condo, remember? There is *never* a mess. I think there are elves that come in and clean the counters at night." I hit the blinker and turned left into the parking lot for Sam's gym.

After signing in, the guy at the desk gave us a brief tour of the facilities, since ostensibly we were looking into becoming members to justify the free workout passes from Sam.

"And in here is our most popular feature," the guide said, pointing to a cement-colored climbing wall with plastic knobs dotting it from floor to ceiling like large colored braille.

"Oh, let's do that!" Anna said with an enthusiasm I hadn't heard since I suggested our weekend together.

"I'm not sure," I said looking up at the fifty-foot wall, intimidated not only by its height, but also by the complicated looking harness and ropes.

"You should definitely try it," our guide said. "I take it that it will be your first times climbing?" We nodded in unison. "Then see Lucas; he'll show you how to harness up and get you on it." He waved to a man standing by the wall with well-defined muscles stretching the confines of his sleeveless shirt. Anna turned her head and winked at me.

"I'll be sure to climb on that," she said under her breath, and I gave her a look of mock indignation and smacked her playfully on the arm.

The tour ended and the guide gave us towels and bottled water. Anna headed straight to the climbing wall and introduced herself to Lucas. I followed hesitantly behind, thinking of all the ways my groom would kill me if I got injured and we had to postpone the wedding. *If I fall*, I thought, *I will pretend to be unconscious until I am fully healed, and everything has been rescheduled.* Lucas explained how to clip in and use the auto-belay system, which seemed simple enough. He gave us some basic climbing instructions, including coming down by 'walking' with our legs perpendicular to our torso, making an 'L' shape. Then, he fitted us into our harnesses, and I couldn't help but notice how his arms flexed as he pulled on the straps to tighten them.

Anna went first and she appeared to start off easily enough, her long limbs stretching high, but when she was about fifteen feet off the ground, I could see her arms and calves straining. She looked for her next foothold and tried a few times to find purchase on a knob to her right, but her foot slipped off and she couldn't pull herself any higher. She straightened her legs parallel to the wall and began descending as Lucas had showed us.

Reaching the ground, she breathed heavily and said, "Whoa, that is way more intense than it looks! Okay, Amy, you're up." She handed me the carabiner attached to the belay rope and I clipped it to my harness. As I began climbing, I felt my balance shifting and I adjusted my feet. My legs took most of my weight as I moved my foot around, searching for solid footholds before standing up and reaching for the next knob overhead. Soon I was ringing the bell at the top, surprising myself. I looked down over my shoulder to see Lucas and Anna, both of whom seemed a little stunned, Anna's mouth hanging slightly open. I gently lowered myself, walking down the wall, exhilarated and breathing heavily.

"Great job!" Lucas said.

"Thank you."

"Let me try again," Anna said, hooking herself in with determination. But again, she faltered at about fifteen feet, simply unable to go any higher. On the ground, Anna unhooked herself, her frustration apparent in her jerky movements. Lucas turned to me.

"You seem comfortable with the heights and the harness. Have you ever tried outdoor rock climbing?" he asked.

"No, but I mostly used my legs to get up there. I'm not sure I have the upper body strength," I admitted.

"Well, legs are important, that is what you are supposed to do," he scanned my legs appreciatively. "But don't discount your arms.

For someone so petite," he ran a hand up my arm and squeezed, "I feel some muscle there. Maybe I could take you?"

"Oh," I said, backing away. "I can't. I don't think my fiancé would approve." I meant to sound lighthearted, but seeing the look on Anna's face, I thought it might have come out as boasting, although Lucas let it go with a good-natured shake of his head.

"All the good ones," he said smiling.

• • •

Back at the condo, Anna and I sipped gin and tonics through straws, mashed avocado mixed with olive oil and chunks of sea salt covering our faces. I went into the kitchen to pour our second round of drinks from a glass pitcher.

"Lucas was so into you!" Anna said, turning her head around to talk to me from her seat on the living room couch.

"He was a hottie," I admitted without necessarily agreeing. "But I saw you talking to him when I was coming back from the bathroom. You were writing something on a piece of paper. I assumed you were giving him your number." I absently scratched my face and was rewarded with avocado goo.

"My number? No," Anna replied as if this were obvious. "He seemed kinda perfect for you." She pressed. I paused, feeling a little stunned.

"Anna, what are you talking about? I'm marrying David." I laughed a little to hide my dismay and I wiped my slimy hand on a paper towel with a little more force than was necessary. I had an uncomfortable feeling that Anna was building to something. She looked up at the ceiling before continuing and drew in a sizable breath.

"But, well, do you think you and David, like, totally fit?" She turned around fully to face me, looking over the back of the couch.

I couldn't believe Anna had just said that. Seeing the look on my face, she added quickly, "It's just that marriage is such a huge commitment and I learned from my experience that you have to be sure, completely sure, that you know a person. I mean, I wish someone had talked to me before I married Paul. I'm just trying to let you know, it is okay if you need more time to be sure you know everything about David, so you are confident that he's the one."

"I absolutely know David is the one! My wedding is in *two weeks*. I'm marrying him." I said steadfastly. I poured the gin and tonics into tall delicate glasses and added extra sprigs of mint garish that I had bought to make the drinks look picture perfect but now felt completely unnecessary.

"Yes, yes, of course," Anna backed off and seemed to let the subject drop, but then she added, "Well, I should warn you. I did give Lucas a telephone number. I gave him yours."

"What?" I hoped I had heard her wrong, but somehow, I knew I didn't. I picked up the drinks, but my hand was shaking and slippery with olive oil. One of the glasses slipped through my hand and smashed on the floor into a million slivers, glittering like crystal toothpicks on the black tile floor.

"Oh shit!" I grabbed a towel and began wiping at the mess. Anna jumped up to help me, quickly coming into the kitchen.

"Calm down, it's fine," Anna said, but whether she was talking about the glass or giving out my phone number, I wasn't sure. I saw some glass in the small gap under the stove and instinctively brushed it out with my bare hand.

"Ouch! Oh god, I cut myself," I said as I felt a pinching like fire ants on the pinky side of my hand. Anna handed me a paper towel from the roll on the counter. I put it over the tiny cuts, careful not to press too hard until I could remove the splinters.

"Is it bad?" she asked, looking over my shoulder as blood burst through the paper like red poppies blooming. I didn't answer her. "I'll get the dustpan," Anna said, confidently opening the correct cabinet on the first try as if she knew just where David kept it.

"Oh, there are so many little cuts!" I said, looking at the side of my hand as another pop of red appeared. The avocado mask dripped into my eyes, making my vison hazy. "I'm going to go wash this mask off." I hurried into the bathroom feeling miserable. Alone, I put my face under the running faucet and scrubbed off the avocado one-handed, blaming my tears on the homemade mask. The avocado made a thick brown puddle that clogged the sink. I cupped water in my uncut hand and covered my eyes, one at a time, blinking rapidly and wondering how long it would be until I could see clearly again.

CHAPTER 18

March 2002

Chaos. Complete chaos. That was the only way to describe the hotel room that was strewn with clothing, makeup, and hair products. Sean was standing behind me, curling my hair with an assortment of irons in different sizes. He had brought so many with him that we had to ask the front desk for an adapter to plug them all in. I was surprised that my steaming hair didn't set off the smoke alarm. He wanted to create a 'cascade of curls,' which I found highly ironic since he had been flattening my hair ever since we met. When I told him about the wedding, he had let out a squawk and insisted that we start growing my hair out immediately. He made me swear to start taking prenatal vitamins *that day* to help my hair grow. I drew the line at hair extensions, though, and this morning he had looked at my shoulder-length hair and reluctantly said he would do his best.

My mom walked over to my wedding gown, where it was hanging from the curtain rod. She picked up the hem, fluffing air into the dress like the sail of a boat catching the wind. I glanced fondly at the expanse of white. It was a full-length gown with a small train. The bodice was simple, off the shoulders with small crystals around the neckline and matching crystals just below the waist.

A tray of half-eaten bagels sat on the bed. Sam, Gail, and Kate looked beautiful in their cornflower-blue bridesmaid gowns. The gowns were simple, off the shoulders as well, trimmed with subtle beaded pearls and long, straight skirts. The girls had opened a bottle of champagne and added copious amounts to their orange juice. Even Anna seemed to be happily in the moment, sipping her mimosa quietly, while the other bridesmaids joked around, excited about the day ahead. Anna's dress was a shade darker than the other bridesmaids' dresses, and she stood at the window, careful not to wrinkle the delicate fabric by sitting. The last few weeks had been so busy that I had completely forgotten about Lucas, who never called. And I realized that I had been worrying so much about Anna's mental state today that I had been able to ignore my nerves until this morning. Now, my heart kept beating out of control in little spasms that came and went. *Anticipation*, I told myself.

"Watch me!" my niece and flower girl, Emily, said as she waltzed to the center of the room and spun dramatically, making her dress twirl.

"Aw!" we said in a unified squeal that could probably be heard three doors down. The fact that Emily had been doing this roughly every five minutes for the better part of an hour had not dampened our enthusiasm.

Sam put her glass on the nightstand and stood behind me, next to Sean. Looking at us in the mirror, I could see traces of the family resemblance: our small eyes obscured by large smiles; our lips, naturally full even without the final touches of makeup. Something in the background caught Sam's attention and her expression changed to panic.

"No, no, Emily, no, no. That is Mommy's juice. Mommy's juice!" She quickly rescued her glass from Emily's tiny hand before her daughter could take a sip. "Your cup is over here, the sippy cup."

"I thought she was too old for sippy cups," I said.

"With your wedding gown hanging in here, I think you should all be using sippy cups," my mom interjected, looking sharply at Sam and Gail, who giggled guiltily.

"I'm just about done," Sean murmured, bobby pins between his lips. Several minutes later he stepped back and looked critically at me, his face more serious than I had ever seen it. Then he broke into a broad smile. His eyes started to glisten.

"Oh, Sean," I said, feeling my own emotions well up.

"It's just"—his voice broke a little—"that I am so damn talented." I pretended to pout. He checked his watch. "It's time for the dress. Can you call the photographer in?" Sean asked the room, and Anna moved to the door. My mom looked at Sean with a questioning glance. "This isn't my first rodeo," he told her. "The photographer will want pictures of Amy getting dressed. They are so picky!" Behind him, Sam rolled her eyes at the absurdity of Sean calling anyone picky.

My mom carefully helped me into the dress while the photographer captured the moment, asking my mom to pause while fixing the long row of buttons on the back of the dress. He adjusted my mom's face so that she was looking at me and told me to look at my own reflection in the mirror, tilting our heads with his hands until he got the angle he wanted. I found these posed pictures ridiculous, but I was too overwhelmed to say anything. Then, he asked if I had a veil, and I nodded. It was Sean who did the work of attaching it to my head, but the photographer staged a photo with Anna standing behind me giving it a final adjustment. I looked at Anna over my shoulder. Anna was barefoot, but I was already wearing my heels, making us almost the same height. She looked at me and in her eyes I saw the years turning backward like pages in a book. Past David, past Paul, past high school, past learning to drive and countless sleepovers to the time when we first met. When I found my first, truest friend.

"That's good, that's good," the photographer remarked encouragingly as I felt my face relax into a natural smile as he continued to take pictures.

• • •

Standing in the back of the chapel, I watched as Emily and Robbie walked down the white plastic runner toward the altar, holding hands to a chorus of delighted guests. At home, Emily had made Robbie practice 'wedding walking' over and over. At less than two years old, Robbie was a little young for such an important role, but his complete idolization of his older sister meant he would go anywhere with her, and they made it down the aisle without incident. Kate led the procession of bridesmaids, followed by Gail, then Sam. Anna gave my hand a final squeeze before following suit, and I linked my arm through my dad's waiting elbow.

"It's time," he said sweetly, giving me a kiss on the cheek as "Trumpet Voluntary" sounded from the organ. As we started down the aisle, I had my first glimpse of David standing regally at the altar, looking as calm as an actor who knew his lines by heart.

• • •

The cocktail hour started before the wedding party arrived. We had walked the grounds of the club, posing for pictures. By the time we entered the dining hall, we were all ready for a drink or two, and unlike other weddings I had attended, David insisted we keep the bar open during dinner. David and I didn't have much in the way of extended family, and the average age of the guests was around twenty-six, which made it feel more like a college formal than a wedding reception. The guests were in high spirits by the time dinner was cleared, so they took to the dance floor with little encouragement.

After several songs, the band announced it was taking a short break and abandoned the stage. People returned to their seats from the dance floor chatting happily. Out of the corner of my eye, I saw Anna stumbling up the steps to the stage, holding the hem of her gown in an attempt not to trip, revealing her bare feet and fire engine–red toes that clashed with the color of the bridesmaid's dress. Her hair had started to come loose from its delicate twist and hung flat on the sides of her face. When she reached the top of the steps, she released the gown from her grip and walked unsteadily to the middle of the stage, narrowly missing an upright guitar.

I watched Anna warily. She had drunk way too much and I worried about her embarrassing herself in front of everyone. Everything had been flawless so far. I started walking with urgency toward the stage and bumped into my aunt Caroline.

"You are the most beautiful bride!" she exclaimed. "Let me see your ring." She took my hand. *Not now*, I thought, but I didn't want to be rude.

"So, what are your plans for the honeymoon?" Aunt Caroline asked.

"Oh, we are heading to Lancaster and staying at a bed and breakfast." I smiled at my aunt and leaned backward desperate to get away, but to no avail. My aunt held firmly to my hand and adjusted her glasses to take a better look.

"That sounds lovely. And your ring is stunning."

"Thank you," I said distractedly. Panic rose in me as I looked over my aunt's head to Anna, who made a clumsy attempt to grab the microphone from its stand. She swayed a couple of times, trying ineffectively to still her body as she squinted at the microphone like a hunter eyeing its prey. She made a second grab for the microphone and caught it in her right hand, then pulled the entire stand toward her, scraping the metal base on the wood floor. After righting the stand, she hung on it for the briefest of moments. With effort, Anna pulled the microphone free from its holder. I wondered what she was going to do. All the while, guests continued to socialize, mostly oblivious to Anna's actions until she flipped the switch that turned the microphone on. It emitted an ear-piercing screech of feedback that got the room's attention. Raising the glass of champagne in her left hand above her head, Anna indicated to the wedding guests that she wanted to make a toast.

"Lookit me, everybody, lookit me," she said, putting the microphone too close to her mouth and distorting her already slurred speech. She backed up slightly, off balance. "It's time for a toast." Her words bumped against each other sloppily. She was in no condition to be the center of attention, but now I felt that interrupting her would make it more of a spectacle.

I felt David come up behind me. "Did you ask her to make a toast?" he whispered accusingly in my ear.

"No!" I whispered harshly back as I started moving forward again, but David put his hand on my shoulder. I was too late; I had to let this play out.

"Let her go," he said. For a moment, his face took on a resigned expression. Then he straightened up and puffed his chest out slightly, ready to handle whatever Anna had to say. If I had known the implications behind her words, I would have done anything to stop her, but at the time, I let her go on.

Anna spoke into the microphone again. "I wanted to say how very happy"—she exhaled the word 'happy' like she was trying to expel something unpleasant with her breath—"I am for my very, *very* best friend." She gestured to me with her champagne glass, sloshing liquid on the stage. "And for David, he certainly knows what he wants." Something in her tone made it sound like nothing could be farther from the truth.

She started to walk to the edge of the stage and slipped a little on the puddle of champagne she spilled on the floor. She caught her balance and looked behind her at the puddle, her expression puzzled, as if she had no idea how it got there. "Hey!" she said suddenly, looking at her hand as if just realizing she still held the microphone. "I should sing," she said with a thick-sounding tongue. She closed her eyes briefly, bringing a tune into her head and swaying recklessly as she started singing a verse from somewhere in the middle of the song "Daisy Jane." The drunken crowd cheered her on.

"All right, that's enough," said Charlie, coming to my rescue. He stood up and threw his cloth napkin next to his half-eaten piece of wedding cake. He dodged tables and guests to get to the stage.

She continued singing in time with music only she could hear. She paused, opened her eyes, and focused on David and me with a stony stare. Blame was the last word she sang, giving it more force than it deserved, as Charlie climbed the stairs. He took the microphone from her drooping hand and replaced it on the stand.

David broke Anna's stare and looked admonishingly at me. "How much did you let her drink?" he asked me in a whisper.

"I…" My voice trailed off, and I watched Charlie put Anna's arm around his neck and escort her off the stage.

"Here you go, Anna. Time to get you to your room." Charlie gestured with a nod of his head for the band to return to the stage. Anna stumbled as Charlie half carried her to the door, the unyielding expression gone so completely that at the time, I wondered if I had imagined it.

• • •

The next morning, Anna found us as we were loading the wedding presents into the trunk of the car. David and I had spent the night in the country club's honeymoon suite. We had brunch with the wedding party and our parents. Now, we were heading to the B&B in Lancaster. Anna hadn't been at brunch, and as she sheepishly approached the car, it was obvious that she had slept through it. Her hair was clinging to the last vestiges of the French twist, and her cheeks were blotchy.

"Amy," she said guiltily, "I'm so sorry. I understand that I got a little out of control yesterday?"

I didn't answer.

"Charlie told me that he had to practically carry me to my room. That I was trying to sing at the reception. I'm so, so sorry. I hope I didn't ruin it. I honestly don't even remember doing it."

"It's okay, Anna. We were all drunk at that point. It's fine," I lied and smiled tightly.

"Okay, if you're sure."

"Yes. I'll call you soon." I turned to David. He nodded and closed the trunk of the car. He walked to my side and opened my door. I looked at Anna across the hood of the car. She was starting to cry, her face in her hands.

"Anna." I walked back around and gave her a genuine hug. "It wasn't that bad. Listen, we were all drinking, so don't worry about it, okay?" She nodded through her tears. "We really do need to get going. I'm exhausted, but I will call you. Maybe we can have lunch later in the week?"

"I'd like that," she said. I got into the car and drove off with David, watching Anna growing smaller in the rearview mirror.

CHAPTER 19

April 2002

Sitting on the velvet seats in the Walnut Street Theatre as a beautiful Liesl von Trapp sang about being sixteen, my mind drifted stubbornly back to the beginning of the night. Noelle, a theater critic who occasionally contributed articles to *BTB*, had invited David and I to join her for opening night at the Walnut Street Theatre's production of *The Sound of Music*. The evening started with a cocktail hour at Noelle's Center City brownstone. Anna was the only other person from the magazine that Noelle invited. Anna brought a date—she would never go to a party like this without a date—a computer programmer she'd met on the metro after exchanging glances for a week on their daily commute. The rest of the small party consisted of Amanda, the producer of a Philadelphia morning show, who came alone, and Julia, a vascular surgeon, who came with her partner, a woman who worked in finance. As Noelle introduced me, I noted that mentioning their job title seemed to be as important as their name. Immediately, I felt uncomfortably young, not just because the average age of the other guests seemed to be over thirty, but because when Noelle said 'nurse,' she rushed the word at the end of the sentence with an unconscious flick of her hand, as if my current job was just a steppingstone and, if given enough time and hard work, it would somehow mature into doctor.

Amanda and Julia were talking in the kitchen when I went to refill my wine. I was about to open the French doors when I heard my name and stopped to listen.

"I did a double take when I first met Amy. David certainly has a type, doesn't he?" Julia said. *A type*, I thought nonplussed. I wondered who else David had brought to one of these gatherings that made them think he had a type?

"I know! There is just something about her. Did you notice, she and Anna were both wearing chokers. At least Anna's looked like real jewelry, Amy probably made hers." Amanda commented with a snide laugh, and I pictured them huddled together as they gossiped. *Anna?* I knew that Anna had come to opening night parties before, and David too, but not as a couple. These women must have misread the situation.

"I'm surprised it isn't made of macaroni!" Julia shrieked meanly. I touched the beaded choker around my neck, a turquoise stone on a leather strap that tied into place. I borrowed it from Sam and thought it was funky, but in an upscale way. Together, Sam and I had spent an afternoon shopping for a dress that would complement it.

"You're awful," Amanda said in a tone that implied she was anything but. "I ran into Amy and David at brunch when they first started dating. She was wearing this sweater that was kind of nice, I guess, but she has on high-waisted jeans. I mean seriously? I didn't know they still *made* jeans like that. You'd never find those at Neiman's."

"Maybe *My Fair Lady* would have been a more appropriate production to see tonight."

I heard shuffling that meant they were heading back into the living room. I quickly ducked into the hallway and composed myself as well as I could in the bathroom down the hall.

When the production eventually ended to uproarious applause, I breathed a sigh of relief. Our group was planning to go to a bar where it was rumored the cast liked to hang out after the show.

As we followed the slow tidal wave of people leaving their seats and climbing the stairs, I put my hand on David's shoulder and spoke in his ear.

"Do you mind if I skip the after party? I'm not feeling well." I lied.

"Are you sick?" he asked, turning his head to look at me concerned while still following the steady line of people trudging slowly to the exit.

"No, it's just a headache. Too much pre-partying, I think."

"Oh, okay. Do you mind if I stay out a little longer?" David asked and I shook my head.

"No, stay with them. Have fun."

Once outside, I made my apologies to the group and David signaled for a taxi to take me home.

In the condo, I untied the choker and put it in a jewelry box, wanting to return it to Sam as soon as possible. I threw the damask printed dress that I had been wearing, a blend of turquoise that matched the necklace with a hint of coral, in the laundry and thought of the muted colors Anna always wore. Blacks, browns, and grays that looked classy rather than tiring. I opened my closet and began pulling out my clothes, making a colorful pile I would donate to Goodwill the following day. I put the rejected clothes in a large trash bag and set it by the door, then I made myself a cup of chamomile tea and waited anxiously on the couch for David to come home, promising myself I would try harder. *The next time I saw them*, I vowed to myself, *I would make their jaws drop*. And at a small dinner party hosted by Julia two weeks later, wearing a gray Chanel dress, that is exactly what I did.

. . .

May 2002

I was lying half-awake in bed enjoying the feeling of a lazy morning when I felt David stirring next to me. I briefly wondered why his alarm hadn't gone off yet, then remembered happily that it was Saturday *and* my weekend off. I curled my body next to his, waking him further.

"Morning," I said softly so as not to disturb him in case he wanted sleep longer.

David cleared his throat and answered me with a 'morning' that was half caught in a yawn. "Amy Garrison," he added with a sappy smile, his eyes still closed. He'd been teasing me by calling me by my full name ever since he found me practicing my new signature after the wedding.

My mind was already racing ahead, thinking about the day. "Do we have anything going on today?" I asked, realizing I had been putting off telling him that I had made plans to see Kate. I had called her a few days after the dinner party. Even though I had achieved my goal—Julia had looked approvingly at the dress—and as proof that I now met her standards, she insisted David and I sit next to her at the head of the table. But the warm blush of victory that infused me then turned cold when I opened my credit card statement. I was feeling stung, like I had been duped into spending more than I could afford. Anna had been at the party as well, but instead of telling me on the sly how great I looked, something we never failed to do when one of us had a new outfit, she simply gave me a look I couldn't quite interpret, something between shocked and annoyed. In any event, I was longing to hear a friendly voice and since I wasn't sure what was up with Anna, I called Kate. We only talked for a few minutes—she was rushing out to a Mommy and Me class—but even that small chat had lifted my mood. Later that week, when I heard about a book reading that sounded interesting, I decided to invite her. I needed the ease of an old friend.

"What did you have in mind?" his voice had a sexy growl.

Missing the implication, I hurriedly added, "Kate asked me if I wanted to go to a book reading with her today." It was a little white lie. The truth was that I had asked Kate to come with me to the reading. I wasn't quite sure why this mattered in telling it to David, but I said it that way anyway.

"Oh, talk dirty to me," David said jokingly. "Kate and book readings, you know how to tease a man."

I snuggled up to him, lying on my side with my back against his chest. "Well, I don't *need* to go," I added quickly, hoping he would say I was being silly, of course I should hang out with my old friend, it was what I would have said to him. I was careful not to be possessive of his time.

"Good," David said. "Let's stay home. Maybe later we could order in. We need some downtime."

"Okay, don't go anywhere," I said as I squirmed out of his arms, suddenly completely content to cancel my plans. David had that effect on me. "I'll be right back. I need to go to the bathroom," I admitted sheepishly, still shy around David about these things, even after the rings were on. But when I returned from the bathroom, David was already up, and I could hear him starting the coffee in the kitchen. I grabbed the newspaper from outside the condo door and brought it inside as the telephone rang.

"If that is Kate," I said as David reached for the phone in the kitchen, "let the answering machine pick up, please. I'll call her later."

David looked at the caller ID on the phone on the bedside table. "It's Anna," he said and handed the phone to me without answering.

I pushed the talk button. "Hey, Anna," I said into the receiver.

"Hey, Amy, is David around? I was calling for him, actually. It's about work."

"Sure, hang on." I handed the phone back to David. I overheard enough snatches of conversation to know that they were talking about next month's issue. I poured myself a cup of coffee and put it on the table in the living room as I unfolded the newspaper and settled on the sofa.

"No, Amy won't mind. See you in a few." David ended the conversation.

"What's going on?" I asked, turning my head to look at him as he replaced the phone in its cradle.

"Anna's having second thoughts about Teri's article on vegetarianism. It's a little off-putting, and Teri included a lot of graphic information and pictures. I agree with Anna. I don't think the magazine is ready for slaughterhouses next to homemade cleaners, so I'm going to meet her at the office for a few hours. We're going to soften the article up a bit before it goes to print." David swallowed the last of his coffee and rinsed out his mug before putting it in the dishwasher.

"You're okay with me going in," he said, more of a statement than a question. He brushed past me, touching me briefly on the top of my head.

"I guess." Something didn't feel right to me. Although it wasn't unusual for David to go in the office on a Saturday, he usually knew in advance.

"Hey, maybe you can still make that thing you were talking about earlier. What was it? A book reading?" David said distractedly as he headed toward the master bathroom.

"Yeah, it was a book reading with Kate," I yelled at our open bedroom door, but the shower was already running, and I knew he didn't hear me. I dialed Kate's number to confirm our plans, positive that spending the afternoon with her was exactly what I needed. I could even talk to Kate about my misgivings about David meeting Anna at the office, the two of them alone, on a Saturday. Kate would put it all in perspective for me. She'd tell me everything was fine because it was fine. *This meant nothing*, I reassured myself. And it would be such a relief to hang out feeling comfortable in my own skin for a while. I knew that Kate would be casually dressed and grateful for a cheap bookstore coffee even if it only came two ways: regular or decaf. She'd be happy with a lunch cart meal, if it meant a little girl time to talk uninterrupted. We could eat on a bench in the park. I would even tell her about the catty people I'd overheard on opening night and Anna's peculiar behavior at the dinner party. It would feel so good to talk uninhibited.

"Hey, Kate, it's Amy. Still up for that book reading today?" I said assuming she was.

"Oh Amy, I'm so sorry, I totally forgot. Tyler has been throwing up all night. He got the stomach flu that is going around his daycare. Raincheck?"

"Sure, of course."

"I'll call you," she said, but somehow, I knew she wouldn't, and I was disappointed far more than I anticipated. The truth was that I hadn't really been there for her, or my other friends, since I met David. I thought about the times I backed out of things last minute because David wanted me home or didn't respond to phone calls. Even at the time, I had felt torn, and I knew I might regret it some-day, but I didn't expect that day to come so soon.

• • •

June 2002

In the lobby of our condo, I turned the key in the rectangular door to our mailbox and opened it. Inside, as reliable as the sunrise, was Anna's birthday letter to me. I paused for a moment, feeling grateful. I was looking forward to this evening when the three of us were going out to dinner to celebrate my birthday. David wanted to have a party, but after planning the wedding, hosting a party didn't sound like fun, even when he promised he would put the whole thing together. I wasn't up for seeing his friends and I didn't feel right inviting old friends to celebrate my birthday when I hadn't celebrated any of theirs in the last year. Since there was no one except Anna that I was comfortable inviting, a small dinner sounded like a good solution. Even if Anna had been acting strange lately, we always celebrated our birthdays together, and this was something I swore to myself I wouldn't let change now that I was married.

"All I want," I told him, "is a nice dinner with my two favorite people in the world." I realized as soon as I said it that it was a mistake, but a small one. David seemed to have accepted that Anna would always be a huge part of my life.

"Two people? First of all, I'm ranked higher than Anna in your favorite people scale. We don't want to have that argument again." I nodded, confirming this fact when David added, "So, does Anna really need to be there? Won't it be awkward? Three's a crowd and all that." Maybe David hadn't moved past the argument quite as much as I thought.

"Three people will be perfect. I know it's a little odd, but David, I've told you this. This is the last chance we have before Anna's trip to Italy." I said defending my position. Anna was attending a work conference in Rome. I was the only person besides David who knew that she was paying for it out of her own pocket. "She'll be gone for five days, and then we'll be on our honeymoon in St. John. I don't want to wait, and this is the only date that works for us. There just aren't two free nights."

"That's why we should have a party," David retorted. "Then we'll have more people, and it won't be uncomfortable for anyone." But me, I added silently, thinking of his friends, wondering what else they had said behind my back even though I had been meticulous about my appearance. I wore only fine jewelry and name brand clothing, keeping to classic styles and colors. I made sure that my brown hair never showed at the roots, gradually going an even lighter shade of blonde, and if the scale moved more than a few pounds, I immediately went on a cleanse. I had even started getting manicures and pedicures at the nail bar Anna used and I always asked the manicurist what color Anna had chosen so that I could select something similar. My appearance was impeccable quite literally from head to toe. I hardly recognized myself anymore.

"But this *won't* be uncomfortable," I assured him. "It'll be fun. You and Anna get along, and it's everything I want, really."

David finally gave in. La Caravella in Manayunk at seven thirty. It was already past six and I knew I needed to get in the shower, but as I took the mail upstairs to our condo, I decided to read Anna's letter first. I walked out onto our balcony. The sky was darkening with an oncoming storm, but there was still enough light to read. Lights were visible in the building across the street, and I could see into a handful of windows whose curtains were still open. People making dinner, watching TV, living their lives. Below, the cars crawled through the streets, the rush-hour traffic producing a steady hum of engines and the occasional honk of a horn. The comforting sounds of my city.

I began reading the familiar handwriting, which began with "Sweet Amy." The salutation that Anna always used made me feel pleased.

Unexpectedly, the wind picked up, and the first crack of lightning shot across the sky, leaving a white streak in its wake like the blinding spots of a flashbulb. I decided to take the letter inside to finish reading it, smiling in anticipation.

CHAPTER 20

July 2002

I had been staying at Sam's house since the accident. Sam and Charlie went to the condo, gathering my things as we had once done for Anna. They put most of my belongings in the attic and settled me in their guest room, Sam arranging my clothes in the drawers like she did with her children's clean laundry. I woke up every morning feeling confused by the unfamiliar sounds of a family, until the memories came crushing in. Some mornings, I could force myself back to sleep, the sweet reprieve of unreality taking me under. But often, I lay in bed, eyes open but not seeing while my brain whirled, talking to me about things I didn't want to hear. I would force myself to get up to make it stop. I'd get through the day, showering without feeling clean, eating without tasting, talking without engaging, until I could return to bed alone and surrender to nothingness.

Sam's kitchen was overly warm heated by the summer sun that streamed in the windows. Sam and Charlie were sitting at the table in the breakfast nook, drinking coffee and sharing the Sunday paper. I could hear the TV playing in the background, a video we all knew by heart that kept the kids mesmerized, sitting cross-legged on the rug, their heads turned upward toward the screen. I walked into the room as if walking through water, my limbs dragging behind me, holding invisible weights.

"Sam, could we go to visit Anna's grave?" I asked. Since the accident, my voice was monotone, strange and dull sounding, like a computer voice. The small act of inflection seemed like too much effort. Sam gave me a surprised look. "It is almost her birthday, or it would be…."

"I guess?" Sam said. She looked at Charlie, who shrugged.

"Now?" I asked. Sam and Charlie exchanged looks again.

"Go," Charlie said finally. "It might be good for her. I've got the kids."

I got into the passenger's seat of Sam's minivan. My hand shook as I clipped the seat belt around me. Sam started the motor and I felt myself beginning to sweat. I couldn't help but remember squealing breaks, grinding metal, splintering glass. I put my head in my hands.

"We don't have to do this," Sam said looking at me, her eyes wide and concerned.

"No, I need to go. Please, just drive." I took deep, calming breaths and focused on the dashboard.

Sam twisted around to look behind her, bracing herself with her arm around the back of my seat to steer the car down the driveway. When we got to the road, she pulled the wheel hard to the right and straightened the car to face forward.

"Relax," she told me, patting my knee and sighing wearily. "We'll get through this."

Sam and I were quiet on the rest of the drive to Bell's Lake. The cemetery was on the north side of town, about a thirty-minute drive south of Philadelphia. The drive was mostly highway. I knew every curve in the road, having driven it so many times. I knew without looking that tree-covered hills scrolled to my left, their leaves achingly heavy, filled with green as dark as envy, almost ready to turn. I knew when we passed by the blue-and-white exit signs indicating where to find gas and fast food. I knew by the change in the sound of the tires that we were on the bridge crossing over the Susquehanna River. In my mind, I could see the river moving swiftly, splashing white against the rocks that were scattered along the shoreline and clustered in the riverbed where it was shallow. I could see it all, though my eyes never left the dashboard.

When we got to the cemetery, Sam drove through the large iron gate and parked on the road near the top of a hill.

"I can't believe I missed her funeral," I said with tears in my eyes. Sam didn't answer; she just nodded slightly in response. Her eyes were also filling with tears, and I looked away, unable to add her pain to my own. I got out of the car first and walked across the grass, navigating my way among the graves, knowing Anna's grave would be next to where we buried her dad. Behind me, Sam shut her car door and locked it with the key fob. The car's single beep was the only sound in the lonely silence. The air was hot and sticky. It unnerved me to think of the bodies we were walking over. I thought about the coffins under us, filled with decaying remains. I had a flash of Anna's face in the rearview mirror after the crash. It was bloody and lifeless, her head hanging at an impossible angle. I stopped short, leaning on a bench, trying not to get sick.

"Are you okay?" Sam asked, coming up quickly behind me.

I took a minute to respond. "Yeah," I said quietly, and I continued walking.

I stopped when I reached the gravestone marked Kildare. It was a simple gravestone made of granite with precisely carved letters and curved corners, rising tall and straight out of the earth. The grave was well kept, but there were no fresh flowers around it, as there were with other graves.

"Flowers," I said out loud. "We should have brought her daisies." I began to cry and fell to the ground, putting my arms around her gravestone. The granite had warmed under the strong direct sun and felt comforting against my skin, which had turned clammy and cold. "Oh, God," I said. "Anna, I miss you so much."

• • •

It had been weeks since the accident. Exactly how many, I wasn't sure. Five? Maybe six? My days had become a monotonous routine, waking to the sounds of Emily and Robbie calling for their mommy, listening to them noisily babbling while going down the stairs outside my bedroom. I would hear the water rushing through the pipes as Charlie took his shower. When the garage door opened, rattling the floor of my bedroom, I knew he was leaving for work. I feigned sleep so I wouldn't have to join them, waiting until I heard Sam leave with the kids to run errands or to meet with friends at the neighborhood swimming pool. Only then would I go downstairs to reheat the leftover coffee in the microwave and stare anxiously into the backyard. I felt afraid for them, my family, vulnerable, on the roads.

Sam usually came home around noon to give the kids lunch and put them down for a nap. Day after day, I helped her make lunch. The days blended into each other measured by sandwich crusts and leftover chicken nuggets. Sam was consistently pleasant and chatty, telling me details about their morning adventures. I didn't say much. There was nothing I wanted to talk about.

"Guess what!" Sam said with forced enthusiasm as she boiled water for macaroni and cheese. "My big girl, Emily, blew bubbles at the swimming pool!"

Emily smiled and looked at me. "I did, Aumie. I put my whole face under like this." She bent forward, making her light brown curls bounce like miniature coils. "And I had to blow really hard." She shook her head from side to side, blowing into the imaginary water. From his booster seat, Robbie laughed at her antics, kicking his feet, and she did it a few more times for his benefit. Sam twisted open the cap on a bottle of Sprite, the clicking noise of the plastic snapping apart seemed unusually loud and echoed in my ears. Sam took a long drink from the bottle and absently put the cap on the table within reach of Robbie.

Sam looked around the kitchen. "I must have left the sippy cups in the car. I'll be right back." She tickled Emily's belly as she left the room.

In my mind, I had a vivid image of Robbie grabbing the bottle cap, putting it in his mouth, and choking on it. The thought became stuck my imagination, pressing into my brain with unrelenting force. I tried to remember what to do, but all my medical training was trapped behind a wall that my brain was too sluggish to break through. I could see Robbie's face turning pale and then purple as he became deprived of oxygen, making hollow, gulping noises as he tried to get air. The image flipped, and I saw Anna being choked by Paul. I felt the same paralysis overcome me, too panicked to act. I blinked hard, my stomach tightening, and it was Robbie again, but he was helpless now, slumping soundlessly over. My brain stuttered and Robbie became David, after the accident, lifeless and still, his head crushed against the dashboard. I forced myself to look away and told myself to stop, that this was not actually happening, but I could see it, over and over. The image of Robbie slipping farther down in his chair, overlapping the real world in my vision. Emily ate a round cracker from her plate; the water on the stove reached a boil. Robbie, dear Robbie, happily banged a plastic spoon on the tray of his booster seat. Sam came back in the kitchen talking about how stuffy it was inside the car. I had trouble breathing. Inwardly, I told myself to leave the room. Everyone would be better off without me. Paul's comment from long ago echoed and expanded in my head. I was useless. I should go. Without explanation, I took the bottle cap off the table, put it in my pocket, and walked out of the kitchen.

• • •

I see their ghosts again. This time, they are a couple walking arm in arm on the sidewalk across the street from me. They stop at a car that is parallel parked on the street. The man walks around to the driver's side, opens his door, and slides in. A red Chevrolet, like David and I used to own. I know that I am staring, but I can't stop. The woman opens her door and is about to sit down when she catches my eye over the roof of the car. Her blue eyes widen slightly. They are the eyes I have seen in my childhood nightmares dozens of times. The eyes of Anna, wide with fear, heading over the second, snowy slope on Farmer's Hill. The woman quickly drops behind the car, sits, and shuts the door. I feel myself falling, an unseen force pulling my head back and I stumble to catch myself. A passing stranger calls, "Hey, are you okay?" Then louder, "Miss?" I stop myself from falling by leaning on the bus stop's bench.

"Yes," I say, shaking my head to clear it. "I'm fine," I add and look down the block at the approaching bus.

CHAPTER 21

August 2002

Sam entered the kitchen as I was rinsing out my empty coffee mug. I opened the dishwasher door and put my mug on the top rack.

"You're up early," Sam said surprised. "I heard you in the shower." Her voice held a note of something hopeful. I walked out from behind the counter, and Sam looked at what I was wearing. "Why are you wearing scrubs?" She asked. Her voice had grown unmistakably hard, the hope dissipating like steam.

"I'm going back to work today," I told her matter-of-factly.

"No. No, you're not," she said without thinking, sounding like my sister again. The forced gentleness she'd managed to hold over the past few weeks was gone. Sam looked at me and took a deep breath. "Listen," she started again, talking between clenched teeth, but she was interrupted.

"Mommy!" Emily called from upstairs. "Robbie took my pony again." The whine was followed by little girl sobs.

"Hang on!" Sam yelled to the ceiling, exasperated. Turning to me she said, "We need to talk about this."

"*Mommy!*" Emily called louder and more desperately. "He won't give it back."

Robbie joined in the crying, saying, "Mine! No, mine!"

Sam hesitated for a second, then called out sternly, "I'm coming," to the ceiling. She put her hands on my shoulders and looked me firmly in the eye, getting my full attention. "Stay here. Do not go anywhere, okay? I'll be right back." Sam disappeared up the stairs. Her footsteps fell away, and I heard her muffled voice, talking calmly to the children above their duet of crying.

"But I have to leave," I said to the empty room as if stating an obvious fact "I don't want to be late for work."

I grabbed the keys to Sam's minivan from the hook in the kitchen and went to the garage. Once in the car, driving felt as natural as breathing. Keys in the ignition, seatbelt on, moving the gear shift to reverse down the driveway, foot on the gas. I passed the mini mart on the corner. I slowly braked as the light in front of me turned from yellow to red. Thirty minutes later, I arrived at the hospital and pulled into the garage, using my badge to open the gate marked 'Hospital Parking — Staff Only.'

I entered the hospital through the emergency room doors, intending to take a shortcut to my floor, but as I crossed the ER lobby, a code blue was called over the hospital intercom and a crash team began to assemble. Bits of information in the mix of voices made me stop abruptly and listen.

"Car accident…"

"… multiple victims en route."

"Two females, one male."

"… one critical."

Urgency hung in the air as the crash team stood by the automatic doors, studiously inspecting their equipment. The ambulance siren signaled the emergency crew's approach. Everyone stopped and watched the doors slide open, anticipation silencing the room. A girl was brought in on a gurney, clanging noisily over the metal thresholds, like water breaking over a dam, causing the room to burst into action. Machines beeped to life, and the EMTs quickly relayed information: blood pressure, vital signs, fractures. Without stopping, the crash team took over and wheeled the girl forward with controlled haste. I caught a glimpse of the girl's head. Familiar long blonde hair, partially matted with blood, covered the brace holding her neck in place. Her blue eyes darted wildly back and forth. Looking at the girl's face, I could see that she was fully conscious and very scared. That is when recognition hit me.

"Anna?" I said, running to the gurney. "Anna," I said again as the young girl's eyes met mine and narrowed. She was trying to answer me, attempting to tell me no. The girl was panicking, straining unsuccessfully to shake her head, unable to speak because of the intubation tube in her mouth. The ventilation machine was beeping in an irritating high pitch as it struggled to regulate her rapid and uneven breaths. I tried to calm her by brushing her hair back with my hand before being roughly shoved out of the way by a doctor, who continued pushing the gurney forward, calling out orders as he ran.

Anna was being torn away from me. I looked down at the girl's blood on my hands.

"Move!" a stern male voice said, and I was jostled even farther away from the girl.

"Anna, you're here," I said in a hushed tone, my soft voice a sharp contrast to the gravity of the room. "I knew you wouldn't leave me," I said in a whisper that was lost in the turmoil.

My thoughts were interrupted by a man in a suit and tie, running breathless into the emergency room. He yelled frantically, spinning around looking for help, making his suit jacket fly open around him.

"My daughter! I got a call about my daughter," he said, panic distorting his voice into a high-pitched plea. He caught sight of the blonde girl being pushed through the swinging metal doors at the other end of the room, and he cried out in agony. "That's her! You have to help her!" he shouted to no one in particular, his voice breaking with tears as he ran after the gurney, but he didn't reach her in time. The girl, surrounded by a team of medics, disappeared through the doors. The man stopped as the doors swung back toward him, slowing like a pendulum losing momentum and finally resting closed, blocking his path. The doors clicked and locked into place. A nurse carrying a clipboard hurried toward the man.

"Sir! Sir!" The nurse waved her arm, trying to get his attention. She reached him and tugged on his sleeve, but he was still focused on the locked metal doors. Bewildered, he wiped at the sweat on his forehead.

"Oh god. Oh god," he said desperately. Our eyes met. I looked at him with recognition. His face was familiar, a long-forgotten face.

"Jack?" I said, and the man's face relaxed, all traces of desperation gone.

"Hey, baby girl," he said in a slow Southern drawl, his easy smile lighting up his handsome young features. It was the Jack of my earliest memories walking toward me in his familiar crooked strides.

"Anna's alive," I told him.

"Yes." he confirmed in a whisper. "It's time to finish the song." He started singing the last verse of "Daisy Jane," his voice a melody that clung to the air as his image faded. The song that I heard in the background of my childhood memories of Anna played its final notes as my mind wrapped around the truth.

Other people's voices swelled like a fog around my ears, but their meaning never fully broke through my consciousness.

"… Amy Sheppard."

"… old roommate works… third floor…."

"… calling her now."

Behind me, Gail pushed through the elevator doors before they were completely open. She looked around the emergency room, her head scanning left and right as she rushed forward and stopped dead when she saw me. I was swaying as if dancing to a song no one else could hear, then abruptly, I collapsed to the floor, covering my face, crying into my bloody hands.

• • •

"Do you know where you are?"

I looked at my sterile surroundings. It was obviously a hospital room, but I couldn't recall how I ended up there. I was wearing a printed light blue and white hospital gown, made of fabric, not paper, but the material was worn thin from its many washings in harsh detergents. Still, I didn't remember putting it on.

"Philadelphia Hospital?" I said tentatively.

The nurse affirmed that this was correct. "Do you know what day it is?"

"No," I told her honestly.

She smiled, reassuringly brushing off my answer as inconsequential. "Do you know the year?"

"It's 2002," I answered. "What happened?"

"Just relax" was her non-answer.

"I'm going to get your blood pressure and temperature," she said, putting the thermometer under my tongue. "98.4." She took the plastic-covered thermometer from my mouth and wrote my temperature down. Then she expertly wrapped the blood pressure cuff around my arm and pumped it up, stopping when it was full and twisting the knob to release the air with an audible hiss. "120 over 79. Perfect," she said. The noise of the ripping Velcro filled the otherwise silent room. "Dr. Riley will be here in a few minutes to talk with you. Do you need anything before I go?"

"No, I guess not," I conceded, knowing she would not tell me anything further. I closed my eyes and confusing images filled my mind. The emergency room, a bloody girl, a frenzied father. The image of Jack. Anna.

• • •

Dr. Riley entered the room. She looked out of place in the white lab coat that reached past her knees, an indication of her status at the hospital. She gave me a sympathetic tilt of her head and sat down in the chair next to the bed. She pulled her familiar yellow notepad out of her leather bag and laid it on the bedside table. Then she reached in her bag again, this time taking out an envelope, folded and wrinkled. The envelope was once white, but it had turned a dingy gray from being carried for more than eight weeks in my purse. It was Anna's last letter.

"Your sister gave this to me," she explained. "It was in your purse." She sat perfectly still waiting for me to respond.

I stared at the letter, remembering, understanding. It was all clear to me now.

"Are you ready to read it?" Dr. Riley asked me.

"Yes," I told her, my voice subdued but firm. She handed it to me. I carefully took the letter out of the envelope, which had no postage stamp, and started to read it out loud.

Sweet Amy,

I've written that salutation to you in many letters over the years, but I still remember the first time. How I struggled to come up with the right opening words. 'Dear' was too formal; just 'Amy' wasn't special enough. Sweet. That is how I have always thought of you. Like the sugar we devoured as kids, but now, best in smaller portions; too much is overpowering. My Sweet Amy.

How do I begin to tell you this? I don't know when things got so far off track, but what I am going to say is simply a matter of putting it right. Do you remember the first time you met David? It was right after I helped you get a makeover. You looked like me. You met David at my party; you were even dressed in my style that night. At the time, I was flattered, thinking you would find your own style eventually. But it didn't end there. You continued to imitate me, down to the smallest detail, and taking what should have been mine. You even bought the same Chanel dress you knew I owned. That was the last straw.

David knows he made a mistake choosing you. When I told him how I felt, he realized you were just a stand-in, a substitute, for me. David and I were always meant to be together. And now, we are.

Anna

I folded the letter back into its original creases and put it carefully on the bedside table.

"Do you understand the letter?" Dr. Riley asked.

"Yes," I whispered.

"Amy, tell me what happened the night of your birthday."

I closed my eyes as I started retelling Dr. Riley the events of the night of my birthday for what would be the last time.

"I worked the seven-to-three shift at the hospital, and I stopped to do some shopping on the way home. I bought an expensive bottle of wine that I thought that David and I could share after we got back from dinner with Anna. I was running late, but I stopped to get the mail because I hoped that Anna's letter would be there. And it was.

"I took the letter upstairs and I started reading it on the balcony, but it started to storm, so I went inside. I read the letter. I had to read it a few times. At first, I thought it was some kind of awful joke, that Anna and David were going to jump out from a closet. But that didn't seem right. I mean, who would pull a joke as cruel as that? When I realized no one was watching me, I just stood there. I couldn't move."

I looked at Dr. Riley with questioning eyes. I wasn't sure what to say next.

"Okay, you read the letter and you were in shock. Can you remember what you did after that?"

"I don't know. I….." My voice faltered. "I somehow ended up in my bathroom. I looked in the medicine cabinet. David's razor and his deodorant were gone. I looked at the toothbrush holder, and it only held my toothbrush. I remember thinking that this couldn't be happening." My voice started to shake, but I felt oddly numb. "I looked at the bottle of Tylenol, and for a moment, I thought about swallowing all the pills." In my mind, I remembered being in the bathroom, contemplating suicide for the first and only time in my life. "Somehow, I knew I wouldn't. I just stared at the bottle, but I never picked it up."

Dr. Riley made a note in her notebook. "Go on."

"I went back in the bedroom, and I sat on the bed. I called Sam. I remember I had to dial the number five or six times; I kept messing up the sequence of the numbers. Sam came over. I heard the doorbell ringing over and over for a long time before I could figure out what the noise was. By the time I walked to the living room to let her in, she was banging on the door and yelling my name at the top of her lungs. I don't—" I felt an intense aching in my chest and unconsciously rubbed it with my hand. I was rocking back and forth, nursing the pain. I felt tears running down my face in ragged tracks. "I really don't remember what happened next," I blurted out at last. That was as much of that night as I could recall.

"Okay, Amy, okay," Dr. Riley soothed. "Just a few more questions. Amy, did you go out to dinner the night of your birthday?"

"No," I croaked quietly, shaking my head.

"Did you have a car accident?"

I shook my head vigorously. "Stay with me, Amy. I want you to say it out loud. Did you have a car accident?"

"No," I said, my voice barely audible. My breathing was hard and heavy. I was staring through watery eyes at the tile floor, a checkered print of blurry white squares.

"Amy, are Anna and David alive?"

I looked up into Dr. Riley's eyes.

"Yes."

CHAPTER 22

September 2002

Sam peered around the doorway into my hospital room. Seeing me, she entered without saying anything and hugged me gently as if worried I might break. When she pulled back, she rubbed her forehead and closed her eyes tightly. Tears trickled through her lashes. She looked down at the plastic grocery bag she was holding, and she handed it to me.

"Here," she said, taking in a deep breath. "I brought you some clothes from the house. You can get dressed and I can take you home. I checked at the nurses' station, Dr. Riley signed the release forms, and you can come with me. You don't need to stay at the hospital."

"Okay," I said. I took the bag and walked slowly to bathroom. Sam collapsed in the chair next to the bed, pressing her palms into her eyes. I closed the bathroom door and tried to avoid my reflection in the mirror, but not before I saw the mess I had become. Dark circles ringed my swollen eyes. My face was pale and taunt. My hair was disheveled and needed to be washed. The blonde highlights had grown out, leaving more than an inch of dark brown at my roots. I dressed myself with agonizing slowness. The light summer clothing Sam had packed for me still felt heavy on my skin.

Sam and I were quiet on the way to the car. The humid August heat made it difficult to breathe. I opened the passenger-side door and the sweltering air that was trapped inside the car hit me like a wall. As I sat, the scorching leather seat burned my thigh below my shorts. Sam got in and started the engine, rolling down the automatic windows to let the hot air out.

"Do you want anything, Amy? We could stop at the store. I'm not sure…." Sam looked at me. She turned the air conditioning on high and the stale air from the vents, which was not yet cool, felt like a furnace blast on my tender tear-stained face.

"Sam?" I said, "Could we maybe go somewhere to talk? Before we get to the house?"

"Sure. Let me just call home. Mom and Dad are waiting for us."

Sam reached in the back and pulled her oversize purse over the top of the seat. She dug through the contents for a few minutes, pulling out diapers and children's books, setting them aside. She found her flip phone and opened it. Sam stepped outside the car to talk privately, leaving her door open. She leaned back on the car as she spoke.

"Well," she said, faking a smile when she got in the car again. "Where should we go?"

"Let's just go to the park," I said, referring to the community park near Sam's house. I looked at the clock on the dashboard. "It's about dinnertime, so it shouldn't be too crowded. I just don't want to be around a lot of people."

At the park, I sat on a bench under the shade of a tree away from the large castle-like, wooden play structure. Sam went inside the small coffee shop on the corner and bought us each an iced coffee.

"So," she said, handing the cup to me. The liquid inside was light brown from the generous amounts of cream and I suspected Sam had added ample packets of sugar, too.

"So," I echoed. "I have some questions."

"Dr. Riley said you probably would. She told me to answer only what you ask, not to inundate you with information." Sam stopped. "Maybe I wasn't supposed to tell you that."

"Oh, Sammy," I said, putting the coffee on the bench and reaching for her. She put her coffee down too, and we hugged, really hugged, for the first time since she had picked me up. "What I must have put you through! You're treating me like the good china. Just how fucked up was I to get the gentle treatment from you?"

Sam laughed with relief and hugged me tighter.

"Pretty fucked up, little sister. Pretty fucked up."

"Well," I said, pulling back, "I'm better now, kind of, so you can stop it."

"Thank God. It wasn't as easy as I made it look." Her sarcasm relaxed me, letting me know that somehow, I was in fact doing a bit better.

"All right," I said, taking a breath. "Here is where I am. I know about the letter. I remember you coming to get me and taking me back to your house. I remember crying for a long time in your guest room. But then, my god, the last eight weeks, I don't know. It's all a blur. I'm trying to piece it together." I paused and decided to take a more direct approach. "You knew the whole time that Anna and David weren't dead and there was no car accident." Sam nodded. "What did you think I was talking about? I couldn't have been making sense to you." I gave Sam a minute to collect her thoughts. Sam picked up her coffee and took a sip through the straw.

"Well, at first, you were reacting like anyone would. You showed me the letter and I read it. I couldn't believe that they would do this to you. I was so mad, Ames. I still am. I could strangle them both. I mean, they left you on your birthday! David must have put the letter in the mailbox for you to find, knowing you would check the mail before going upstairs to find a half-empty condo. That's so cowardly." Sam's face flushed with anger, and her grip on the coffee cup caused the lid to pop off. Coffee leaked out and ran down the side of the cup onto Sam's hand. She moved the cup to her other hand and flicked the spilled coffee off her fingers, taking a minute to calm herself.

"Anyway." She sighed with resignation, carefully replacing the lid, and snapping it into place. "Let's see. It was Monday night when I brought you to my house, your birthday. Tuesday, you were despondent, walking around in a daze, not saying much, not eating. You didn't want to talk about it, which I totally understood. The kids tried to make you smile; they didn't understand what was going on of course, but even then, you looked like you were far away or sunk inside yourself. None of us could reach you. You barely talked, and it scared me. At first, I tried to give you some space, but it didn't change, day after day. You slept for long periods of time and when you were awake, you seemed to mentally drift in and out. I'd never seen you like that." A car passed us with the radio turned up, and Sam waited for it to go by before continuing. "By the end of the week,

I was freaking out. I called your doctor and she recommended that I make an appointment for you to see Dr. Riley. When I called Dr. Riley's office, I explained that you'd had a great shock. I described the way you were acting, and she agreed to see you right away. We took you in on Saturday. I told her about the letter, about Anna and David." Sam paused and took another sip of her coffee. "I took you to her office. Do you remember? She talked to me after your first appointment. That's when she told me that you thought that they were dead. I asked her if she was sure you didn't mean 'dead to me' or anything like that, but she said you didn't. Your mind invented the car accident. You believed it to be true."

"Why didn't you just tell me the truth?" I asked, but I already knew the answer.

"I probably would have, if I had figured out what you were thinking before I met with Dr. Riley. She said that you were perpetuating a delusion to deal with the shock of Anna and David's actions. She gave me some information on dealing with a family member with delusions that I shared with Mom, Dad, and Charlie. Dr. Riley told us to be honest with you, especially if you asked specific questions, but not to argue with you. She said that trying to convince you of the truth by arguing wouldn't do any good. You had to figure it out on your own. I would have been honest with you, Amy, but you never wanted to talk about it. You never asked me any questions. Dr. Riley wanted to try therapy before medicine. I agreed with her. She talked to Mom and Dad too. She really believed that the delusion was temporary and that you'd figure it out when you were ready to deal with it."

I let the information sink in.

"What about taking me to see Anna's grave?" I asked.

"I took you to the graveyard because you asked to go. I thought it was a good sign, you know? That if you were looking for tangible signs of their deaths that maybe you were starting to come out of it. I hoped that when we got there and you saw that Anna didn't have a grave, you'd start talking about what really happened and I could help you. That we could get back to normal. But when we got there, you went to Jack's grave. You never questioned that it was Anna's. You were so upset that day. Do you remember I took you directly to Dr. Riley on the way home?"

"I remember having an emergency session, but it seemed like all the other sessions to me. She just wanted me to talk about the accident again."

We sat in silence for a moment. I looked across the playground. A young mom with a toddler had arrived. She unbuckled him from the stroller and put him in the sandbox. The mom handed him a green plastic pail and shovel from the basket under the stroller, and he began digging happily in the sand.

"I just can't believe how long it has been. I don't really remember what I did with all that time."

"For the most part, you just seemed depressed. I couldn't stand seeing you so listless. Mom and Dad came to the house a lot. Mom wanted you to move back in with them, but we decided that it would be better if you lived with me, closer to Philadelphia. That maybe being here, you'd remember the truth sooner. Plus, it was closer to Dr. Riley's office." Sam paused, deciding whether to bring up the next subject. I could see the indecision on her face.

"What is it?"

"I talked to the hospital, too."

"Oh no, my job," I said. I honestly hadn't thought about how this would affect my work until now. How could I have forgotten?

"Yeah, you are on a leave of absence. They were understanding, but you'll have to be medically cleared before you can go back. Let's just take it day by day, okay?" Sam said, worried that she was overwhelming me. I was suddenly unbelievably grateful for my sister.

"Thank you," I said, "for everything, Sam. I know I interrupted your household."

Eight weeks. It was still unbelievable to me how much time had passed. I felt like there were holes in my memories, the feeling of backing down the driveway trying to remember if you locked the door. "I remember leaving the house...." I didn't know what else to ask or even what else to say. Thankfully, Sam filled in.

"Yes, you started going out during the day. I asked Dr. Riley if that was okay. I worried myself to pieces every time you left, but she said to let you go. You never drove, as far as I could tell, until the day you went to the hospital. You never went anywhere in particular. When you'd leave, you wouldn't even say where you were going; you would just leave. I followed you once. You went into Philadelphia. You rode the metro to the end of the Broad Street Line, and then you rode it back. You didn't talk to anyone. You didn't get off. You looked like you were in a trance, sitting on the metro, just watching the people. Then you came home."

• • •

I settled myself on Dr. Riley's sofa. It was strange to be back in the office. The room was familiar to me, but I felt as if I was seeing it for the first time. I had never noticed the painting on the wall behind the sofa, a branch of a cherry tree in full bloom, stretching up and out, against a pale blue sky. I took my usual seat near the center of the sofa, and I noticed that the fabric was a plaid pattern, a blend of pastel colors so light they were barely discernable from one another. I noticed marks on the walls, stains on the carpet that I could have sworn weren't there before. The sofa felt solid and stiff, not the suffocating softness I remembered.

"You look good, Amy," Dr. Riley commented. "How are you feeling?"

"Fine," I said, impatient to begin the session. What Sam had told me weighed on my mind and I started talking immediately. "Sam told me that before the incident at the hospital, I would leave the house and just wander. I don't remember that at all and it scares me. Sam said she followed me once, and I looked like I was in a trance. Why would I do that?"

"Why do you think you would do that?" She volleyed the question back to me.

I rolled my eyes, annoyed. I felt anxious and I wasn't in the mood for a deep exploration of my psyche. I just wanted a straight answer. Seeing my agitation, Dr. Riley spoke seriously.

"To be honest, I do have an idea as to why you did that, but the only way to know if my theory is right is to let you get there yourself. Otherwise, I could plant a notion in your head that doesn't fit and that wouldn't do you any good in the long run. So, indulge me, why do you think you chose to leave the house, but not go anywhere specific?"

I sighed. "Maybe I felt lost," I said, but even as I said it, I could tell that wasn't the reason. "Or maybe I was trying to run away like they did? Or trying to run away from myself?" I could feel that I was guessing, grasping at straws. I started again. "Maybe I was attempting to get lost in a place that wouldn't remind me of them?"

"Do you think that is true?" Dr. Riley asked. "Does it feel right when you say it to yourself?"

"No," I said flatly.

"Let's go back. You started out by saying that maybe you felt 'lost,' and you used that word again. I think your choice of the word 'lost' is key. Tell me, Amy, what did you think you lost in the accident?"

"My best friend and my husband," I said as if this was obvious.

"But they weren't really gone, right?" I nodded and Dr. Riley continued. "And on some level, your subconscious knew that. Right?"

At last, I had an idea of where she was going with this line of questions.

"You think I was looking for them." It was so clear to me now, as if I had broken through the surface of the murky waters that had been drowning me for weeks.

"I do. I think on some level your subconscious knew they were alive and wanted you to find them, so that you could stop pretending that they were dead."

"I was looking for them. They were lost to me, and I wanted to find them," I said conclusively.

A memory popped into my mind. I was waiting for the bus. I saw them on the other side of the street. Anna and David, walking arm in arm. I saw my car, the red Chevrolet. I saw Anna's face. She looked at me. I saw fear in her eyes. It was her nightmare coming true. She was facing me. She hurried into the car.

"Amy?" Dr. Riley leaned forward, concerned.

"I saw them," I whispered. I put my head in my hands. It was all coming back to me in a rush. "I actually saw them."

"You did?" Dr. Riley's surprise was genuine.

"Yes. The day before the incident at the hospital."

• • •

The lobby of Dr. Riley's office felt unusually warm. There was a sign on the wall explaining that there was no receptionist on duty and that patients were kindly asked to wait until their doctor came out to escort them to their office. I felt like I had read that sign a hundred times, reading and rereading it simply because the words were in my line of vision. The room was dimly lit by two table lamps with dark brown shades. A white-noise machine emitted sounds of a waterfall and faintly chirping crickets. I reached over and turned it off with a harsh snap.

"I'm sorry, Amy," Dr. Riley said as she opened the door to the reception area. Her hair was pulled back into a half-hearted bun. She pushed a stray strand of hair away from her face and tucked it behind her ear. Her face was glossy with a thin coat of perspiration. "The air conditioning is broken. We have someone coming this afternoon. Do you want to reschedule?"

"No, I'll be okay," I said. I stood and followed her into her office.

"What's going on today?" Dr. Riley settled in her chair. I took my usual spot on the sofa.

"Honestly, I'm just so angry."

"You should be," she said, and I felt as if she were reading from a script. *The doctor validates the patient's feelings.* "Tell me about your anger." She continued speaking on-script. Dr. Riley had set up a plastic rotating fan facing the sofa. She reached over and pulled the tab upward, allowing the fan to cycle back and forth.

I sighed, thinking, *I don't want to talk about this. Talking makes it real. I just want things back the way they were.*

"My life was so perfect, and then it all went to shit! I still don't understand why. Why would Anna do this to me? Why would David? What did I do to deserve this?"

"It's not a matter of what you deserve or don't deserve. Life doesn't work that way."

"But it happened! How could they betray me like that? I was always there for Anna! For years, I built her up, applauded her successes, and she couldn't let me have one thing? One man?" I tried to control my voice, but I heard myself getting louder.

"And David. He said he loved me. He married me. Why would he do this to me? Why would he pretend to love me if he really loved

Anna? I would have been fine if he was with her from the beginning. But he chose me. Me! And then they ripped the rug out from under my feet! Why did they have to involve me at all? They could have had each other the whole fucking time! It's what I would have expected!" I was yelling now, but I didn't give a damn if people outside the door could hear me. I felt sweat soak through my clothes, pooling under my arms and between my thighs. The fan wasn't cooling the room; it was just pushing the hot air around, its round face slowly shaking its head no, mocking me. I tried to take deep breaths to calm down, but the air felt so dry, I was choking on it. "I can't even cry anymore." I threw my hands out in front of me. My head and arms were shaking with rage. "How could they do this to me?"

"Amy, listen. David and Anna didn't wake up one day and decide to betray you. There must have been more going on than you saw on the surface. Figuring out how and why this could happen to you is what we need to do. What they did to you shouldn't happen to anyone, and you can't blame yourself; it wasn't under your control. But it is important that we figure out why you were so vulnerable because that is something you *can* control, if you understand it. I know that you want to rant about them, hate them, resent them, and you certainly can, but in the end, therapy is about you. You are the single most important person in these sessions, and I want to see you emerge from this stronger and happier. This won't break you. This is not the end of your story."

With the door to the office closed and the air conditioning broken, the room felt as confining as a prison cell. Dr. Riley put her notepad down and laid her pen on top of it. "This is completely unorthodox, but would you be comfortable talking outside?"

"Yes," I said, standing and practically running out the office door. We walked through the empty lobby and outside the building. Dr. Riley's office was in the last row of an office park surrounded by tall oak trees. Tucked back in the shade of the trees was a short brick wall, and we walked toward it, relishing the slight breeze. We sat next to each other, and I felt myself gaining control.

"This is better," I said, calmer now.

"Your anger, Amy, it is justified, and it isn't going to go away all at once. But I don't want the anger to own you. When you are ready, recognize it. Label it. It is a natural stage of grief, and even though they aren't dead, you are grieving. You've suffered a huge loss."

"Grief. The Kübler-Ross model," I said, referring to the five stages of grief I remembered from my days at nursing school. "Well, we can cross denial off the list," I said and smiled wryly.

My comment took Dr. Riley off guard, and she let out a sharp laugh. "Check." She made a checkmark in the air with her hand. "Actually, the stages of grief in that model are under debate in psychiatric circles. Not everyone goes through all of them and there isn't a specific order, but in my experience, I've found that in dealing with loss, anger is pretty much unavoidable."

"So, say we go by the model. I have bargaining, depression, and acceptance left." I ticked them off on my fingers. "Oh, the fun I have to look forward to."

"Acceptance," Dr. Riley said. "I've never liked that term. It sounds defeated."

"I agree," I said.

"I want to think of a new term, something that is less negative, less humbling. The *idea* of acceptance is a good one, but I've always thought that term internalized a feeling of despair."

We sat in silence for a moment.

"What about 'acknowledgment'?" I suggested. "You can acknowledge the event for what it is and move forward without bringing all of it with you."

"Acknowledgment," she repeated. "I like that. What do you think? Can you acknowledge what happened to you? Put it in its place as your personal history and start to move forward?"

"Hang on," I said. "I'm not finished being angry." I said it derisively, but there was absolute truth to it. Dr. Riley ignored the quip.

"I understand. And anger itself isn't bad. As women, we are taught to suppress it. It is unbecoming." She rolled her eyes at the word. "But it can be useful. Let's use your anger constructively. One of the best ways to guide your anger is to write about it. You can examine your anger as a response to a situation and make positive actions to protect yourself from being in a similar situation in the future. Would you be willing to keep a journal of your feelings?"

"I guess," I said, although the idea of writing did not appeal to me. I didn't want to explore anything. I wanted to hide from it. I wanted to keep it from being too real.

As if reading my thoughts, Dr. Riley said, "Remember, this is for you. Putting yourself first, that is something I feel that you will have to learn to do. Maybe for the first time." I let her words sink in as we continued the session.

CHAPTER 23

October 2002

I exited the train at Thirtieth Street Station, the closest stop to Dr. Riley's Center City office. When she called and asked me if I could meet her at her firm's downtown office, I agreed with a little reluctance. It was the first time that I had gone back to Philadelphia since I came to terms with Anna and David's betrayal. I would be near my old apartment with Gail, painfully close to the condo I shared with David, and within walking distance, albeit a healthy walk, of Anna's apartment. I wondered if she still lived there. Had she and David moved in together? Had they moved out of the city? Did they still work together at the magazine? I honestly didn't know. I took the stairs from the platform and entered the main concourse with the high coffered ceiling and stunning art deco chandeliers hanging above me. This morning, I decided that I needed to get out of my sneakers and running shorts. I borrowed a pair of Sam's wide-legged palazzo pants that made my legs look long and slender. I wore comfortable ballet flats and a simple top. I even put on makeup. Although I hadn't been back to Sean at the salon, I did go to Sam's stylist. She colored my hair closer to my natural color to even out the regrowth and suggested that I let my bangs grow out fully. She also gave me some sample products to help control my curls. No more straightening irons for me.

That morning, as I had stood looking at my reflection in Sam's full-length mirror, I felt rejuvenated. Without bearing the weight of anyone's expectations, I was growing stable and strong in my own unique way. I was beginning to understand the whole picture of who I was, who I became, and why it destroyed me. Now, it was time for me to acknowledge and go forth.

"Hi, Amy, follow me," Dr. Riley greeted me and led me back to a small room that was generically decorated. The slot on the door that would have held a nameplate was empty.

"So, here we are. Our last session for a while. What would you like to cover? Let's start with how you are feeling," Dr. Riley said.

"I'm feeling good," I told her, then admitted, "Well, a little scared, actually. I decided what I want to do from here. I am going to travel for a while before going back to work. I booked a flight to San Francisco and rented a car. I started looking at places that I want to see on the West Coast."

"That's wonderful! You seem excited, but tell me, what are your concerns about this trip? What worries you?"

I scoffed. "What I'm *not* worried about would be easier to answer." Dr. Riley waited for me to continue. "I guess I'm afraid of getting lost. I'm afraid of getting hurt or mugged or the plane crashing or…," I faltered. Dr. Riley continued to wait. "What if I starve?" I said with purposeful exaggeration.

"If you get lost, you can ask for directions. If you get hurt or mugged, you'll go to the hospital or the police. If the plane crashes, there is nothing you can do about it." I raised my eyebrows at her, surprised by her bluntness. "Well, there's not. And as far as starving, there are these restaurants all over the United States. You can identify them by the big golden arches out front. C'mon, Amy, no jokes, tell me, what are you really afraid of?"

My smile faded. "I'm afraid of doing this on my own," I whispered.

"I understand," Dr. Riley said. "Without a doubt you are scared! You've been through a lot. We've talked about this, and *I* think that you are ready, but the question is, do you?"

"Honestly, I don't know, but I am ready to find out. It's just… I miss them, I hate that, but I do. Anna was a part of my life for so long. I'm not sure who I am without her. Or without David." Over the last few sessions, Dr. Riley had guided me through the process of healing. Although she cautioned that I wasn't finished, I felt now I could see how easily manipulated I had been. I could see my dependency on friendships and marriage to define who I was. My insistence on controlling Anna's life to the point of neglecting my own. My efforts to be the wife I thought would meet David's standards instead of myself.

"It's natural for you to feel that way, but now is the time for you. You need to take care of yourself. Figure out what you really want from life. It's a hell of a big lesson, but step back. Learn from it. Focus on yourself."

"So, I guess I still have to risk death by airplane, huh?"

"Your plane will be fine."

"If not, I'm blaming you."

"I can live with that."

We spent the rest of the session talking about some of the things I had written in my journal, as she suggested. I read some passages out loud to her, feeling my own words telling me what I needed to know. Before I left, Dr. Riley said, "Enjoy yourself. This is a great opportunity! It's been a pleasure working with you, Amy. I look forward to seeing you when you get back." She stood and shook my hand with a smile that held genuine affection.

CHAPTER 24

October 2002

The air was cool, colder than I had expected, as we stood in clusters outside the strip mall, waiting for our group to be called. I looked at the worn green ticket in my hand. It was folded and creased, the lamination peeling off one corner, but the number was clear and intact.

"Green group, your truck is here." A man waved his hand, gesturing for the waiting crowd to follow him to a flatbed truck that clearly had seen better days. He took my ticket, then offered me a hand as I climbed the steps into the back. There were two long benches on the outside edges, facing outward, looking into the plastic windows sewn into the truck's canopy covering. Camera equipment had been stacked in the space between the benches, along with a cooler, blankets, and some worn backpacks.

"Slide all the way to the end," he told me. "Keep sliding in until you reach the person next to you. It's going to be a cozy ride." A man slid next to me as the tour guide yelled, "Three people to a seatbelt."

"Did he just say, 'Three people to a seatbelt'?" the man said with a snicker. His weathered face was framed by blond hair pulled back from his receding hair line into a small ponytail and a beard. He adjusted his round glasses, pushing them higher up on his nose.

"Safety first," I said as I put the seatbelt strap across my lap and handed him the buckle. He handed it to the person on the other side of him, shrugging his shoulders and saying, "I don't get it either." The person next to him turned slightly in their seat, trying to find the latch.

"I wonder if we have anyone on board with medical training, just in case," he said, grinning, as the truck roared into life and made a hard turn into traffic.

"You're in luck. I'm a nurse," I said. The truck made another tight turn and rocked slightly to the right. The passengers made a collective 'whoa' noise that was followed by nervous laughter. "But if this truck flips," I continued, "I don't think it will matter much." I tapped the plastic window with my fingernail.

"Very true," the man said. He leaned backward, trying to give me a little personal space in the cramped truck. "I'm Matt. Matt Thompson. I'd shake your hand, but I don't think I can pry mine free. I can't believe how many people they squashed in here."

"I'm Amy," I said. "Amy Sheppard." My maiden name rolled off my tongue with ease, but the whisper of Amy Garrison was still there, like the black and white picture of two faces hiding in the optical illusion of a vase. The truck hit a bump, and I shook the negative feelings off. We turned off the highway onto a dirt road, and the ride became jolting, knocking us off balance on the vinyl-covered seats. Although the trip was short, only about fifteen minutes, the change in landscape, from the small town of Page, Arizona, with its adobe style houses to the dry nothingness of the desert felt as if we had traveled to the moon. The truck finally came to a stop in a cloud of dust, and we climbed out.

The sharp sunlight made me blink as my group stood outside the canyon in groups of twos and threes, but there was a light breeze keeping us cool. Matt stood next to me. In front of us, the orange rock of Antelope Canyon formed an awe-inspiring wall almost seven hundred feet high. A jagged crack ran from the top to the bottom, a long, lean triangle that formed the entrance to the canyon. As we waited for the rest of the passengers to disembark, Matt smiled politely at me.

"Have you been here before?" he asked.

"No, you?"

"First time."

The guides began unloading the photography equipment and matching it to the people in the group. I inspected mine when it was handed to me. Even though the camera had been in its case, dust had worked its way inside and I blew on the lens to clear it.

"Then I guess you aren't from around here either. Where are you from?" Matt asked.

"Philadelphia," I said. "What about you?"

"New Jersey. We're practically neighbors. Are you traveling with anyone?"

I shook my head. "Just me," I admitted. I thought back to my first few days alone. The night I landed in San Francisco, I had cried long and hard in my cheap hotel room, looking out the window at what was supposed to be a view of the Golden Gate Bridge but was just the pink and blue neon sign for a Taco Bell. I finally fell asleep, a dreamless, heavy sleep, but woke up at 3:28 a.m. unable to sleep any longer. I punched my pillow until my hands hurt. I stayed inside the hotel room until late in the morning. Then, I got up, left without taking a shower, and walked to Fisherman's Warf. I found myself on Pier 58, listening to the barking of the sea lions. I ate clam chowder from a bread bowl while sitting on a bench facing the waterfront, all the while trying to convince myself I was going to be okay. It was almost dusk when I got my first real view of the Golden Gate Bridge peeking out of the fog, the cables looking too thin and fragile to keep the bridge suspended over the bay. I climbed the hill to Coit Tower and stood looking out at the water as the sky faded from yellow to orange to black. I felt a loneliness so acute that it threated to swallow me whole. The city of San Francisco, with its steep hills and colorful houses, looked different from Philadelphia in every way but still held the traces of Anna and David that haunted me. On the crowded streets there were too many happy couples. Too many close friends. Three thousand miles wasn't far enough away. I wanted to call Anna. I wanted her to tell me we could rewind time to when we were friends, before David, before she betrayed me. I wanted to forgive her. I wanted to tell her I was becoming my own person. I wanted David to say he'd be waiting for me at the airport. I wanted to hurt them both. My emotions spun in rapid circles, like the barrel of a machine gun that just kept firing. I called Sam and cried incoherently into the phone. The next day, I left the city behind. While driving across the monotonous barren landscape of the desert, a subtle shift took place inside of me. The wanting for Anna and David began to disappear like the nonstop tears, evaporating in the desert sun.

"I'm here with my wife," Matt was saying, bringing me back to Arizona, "and a couple friends, but they are back at the hotel. We're going to meet up at Lake Powell later. They toured the canyon yesterday and said that it is amazing. I'm the only photographer in the group, so I wanted to wait for this tour."

"Oh," I said. I felt like I should say something else. I wanted to explain why I was there alone, but where to start? I had barely talked to anyone in days.

Dr. Riley's voice came into my head, repeating words from one of our last sessions: "Take some time off before you go back to work. Do something just for yourself. It will be good for you to be alone. Let the rest of the world spin without you for a while, and I think you'll be surprised at how much you can learn about yourself when *you* are the only person you are responsible for."

Our tour group headed toward the entrance of the canyon and stopped when the main guide stood on a rock to gain our attention and started speaking. I loosened the scarf from around my neck. People shifted, excited to get the tour started.

"We are at the entrance of Upper Antelope Canyon. The guides," he said, indicating the people wearing khaki vests over their shirts, "will be stationed throughout the canyon to point out highlights and give advice on taking the best pictures. You are free to set up your tripods and take your time setting up your shots but please be considerate to the other people on the tour. Most of you have already done the sightseeing tour, so you are familiar with the canyon, but if you have any questions, please ask. There is only one path through, so you won't get lost. It is eleven forty-five, and you'll have two hours to photograph the canyon. Please return to the entrance no later than one forty, 'cause we are heading back with or without you, and it is a long walk back to town. Enjoy."

We lined up to walk into the canyon, and I gasped at my first view of the inside. Sandstone walls towered above me, orange swirling with yellow and black in perfect symmetry. The walls appeared to undulate and curve in a silent dance. I touched the wall. It looked like I could smooth it under my fingers, like playing in the sand at the beach, but it was solid and unyielding. I put the camera to my eye and began taking pictures, zooming in on the places where the colors contrasted the most. I followed the tour deeper into the canyon, winding between the walls through cracks so small I had to turn sideways and into areas as wide as my parents' living room.

Two hours later, we climbed back into the trucks, dusty and satisfied. Most people were flipping through the pictures on their cameras, looking at them on their digital displays. I sat with a woman who introduced herself and told me she was from Sedona, Arizona.

"Sedona is about a three-hour drive from here. You should go," she said after I explained I was on an open-ended tour of the southwest. "There are a lot of picturesque views at Red Rock Crossing, great for us amateur photographers. Plus, the town is known for being a spiritual center, a place for healing, if you need it," she said with a wink.

"I have a hotel for the night, and I'm supposed to be heading to the Grand Canyon tomorrow, but who knows?" I said, giving Sedona consideration. It was strange to have no agenda, no one holding me accountable. I breathed in and touched the silver pendant that Sam had given me at the airport. The pendant had the imprint of a hand with a spiral in the palm. It was called a Healer's Hand, an ancient

Native American symbol of healing and protection. Sam bought it at a store in northwest Philadelphia that specialized in Native American crafts and jewelry. It was unlike Sam to give me something that wasn't practical. The fact that she gave me something symbolic, even a bit mystical, touched me deeply.

"I guess we are all trying to learn from this, expand our horizons a bit. Remember to relax and let yourself heal," Sam had said as she hooked the necklace around my neck and hugged me goodbye.

The truck made it back to the strip mall where we began, and I got into my rental car. I had about an hour before my tour of the Lower Antelope Canyon, but I wanted to get there early. I heard the lower canyon had a snack bar with decent coffee, which I desperately needed, and I wanted some time to regroup between tours. The drive between the canyon entrances was short, and the gigantic red and white sign for the lower canyon's tours couldn't be missed from the highway. I turned into the crowded parking lot.

I drank my coffee in the small room while I waited for my tour group to be called. When it was, we walked out the back door and across a vista that led down to the canyon. In contrast to the upper canyon, which was a simple walk on level ground, this canyon had steps leading downward into the canyon and more steps throughout. Whereas the upper canyon was narrower at the top and open at the bottom, the lower canyon was the opposite, giving the sandstone walls completely different lighting and feel. We were encouraged to take pictures, but not to use tripods, and to keep moving though the canyon. Satisfied with my beautiful pictures of the upper canyon, I wanted to take fewer pictures and just enjoy this walk, letting the moments sink in, forming new memories I would always keep but didn't need to share. This was just for me.

Inside the canyon, a small group had formed behind a woman who was taking a picture, waiting in-line to take the same shot.

"What are we looking at?" I asked a guide.

"It is known as 'The Lady in the Wind.' Here." He gently moved me in front of him and put his head next to mine. He pointed upward over my shoulder, and I followed his finger with my eyes. "That is her in profile. Can you see her?" he asked, tracing the outline of the face.

"Yes," I said, moving away from him toward the image created by the rock. Her hair appeared to be blowing back from her face. She looked both as soft as sand and as hard as stone. The lady was featureless, sightless, moving forward and yet perfectly still. She was emerging from the solid rock, renewed and revived. I pressed the button on my camera, capturing the symbol of the woman I was becoming in a single click.

ACKNOWLEDGMENTS

First, I'd like to thank some of my earliest readers/editors, the ones who suffered through the original draft of *Sweet Amy* and gave me the reassurances I needed to keep going. So, thank you to Jennifer Brook, Fran Ireland and Joanne Hutchinson. Thanks to my other early readers and sisters, Janice Burguieres, Susie Serdensky and Mary Secor. You also survived reading the initial draft and I hope you will find the changes to be positive ones. Stephanie Ebbert, you were there with me from the beginning to the end, giving me confidence and advice and friendship and I can't thank you enough.

To my first professional editor, Jessica Hatch (Hatch Editorial Services, hatch-books.com) you did an awesome job of helping me take *Sweet Amy* to the next level and your insights were exactly what the manuscript needed.

To one of my besties, Dianna Miguez, who would like it to be noted that she did *absolutely nothing* to assist in the completion of this book (her words) except living by example and putting creativity first in her life (my words). Strong women who know themselves make the world go around. To the other strong women in my life,

Susan Lambert and Tracy Thomas, you never fail to inspire me with your spirit, and I have learned a lot from each of you. And speaking of strong women, I need to give a shout out to my RPCV sisters, Julie Lamy, Lara Grande and Renée Day, who are all shining examples of great women and friends.

I would not have been able to finish this book without the encouragement of the Book Babes (or Book Bitches depending on our mood) at The Park at Westlake. You have kept me reading, writing, and laughing for longer than any of us care to admit. You girls are da momomomomit and I love you all! Within this group was the special support of Jennifer Gilberti and Katherine Catolico who got me through the last few book edits in the middle of a pandemic, thank you for the friendship and the wine!

Lastly, thank you to my sweet boys, Ryan and Craig, who are my life's biggest joy and to my husband, Kevin, whose never-ending, never-wavering support makes all the good things in my life even better.

DISCUSSION QUESTIONS

1. Real friendships between women are not always as perfect as the quotes on coffee mugs would have us believe and Amy/Anna's relationship is a prime example. When did you feel that Amy overstepped her role as a friend? When did Anna take advantage of Amy?

2. Which character did you relate to more? Are you an Amy or an Anna? Is it possible to be a little of both?

3. We learn about Samantha's difficult teen years through Amy's memories. How did growing up with Samantha as an older sister affect Amy's self-confidence? How did Samantha's character change?

4. How did Anna's father's death affect her personality? Would Anna have made different choices if her father had lived?

5. Throughout the novel, Amy sees herself reflected in mirrors, windows, and other surfaces. How were reflections used throughout the novel to help Amy see herself (and those around her) more clearly?

6. Overall, is David a likable character? Do you think Amy really loved him or just got caught up in the excitement of being loved by someone who she thought was out of her league?

7. When did you suspect that Anna and David were alive? What clues did you get during the retelling of the night to Dr. Riley?

8. Who needs more wine?

9. The makeover sends Amy on a path of changing herself to be more like Anna, but she had been imitating Anna in subtler ways her whole life. Why do you think Amy didn't try harder to find her own sense of beauty and style? Was it fear of not meeting David's expectations or something deeper ingrained in her?

10. Do you think Anna and David stay together? Do they continue to work at the magazine?